Also by Jay P. Newcomb

Visigothic: The Barbarians of Midgard
Visigothic: Wizards and Kings,

VISIGOTHIC

On Destiny's Edge

JAY P. NEWCOMB

authorHOUSE®

AuthorHouse™
1663 Liberty Drive
Bloomington, IN 47403
www.authorhouse.com
Phone: 1 (800) 839-8640

Published by AuthorHouse 12/21/2018

ISBN: 978-1-5462-6223-7 (sc)
ISBN: 978-1-5462-6221-3 (hc)
ISBN: 978-1-5462-6222-0 (e)

Library of Congress Control Number: 2018911617

Print information available on the last page.

CONTENTS

For Joann, my beloved wife

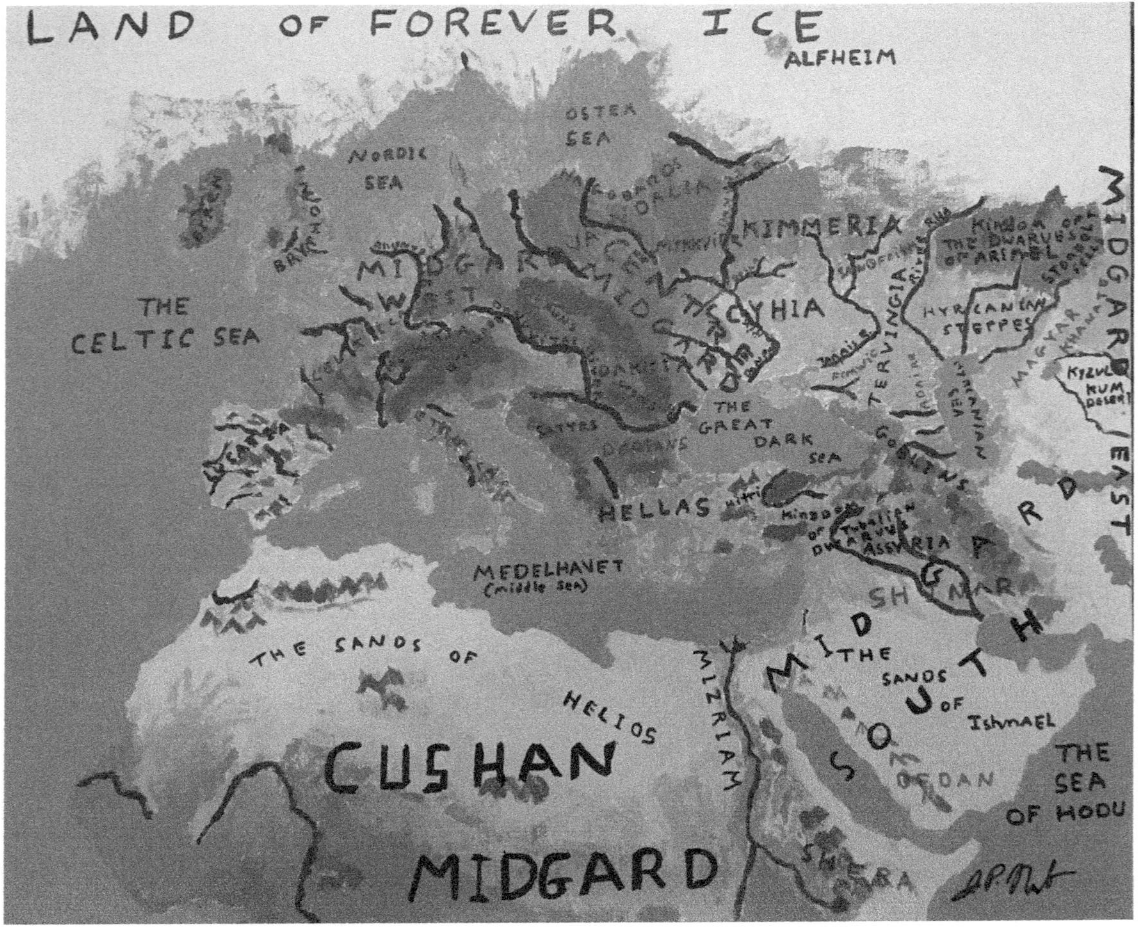
LAND OF FOREVER ICE
ALFHEIM
OSTEA SEA
NORDIC SEA
THE CELTIC SEA
KIMMERIA
CENTRE MIDGARD
MIDGAR WEST
SCYHIA
KINDOM OF THE DWARVES OF ARIMEL
HYRCANIAN STEPPES
MAGYAR
KYZUL KUM DESERT
MIDGARD EAST
TERVINGIA
HYRCANIAN SEA
THE GREAT DARK SEA
GOBLINS
HELLAS
ASSYRIA
MEDELHAVET (middle sea)
SHINAR
THE SANDS OF HELIOS
CUSHAN
MIDGARD
MIZRIAM
MID SOUTH MIDGARD
THE SANDS OF Ishmael
DEDAN
THE SEA OF HODU

BOOK III

The fire flickered; flame wavered, sank to silence slaked and fading. Svart lay the shadow of Sigurd riding in helm of terror high and looming

Volsungakvida En Nyja
Edda Sigurdarkvida en Mesta

A Fallen World

From the Skald's Tale:

From whence cometh evil? Why is Midgard this way?" asked King Roderick of the venerable and aged Skald Lothar, there in the Great Meadhall of Merida, Capital of the Visigothic Kingdom. The Meadhall was filled with guests who took advantage of this chance to hear once more the ancient history of their people at this long winter's fireside tale. Whole families were there gathered and the children listened intently to the long story which the aged old story teller had been weaving for them thus far. And now asks the King, "From whence cometh evil? Wherefore is Midgard such, and why is Wassergard even so, Noble Lothar?" The story teller replied, "Great King, it is written in the books of the beginnings":

And there was war in Asgard: Michael, Thor and Wotan and the Valkyries fought against the dragon; and the dragon fought and his angels, and prevailed not; neither was there a place for them found any more in Asgard. And the great dragon was cast out, that old serpent Loki, called the Devil, and Satan, which deceiveth all Midgard for he was cast out into the earth, and his minions were cast out with him, and these became the Vanierim, dwellers in a dark spirit realm known as Vanaheimr.

How art thou fallen from heaven, O Loki, son of the morning star! *How* art thou cut down to the ground, oh thou of the Vanier which didst weaken the nations! For thou hast said in thine heart, 'I will ascend into Asgard and I will exalt my throne above the stars of *Dan Ene Gud*. I will sit also upon the mount of the congregation, in the sides of the north and the very halls of *Dan Ene Gud* himself: I will ascend above the heights of the clouds; I will be like the most High.' Yet thou shalt be brought down to Halja, to the sides of the pit.

They that see thee shall narrowly look upon thee, and consider thee, saying, '*Is* this the Vani that made all Midgard, the earth of the nations, even all of them, lie in glory, everyone in his own house?' But thou art cast out of thy grave like an abominable branch, and as the raiment of those that are slain, thrust through with a sword, that go down to the stones of the pit into the depths of the halls of the dishonored dead; as a carcass trodden under feet. Thou shalt not be joined with them in burial, because thou hast destroyed the land, and slain the peoples oh Loki, for thou art the seed of evildoers

When the time of Ragnarok has come, the word of *The Most High* shall say, 'Prepare slaughter for his children for the iniquity of the Vanier; that they do not rise, nor possess the land, nor fill the face of the world with cities. For I will rise up against them, and cut off from Vanaheimr the name, and remnant, and son, and nephew, and as for those dwellers in Midgard who have been deceived by the soothsaying words of the Vanier I will also make their lands a possession for the bittern, and pools of water: and I will sweep it with the besom of destruction,' saith *Dan Ene Gud*. *Dan Ene Gud* hath sworn, saying, 'Surely as I have thought, so shall it come to pass; and as I have purposed, so shall it stand, that I will break the Slaughter Wolves in my land and upon my mountains tread them under foot. Then shall the yoke of the Vanier to depart from off of them and Loki's burden depart from off all of their shoulders. This is the purpose that is purposed upon all Midgard and this is the hand that is stretched out upon all the nations. For *Dan Ene Gud* hath purposed, and who shall disannul it? And his hand *is* stretched out, and who shall turn it back?'

Thus my King did Loki fall from his exalted state in Asgard and was cast down onto the earth, our great world of Midgard. All those who followed him became the Vanier, or as the Elves call them, the Vanierim and he their king, even those called the Watchers who in the primordial age, came down and took beautiful women from among the daughters of Adam, mated them and seeded the earth with the race of Titans, called the Nephilim by the Elves.

Smarting from his defeat he said, "*Dan Ene Gud* loves these hairless apes called mankind more than I, his first born! It is better to rule here though than to serve in Asgard!" It was then that his brother from among the Aesir, called Aesirim by the Elves, Thor and Wotan appeared saying, "Thou hast not been cast here to rule, but to taste the bitterness of exile because of thy treason, until the coming of Ragnarok." Loki now took the shape of a black angel, with great crow's wings and all around him there begin to swarm flocks of ravens, squawking and screeching. Midgard all around them was perfect and its beauty was at that time, like no other world which *Dan Ene Gud* had created, and yet a serpent was now in Eden. It came to pass that Loki took leave of his brothers, and becoming a great dragon, he set out to seduce the wife of Adam with soothing and lying words. This story is not told here, but in the tales of the ancient ones, the book of the peoples of Midgard and the forgotten tales of Eden and Lemuria.

Thus began the War of the gods, the Aesir (called Aesirim by the Elves) against the Vanier (called the Vanierim by the Elves) and two thousand years later, the Primordial age of Midgard ended with the great flood of which I have told thee my King in the past—the deluge in which all the lands were destroyed; excepting Noach and his family and their families who survived in an Ark in order to repopulate Midgard. The Titans and all their bloodlines were drowned, and their evil souls became the Jotnar, called the Jotnarim by the Elves, lesser allies of the Vanier even as the Vanier, the so called *Watchers* who had spawned them were imprisoned in the deepest of the darkest gloomy dungeons, called the *Abyss* by the Elves, until the time of Ragnarok. But the War of the gods continues as Loki plots to bring about Ragnarok before its time, so that by a *Gotterdammerung* (twilight of the gods) he may have his final revenge on mankind, the Monkies for whom he burneth with jealousy. And wherefore is he jealous my King? Because he is like unto a child envious of his siblings. For he is falsely perceiving that *Dan Ene Gud* loves we men more than he! Loki was the serpent in the garden that fooled Eve, called Havah by the Elves and sent Lilith the Huldra, the same *jötunn* known by the Celts as a *corrigan* to corrupt Adam by the lusts of her body! Since then man and many other speaking creatures have chosen to follow the path of their evil desires and have walked in the footsteps of Loki!

So my King, this is why there is evil and why Midgard is so. As we few Visigoths sit here today around this warm hearth at the tale fire in the Mead Hall of King Roderick, I Lothar the Skald continue the saga of long ago from the dim times of our people in that first great and heroic age of Midgard and so let thine ears hear more about the days of high adventure! When at the last tale fire I told all of thee about the wizards and kings and of the great battles and quests at the time of Dithranti's march into the east, and of the march of the Elves from out of the Land of Forever Ice. I told thee many things about the love between Sigmund the Volsung and the beautiful and most fair princess of the Dwarves of Ariemel, Eileza Andavarsdottir. You heard the strange tales of Changelings and of the wondrous little people, those brave and noble Leprechauns. Recalling all thus told; hear now more of these things. Commit all that I tell thee to memory, for this is how the memories of our ancient fathers is made alive every single day—for they are not truly dead as long as we remember them.

CHAPTER I

The Scroll of Azetbur

From The Skald's Tale

I Skald Lothar have told thee of the circumstances of the birth of King Ronan at the last tale fire, and of the great celebration that followed. Know that his father saw in him the potential of true greatness, as did his dear mother, the Shield Maiden Queen Gwynnalyn. The child was her glory and the love which she had for him was beyond description. Ye here who are mothers can know the emotions the queen had for the baby Ronan, her firstborn son. It came to pass in those days after the Slaughter Wolves and their allies had been defeated, that one short season of peace came—if only a fleeting one. But by the next year the Tervingians and the Dwarves, even the Elves and Fauns had come to realize that their enemies wouldn't leave well enough alone and that across the great steppes of Midgard and in the west, fear wasn't a thing of the past.

Hister brooded in his fortress, Castle Kul Oba pondering his next move. With him were the Gnome Throostra, the Huggin Argob, Hister's slave-wife Heike and their six month old son Eblilis. They sat at a long table consuming a meal of baked bullocks of goat ram sautéed in a bit of mushroom and black olive gravy; the ingredients having been brought in by a troop black of Satyrs, an evil race of Fauns long split away from the good Fauns of Agara—for they were doers of evil in all the lands into which they ventured.

Heike kept her hatred for Hister concealed very well these days and he was growing to trust her as more than just a slave concubine. Eblilis was bundled up to protect him from the damp chilly air of the dining hall which was barely held at bay by the great fireplace across the room. A group of Gutthiuda Thralls brought in a load of firewood in a two wheeled cart. One of them, an older man who seemed very sore and tired, looked at Heike as she sat at the table feeding a little hot broth to the baby. He of course recognized her as his people's own Gutthiuda Princess whose parents it was said, Hister had turned into trees. She glanced back at him in recognition and he gave her a quick nod and looked away continuing with the other three slaves to stack the split firewood into the wood crib next to the fireplace.

"What is our plan now Master?" asked Throostra. "Spring is upon us." Argob the Huggin sat upon Hister's shoulder as the evil Sorcerer replied, "For now we bide our time. We must continue the construction of the Black Ziggurat. Imperial troops cannot march right now due to the harsh weather still raging here and the spring muds down on the Steppes, and the Sons of Light and the Circle of Spirit Maidens guarding Sigurd's witch queen and their son. Early summer will soon be here and so we must rebuild our strength and secure what borders we have. We are depleted and so for now we wait my young sorcerer's apprentice. Be patient for our strike back at the rebel alliance must wait until the proper moment—even if some years have to pass. What is that to us? We must keep our eyes on the goal as Loki has instructed which Ragnarok is."

He took bites out of his chicken and chewed as did Throostra. Heike spoke saying, "Master, I must go and change the baby. May we be excused?" Hister lifted up his head and she could see his long, wiry black hair and a pointed mustache and goatee with a bit of bullock grease in it. "Yes my wife you may go and tend to my son. When he is old enough he too will learn the black arts for he is the counter balance to Sigurd's son Ronan." Hister motioned with his finger for her to come to him. She rose up just as the slaves pulled the wood cart out of the room and into the dim, lantern lit hallway. And they heard the heavy thud as the great oaken door close solidly behind them.

She handed Eblilis to Hister who kissed the child's forehead leaving a smear of grease and bullock fat. He could smell that the child needed to be changed and with that confirmed, he handed the baby boy back to his mother. A servant opened the door for her and she left the room. Another plate was brought in for the Raven Argob, Hister's *Raven of Huginn's Folk* and the greedy black bird went after the meat eagerly. Argob was there in the service of Hister, having been sent to the evil sorcerer by his father King Svart Svartfjær of Ravenswood. It was this same Argob who had a sister named Morgan Blackfeather, or simply Morgana and she was known the greatest of all the tricksters in Midgard—even running crooked shell games no less and of whom much more will be said later in this saga, as well as their good natured brother Skeletaan.

The hallway was dark as the entire castle was constructed out of black basalt rock, but the corridor was lit by torches and oil lamps, the olive oil of which Hister obtained through his Dorian Merchants in vast quantities. Passing her in the opposite direction were three Gargoyle Wing Troopers and an assortment of Gnomes. Heike soon arrived at her private chamber and was so greatly relieved that Hister hadn't shared her chamber since she had given birth; and this was a blessing for poor Heike in that his unexciting embrace to her was repugnant to her dignity. Except for this thing the Castle of Kol Oba was a comfortable prison, but a prison none the less—at least Morgan Blackfeather was her friend when she wasn't off in Myrkvidr or on some other ill adventure.

She ordered hot water and within a few minutes the servants of her own tribe brought it in. She filled the baby's basin with water and bathed the child while the servants removed the soiled cloth diapers and brought in fresh ones. When the servants had departed she bolted the iron and wooden door securely and soon the baby was sound asleep in his wood bassinet rocker. Heike now crawled under her bed and opened up a secret panel in the floor, removing a leather scroll about two feet long. It had a green cover over it which she removed and sat beside it on her small desk. She untied the rawhide thong which bound it and opened it up. The writing was in Dakkian runes—which she had learned to read as a child, being very similar to Gomerian and Dwarvish runes. How fortunate for her and how unfortunate for Hister not to have noticed that one of his seldom used texts of sorcery had gone missing. This was the *Scroll of Azetbur*.

This scroll was a fowl and evil text being the secret writings of the original Sorcerer of Dakkia, *Fulcrum of Azetbur*. This text was later obtained by the *Coven of the Carpathian Cave Witches* and so Hister had obtained from it his mother sometime in the past, when as a child she nursed his powers to greater infamy. The scroll was inked in blood on pigskin and the powers destruction it could unleash was enormous. Even Hister didn't fully appreciate it. But the unwise Heike in her determination to overcome Hister with evil greater than he could muster was well on her way to becoming a powerful maleficent sorceress. She studied the scroll intently in the lamp light while outside the castle a spring snowstorm was raging, its great wet flakes falling out of clouds most dreary.

Over the next four years Hister, King Idanthrsus and their allies would not let King Sigurd and his people alone, conducting invasions and harassments and much raiding. But through it all the rebel alliance held firm. Many unnamed battles were fought as the armies' criss crossed the steppes during the summer campaign seasons every year. There were fights in the south with the Goblins and swarms of Ogres poured forth from the black land of Morag as Hister made every attempt possible to defeat King Sigurd and slay his son. Many lives were lost during those years. Hister was quite put out by the King of Huginn's Folk during those years, for the wily old King Svart, while sending a few birds out to help the cause, refused to commit his entire force of winged air gladiators to the cause and Hister hated this.

And as for the forces of good, the *Dvärgr* (Dwarves) were there with King Sigurd through it all and in spite of the war the Dwarves were able to finally settle in the Stonebelt Fells and establish their kingdom in the lands explored by King Andavar the Great.

There were other battles in the war west of Dakkia. Invasions by the Nibelungen (who were the Gnomes of Agathyrsi in the land of Myrkheim and ruled by King Throng) against the Faun Kingdom to the north by northwest of the Gnome Kingdom—and the Black Satyrs joined the Gnomes. But the Fauns of Agara prevailed and drove the vile usurpers from the lands during those years and unto Myrkheim did they flee.

Watching it all was the Witch King Thrain of Valland from his stronghold in the Ashen Fells called *Erdemorden* (Murderworld). Now Thrain was no ordinary mortal but a demigod who had been born of an ancient Babylonian sorceress named Kashshaptu and the Watcher called Batraal. Yet he was greater than a Titan of old, for Loki manipulated the spirit of the infant being during its conception as Kashshaptu lay with Batraal and thus created an evil being—which was both of this world and that of Vanaheimr. Now it was said the Kashshaptu was the sister of Zultra, that same Zultra who was the wife of prince Gigan, son of Tammuz. She was the maternal ancestor of Adawulf Hister. Her father in-law was King Tammuz, who was the son of the evil King Nimrod and the Witch Queen Simuramus of Babel.

The title of *Witch Queen* fell to Kashshaptu who was the elder of the two sisters and those twisted sisters were the apprentices of the Witch Queen Simuramus. Thus from this pedigree from Midgard and by the arrogance inherited from his Vani father Batraal, Thrain claimed the title of *Witch King*. In truth Loki knew that Hister being a mortal (yet a mortal of kindred blood to Thrain) couldn't ultimately succeed. But yet the chaos that Hister spread would weaken the world of mortals and pave the way for the rise of Thrain. Now all the Witches of Midgard were under his dominion, even Hister's mother and sister. But the story of his rise to power in an era to come has yet to be told.

Though Hister couldn't bring Sigurd down, his powers of sorcery grew more and more with each passing year, and together with his mother Svetlana and his sister Angrboda, they formed the trinity of evil—even his father *King Radu of Dakkia* fearing the terrible power of his youngest son, joined the axis of evil, even as his lands were garrisoned by thousands of Ogres and his small mountain kingdom was swallowed up by Hister's Empire. Were it not for the Sons of Light and the Circle of the Spirit Maidens and the Druids, all would have been lost.

So that being said I shall turn back the sands of time, before those four years of which I've just spoken to just after the time of the gathering and the great battle of Thorstadt, to speak of how the Dwarves departed unto the Stonebelt Fells. Hear now my tale my Visigoths.

CHAPTER II

Away Unto Ariemel

From the Skald's Tale

All recall the story of young love. Remember that growing love between two young people from two very different peoples? There came a time of separation for Sigmund the Volsung and Princess Eileza Andavarsdottir of the Dwarves—she with the long blue-black hair, twas painful yet not everlasting—though to them it seemed that most surely it would.

ew things came to pass in those days, in the year of the birth of the future Goth King Ronan Sigurdsson in the *five hundred and ninety third year of the first age of Midgard, on the second day of Primilce-mōnaþ (Month of Three Milkings) Harpa and Skerpla*, immediately following the celebration of the season of Walpurgisnacht. The first day of this month was always celebrated by the Dwarves as the *Festival of Thrimilci* in gratitude for the beginning of summer. Thrimilci is a festival of joy and fertility much like Ostara and most of the Northern World is finally escaping from the snow at this time.

Spring was well under way and for most people there in Thorstadt it was a time of joy. Crops were being planted and there were marriages and many births that year. But for two young people in love, the times were not so happy at all. For Togrobeg, King of the Dwarves of the north had announced shortly after Ostara and the incredible events which accompanied the birth of the Crown Prince Ronan that the time had come for him and his people to continue on to their new home in the Stonebelt Fells, up-up and away to the new city of Ariemel, and now that the day had come twas a day of tearful bitterness for Siggy and Leeza.

The morning sun was bright at the ninth hour and all of the Dwarves were gathering together for the journey. In the Dwarf Quarter the people were busily making their final preparations for their journey. Women were busy packing up the last of their belongings and getting them loaded into the dwarfwains, their wagons, some of four wheels and others of two. Packs were being secured by the men to their shaggy *Dvärg mulor*, (Dwarf mules); mules bred from their small donkeys and their long and shaggy haired prairie ponies. These animals were short enough to accommodate the Dwarves quite well and were stocky, muscular and very surefooted, something that would be needed in the mountainous lands into which there were migrating.

Up in the Mead Hall Rutia, the Dowager Queen of the Dwarves was fussing at Elena and Leah, her ladies in waiting saying, "The day of our getting out of this wretched place is finally here and it's come none too soon!" Make sure that not a single thing of mine is left behind. And where's Eileza? She's not here! She's with that toad Sigmund! I hate that bloody little waug! The fact that his father and Togrobeg allowed the two of them tó pledge their troths to one another will never change my feeling about this! Dwarves should never marry outside their race, especially a royal princess!" As the angry Dowager continued to rant and to spew forth her venom her guards, the thick bearded twin brothers Austri and Vestri were ever watchful at the door as Rutia's household servants were closing and locking six great wooden trunks, and carrying them out—two strong young male dwarfs on each end. They carried the heavy trunks from out of Rutia's chambers and outside through the side entrance were they were handed off to others and loaded into Rutia's Dwarfwain, a large four wheeled wagon that was pulled by a team of six strong Dvärg mulor.

In the meanwhile King Togrobeg sat with King Sigurd in the private dining hall enjoying a last mug of pumpkin ale, they twain raised their ale horns and said, "Skol!" Sigmund and Eileza were spending their last precious moments together, alone in the dim light of Osrik's tunnel. Sigmund held her in his arms as the beautiful young lady wept bitterly. There was a lump in the boy's throat as large as an apple, so much so that every time he tried to say something he to begin to weep. Wrapped in each other's arms they leaned against the wall of the tunnel under the wall lamp and slowly slid to the floor. For a few long moments they wept in each other's arms—not balling loudly as if they were toddlers having a tantrum, but softly and quietly.

Sigmund leaned his back up against the wall and she shifted positions so as to lay across his lap with her head under his chin. His long red raven hair hung down around his gentle young face and around his shoulders and onto Eileza's own hair. She could hear the beating of his heart in her left ear and in his nose; Sigmund could smell the soft fragrance of her freshly washed hair. Soft and clean and silky smooth it was and he gently ran his fingers through her long, elegant blue-black hair—which fell over her shoulders loosely, half way down her back. She then slipped down and lay with her head in his lap and as he bent down, their lips met in a deep kiss and both of them were filled with the collywobbles from head to toe.

When at long last they separated to catch their breath she looked up into his eyes and said, "This isn't right Siggy Wiggy. I wanted so much to stay and for us to be married. I thought Toggy would allow it sooner rather than later. But he gave in to mum! I know he did Siggy! She's not fully turned over a new leaf, in spite of what I told you that was going on with her. She's acting like a witch to me again Siggy and now I know that she is up there gloating over my misfortune—in spite of all those things that she said before you and I marched out with the army last year to meet Dithranti and Yoshael. My mum is the kind of Dvärg that looks down upon those that she deems lesser than herself and she believes the Dwarrows (Dwarves) are somehow a better race than all others. I know she's absobloodylutly wrong about that Siggy because thou art a wholly different race than I—yet thou art so loving and kind and my dear heart. Maybe I won't go at all with her or with any of them—so to Halja with Ariemel! My home is with thee Siggy and not in the Stonebelts." Sigmund replied, "I tried to get dah to let me go with thee to the new halls, but he said no. And we both promised never to run away again—at least not now while we're still young. It's a bloody lot of tosh Leeza! I even thought we would be allowed to marry after my rite of passage. But just like your mum and brother said, that you were still too young, my mum and dah said the same thing! Dah said he'd say when I was ready to have a wife and he made me promise not to try and run away like we did before. You're right Leeza, this whole prince and princess thing is highly over rated. The other day when I was out and about with Lilia tagging along, I saw a couple not that much older than we are among the commoners getting married. Priestess Byrnhilda herself performed the sealing. Our noble birth has cursed us again, for now darling, but I vow to wait for thee my love. I shall not love any girl but thee, ever Leeza. Dah says that I have to make sure that I can support a wife, and to be able to prepare a place for you, just like he did for mum back in the old days. Byock the wizard said the same thing and so did Shlomael my Norn. Shlomael said that, 'I must go and prepare a place for you, that where I am, there you can be also.'"

She calmed her quivering lips for she was near to crying again and after a long moment she said, "Well your father does know his onions Siggy so he's probably right. But look at me. I'm supposed to be tough, or so they say. I've been trained as a shield maiden and I've fought in the war—even killed the Ogre that day. But so help me love, this pain here, right now in my heart is like a dagger betwixt my breasts." Eileza couldn't help but weep and Siggy took out a handkerchief and gently wiped away the tears in her eyes. Then a thought occurred to her and she said, "If I were with child, they'd have to let me stay here. They'd have to let us marry or there'd be a scandal. Then there is nothing that my infernal mum could do about it Sigmund." He replied, "I know that sounds like a good idea Leeza but let's think it through." She replied, "Let's make love here, right now in the dark Siggy. We've both wanted it so badly and it so hard to wait for our wedding. This may be our last chance before I have to leave."

Sigmund was burning with fiery collywobbles as their lips met. She sat up and they were quickly in each other's arms. It would have gone too far but for the fact that both of these young people had pledged their troth and wanted to do things the right way. Eileza was lying under him, her stomach burning inside with collywobbles and them twain at the very same time saith, "But we promised each other a wedding night." He rolled over onto the ground beside her and they both stared up at the flickering lamp, hearts still pounding and she said, "I was wrong Siggy. If we can't keep such a big promise as that to one another, we shan't be able to keep any promises to each other of any sort. I'm sorry Siggy, for suggesting it." He replied with a shaky voice and pounding heart saying, "That's right Leeza. I can just imagine what romance will be like if we wait to share it, when we shan't have to sneak around or fill guilty or being caught bang-to-rights. Truly we shouldn't cause a scandal and I don't want us to break our promises to one another—not now and not ever Leeza."

Eileza sat up beside him and looking down at his face she said, "But even so, the passion we feel right now, what I just felt when we were in each other's arms was something so, so stormy a feeling. That's a special thing Siggy and bonds my soul to yours. It was the biggest collywobbles ever and I feel, so loved and so cherished by thee. I promise thee my troth and to never love or to marry any boy but you. I shall wait for thee Sigmund the Volsung, no matter what because I love thee so, so very much Siggy Wiggy Miggy Diggy."

The sound of the trap door being opened and the thud of a pair of booted feet on the steps leading down into the tunnel caused the two broken hearted youth to swiftly rise to their feet. The voice of Sigmund's brother Gedron called out saying, "Sigmund, Eileza, it's time. I've looked on forlornly the door and not allowed anyone down here to interrupt you two love birds but now's the time. King Togrobeg and King Sigurd, everyone in fact is going outside. Better come along on the double mates."

Sigmund and Eileza knew that the time had come and that they had to leave the tunnel and so hand in hand they walked back up the corridor and met Gedron who was standing at the bottom of the stairs. And now Gedry, in even in the dim light of the flickering lamps could see that the two of them had been weeping. Gedry's heart went out for the both of them, for he knew how much in love they were. He placed a hand on the shoulder of his little brother and another down onto Eileza's and said, "I know this is more than difficult for the two of you. I support the both of thee, and I just wish that there was something that I could do to help—but dah has made up his mind. So has King Togrobeg but all isn't despair for they've allowed you to pledge your troths. The time for the wedding will come and until then Eileza, I shall guard Sigmund for thee and keep him from harm's way." She hugged Gedron and said, "Thank you so much Gedry. You're the best big brother a girl could ever have." As he embraced her in brotherly affection Gedry saw the look of anguish on the face of his little brother and gave him a sympathetic smile over her shoulder. "Thanks Gedry," said Sigmund. The three of them walked up the stairs and Gedry closed down the large trap door before they exited Osrik's old bed chamber.

By the time that they exited through the wide open doors of the mead hall, the dwarves were mounting their shaggy ponies. Eileza's was saddled and waiting and as she came outside, Austri and Vestri were waiting there with her armor and weapons—which they promptly helped her into. Soon she was in her hauberk and with her sword strapped on and her Sallet style helm on, her heart was once more breaking as she looked into the eyes and the tear reddened face of her Siggy Wiggy.

King Sigurd was there as well as Queen Gwynnalyn who was holding baby Rony in her arms. She saw the look on Sigmund's face and her heart went out to him. She went to his side and said softly, "You and her will be together again Siggy. Thy troths have been pledged after all." He replied, "I just wish it were now Gwynn. She's not even gone yet and I miss her already." She kissed his forehead, handed the baby to Greta and then followed King Sigurd up the steps onto the platform where they would address the assembly. All of the important people were gathered here to say farewell to King Togrobeg and the Dwarves—for they must away unto Ariemel go. King Yoshael and the Elves were there as well as the Circle of the Spirit Maidens and the Sons of Light (the wizards).

Among the Lords of Tervingia in assembly were Hodbrodd, Radagaisus, the Jarls Gondark, Adaire and Godwin; Lords Raedwald, Randver, Radau, Fridigern, Hjalprek, Sinfjotli, Regin and Snaevar along with Scap Rolf (the King's First Minister and Chief Steward) and Scap Kronos—the time keepers of the kingdom. In short the entire military leadership of the Kingdom was present on that day to honor the Dwarves and see them off to their new homeland.

Eileza came to Sigmund and in spite of all those assembled there they kissed for the last time (for their love was already quite famous throughout the kingdom) just as Volsung and Gerda, the Changelings (in human form) and the five Leprechauns approached from inside of the mead hall. "Until we meet again Siggy Wiggy," said Eileza. "Until then Leeza, forever and always," he replied. They slowly let go of each other and she walked with her head held high and in all the dignity that she could muster, she mounted her pony.

There was a soft breeze blowing and from the top of the platform, King Sigurd and Queen Gwynnalyn could see the proud military formation of Togrobeg and the Dwarves. They could see the Dwarf Lords like Lord Commanders Alesander and Theodah, Count Dunyr and the Margrave Gindalf—Baron Althjolf as well as Lord Azgar and General Kroki and High Priestess Skadi. Warriors like Durin were there as well. Also it was noticed that a beautiful lady dwarf by the name of Araelia, who of late had been seen in the company of King Togrobeg was there and it was thought that he had taken a liking to her. Was this a portent of the future? Only time would tell.

The entire assembly was silent now as King Sigurd began to speak. "I stand here before thee all today, to express the gratitude of myself and of the people of the United Kingdom of Tervingia, to King Togrobeg and the Dwarves, for all the help and assistance which they have rendered to us during this war. We pledge our continued support to the efforts of our brother King Togrobeg to build his Kingdom at Mount Ariemel. This war is far from over, and we are grateful for the warriors which the King is leaving behind here—for the threat of the Slaughter Wolves is still great. But in order for the Dwarrow people to become an even greater power in Midgard, they must go and build a nation for their children and their children's children. To all of the sons of Tubal, you are our friends and allies and we shall never forget the friendships and the comradery that has been forged between our two peoples during this terrible war which was thrust upon by the Scythians and their allies and the Sorcerer of Dakkia. And so for all of us, I bid thee, King Togrobeg, a very fond farewell."

With a salute from King Togrobeg and to the sounds of the horns playing a fanfare the Dwarves departed Thorstadt, marching out of the city in a proud and most grand parade to boats and rafts which ferried them eastward across the wide River Rha. Sigmund climbed the stairwell into the tower where he watched for hours until all of the Dwarves were across the river. The sad young man watched as the Dwarves assembled across the river and marched away to the east in a cloud of dust. As the last elements of the Dvärgr disappeared over the ridges and past the Thorstadt Stonehenge, Sigmund saw a lone rider return to the ridge, sitting upon a pony for a long while. He thought that it had to be Eileza for the figure seemed to wave. He leaned out of the window and returned the wave with his eyes full of tears. Then the rider turned and disappeared and was seen no more. Twas then that Sigmund noticed that Lilia was there as well, ever at his side, looking lost and forlorn—for she had come to love Eileza most dearly. The child looked up at him, with her doll wrapped in a small blanket in her arms, with no words to say. Sigmund picked her up and she put her chin on his shoulder and carried the Wish Maiden downstairs for lunch.

Eileza sat long on her brown shaggy pony there on the ridge, seeing a figure in the tower window and knew in her heart that it was Sigmund. She saw that all of her people, on ponies and in dwarfwains had passed on now, and that she was alone with her thoughts. Her eyes filled with tears and as she waved to Sigmund in the tower she said, "Goodbye Siggy Wiggy—my forever love." Lowering her hand, she tugged on the reins of her pony and rode away to the east.

CHAPTER III

The Grand Halls of King Togrobeg

From the Skald's Tale

Away unto Ariemel doth my tale take thee now oh King Roderick, to the far off times of the beginnings of the rise of what was once the greatest Dwarf Kingdom in all of Midgard, Ariemel under fells most high, into the glistening halls of King Togrobeg Andarvarson, the true heir of Tubal's legacy.

The Dwarves traveled east for many days before turning north, following up the Yural River. The travel was slow due to the large number of families and their dwarfwains. But within four weeks they had arrived at their new home, on *Þūnresdag* (Thunaresdag) on the 2nd day of *Midsumor-mōnaþ (Midsummer Month) or Skerpla and Sól-mánuðr (Sun month) in the five hundred and ninety third year of the first age of Midgard.*

The people who'd gone before them had done a most admirable job in preparing for the arrival of the nation. At the foot of Mount Ariemel, which the late Andavar the Great had named after his beloved maternal grandmother, were the beginnings of a city. A log palisade fortress had been constructed on a hilltop at the base of the mountain and inside of it were a great many rock and log houses. These modest dwellings were intended to house the people until great many pillared halls could be constructed under the mountains—here where the Dvärgr would at last have a comfortable home.

They had discovered the richest mountain in all of Midgard, or so it was later said and so they were doing what Dwarves do best—they were mining. Dwarves were a people of the earth and felt most at home in cavernous halls of their own making. They are also the greatest of all craftsmen and from the ores found here, Eileza's people would be designing the greatest works of artistry known to any race in Midgard. In due time and in years to come as the Dwarrow people played their music under this gem crusted mountain, Ariemel would become the greatest Dwarf Kingdom in all of Midgard.

Eileza saw the workers creating a great stone archway around the entrance to the underground halls and she saw others working the cliff face to the left and right, carving two mighty colossi, statues of their ancestor Tubal on the right, and her own beloved father King Andavar the Great on the left. She saw the smoke of forges burning hot and as she entered the gate of the city with her brother the King and the Dwarf Lords she could hear the sounds of hammering, tinkling sounds metallic in their call. Close behind in her carriage was the Dowager Queen. Perhaps she was the happiest of all there for she said in her heart, "Alas my daughter is away from that dirty Volsung. Here she will at last learn what it means to be a Dvärg."

Rutia, although ill, seemed to be doing better under the treatments of Priestess Skadi during the first year but in the summer of *the five hundred and ninety fourth year* she took a turn for the worse and went into a precipitous decline, finally succumbing to death on the 2nd day of *Midsumor-mōnaþ (Midsummer Month) or Skerpla and Sól-mánuðr (Sun month) in the five hundred and ninety fourth year of the first age of Midgard.*

The details of her demise were unknown until later times and therefore are not told in this part of the saga, but the Dwarves knew as they watched her body being consumed in the pyre in preparation for her entombment that a day would come, that when by the command of *Dan Ene Gud*, Wotan will sound his Gjaller Hörn, and she would come forth from Wotan's Hall as one of the Einherjar to battle against wraiths and all the powers of the dark side at the end of all things. But for now Rutia's bones would rest deep within the newly carved royal mausoleum under the mountain. Twas Eileza herself, with torch in hand who kindled the flames and stepping back watched the pyre blaze high and hot—but in front of her people she showed little emotion other than the redness of her eyes.

A whirlwind came suddenly and pulled the smoke high aloft and Eileza was comforted by it saying, "May you rejoice in Valhalla mum, and if not there then may Freya receive thee into her hall Mum." The funeral drums were pounding and the horns were blown in a long and most mournful dirge. There was weeping and gnashing of teeth and many Dwarves rended their garments. Away went Eileza and Togrobeg to wear sack cloth and sit in ashes.

And so the years started to pass, first one then two then three on into the fourth year, the *five hundred and ninety eighth year* and as Sigmund and Eileza in their two separate worlds continued to mature, they never forgot one another and longed for the day when they twain would be reunited in love's grand reunion. During these years the war continued and Togrobeg kept forces fighting in the war from his base as king under the fells. The mot and baily castle which stood outside of the entrance to the growing maze of underground halls was rebuilt of polished white stone.

Other Dwarves farmed the river valleys surrounding the mountain, and in particular the Dwarrow Downs but alas they found enemies in the region who did not like the presence of the Dvärgr. These were a mysterious race of creatures, apparently some sort of white, carnivorous snow ape or hairy ice trolls. These would attack small groups of woodcutters and even the farmers in the most savage and brutal manner possible. They didn't seem to have a civilization, but haunted the forests, glens and dales of the Stonebelt Fells, eating their meat raw. Traders who journeyed up from Shangra La said that similar creatures existed there called Yetis (Stinking Dirty Snowmen) and so the Dwarves called these monsters by that same name, although King Togrobeg dubbed the first one he saw as the Abominable Snow Man and also the Abominable Snow Monster of the North. This creature stood at least eight feet tall, had face of an ape and the teeth of a saber toothed tiger, feet like a giant man and claws like a bear and covered from head to toe with thick white hair—and it's roar was like that of a dragon. Anyone in his right mind would fear these terrible beasts of the Stonebelt Fells. Eventually the Dwarves sallied forth with their armies and those *Snowmen* that they couldn't kill; they drove north, forcing the creatures to live at the edges of the great glacier marking the southward boundary of the land of Forever Ice.

It was also discovered that there were gigantic boars the size of dragons living in this region known as the *Vildsvin*. These pigs were massive ranging in size from a large bull to that of a wooly mammoth, of which there was also abundance in this new land. Unlike the Elves who follow a diet given to them by *Dan Ene Gud* in which any kind of pork or ham product was not to be touched, much less eaten, the Dwarves had no such understanding and so they hunted these *Vildsvin* and baked their ham in great underground ovens. But Eileza remembered all that she had been taught by the Elves in her youth and so had no taste for such meat.

Eileza helped her brother as much as she could during the three years after the passing of Rutia, and if the legends be true, grew into the most beautiful and honored princesses of the Dwarves that Midgard had ever known. The young shield maiden refused all suitors who sought after her hand, for her heart belonged only to Sigmund the Volsung. The legends speak of Eileza as being a very skilled jeweler, coin etcher and gold smith. She made a special craft, a gift for her far away Sigmund which was a beautiful polished gold coin with diamonds set in its edges round about. It had a hole on the edge through which a woven leather string ran with the two ends tied off with a beautiful golden clasp with her tiny intricate carvings of the Midgard Serpent. The coin was large and was finely engraved with an image of Eileza herself on the head—and on the tail side was a mistletoe plant. She made other items such as rings and ear rings, and broches, but this coin necklace was her special gift for Sigmund—and now more than ever she was growing restless to see him.

And so when it came time for the Baron Althjolf to go to his post as ambassador to Thorstadt, the now seventeen year old Eileza would no longer be kept at home. The King was courting the Lady Araelia in those days and Eileza knew that a marriage would come and an heir would be born, thus she would not have to sit as Queen under the mountain; and so with much determination and a terrible longing for Sigmund the Volsung, Eileza came to King Togrobeg one day as he sat playing chess with General Kroki, determined that the time for her to leave had come.

The royal chambers were still under construction here under the mountain, just off of the giant pillared gallery where sat his throne. Here in the conservatory which was lit by many bright lamps, at a large wooden table sat King Togrobeg and General Kroki where they twain were in an intense mood of concentration—having been at this game for three hours. Eileza said, "I beg your pardon my King, but I must have a word with you—in private." Togrobeg looked at her and asked, "Is it serious Eileza?" She replied with a nod and so the thick bearded old General took the hint. He rose up and with a smile said, "Aye Princess Eileza, he's all yorn. Ye just saved our King from being check mated." Togrobeg laughed and said, "Aye so he says."

When Kroki had departed and closed the door behind him Eileza said, "Toggy, it's been four years since we came here from Thorstadt and three since Mum passed away. I'm seventeen now and I will go and see Sigmund. With mum's passing it's time for me to go home Toggy." He replied, "Home? But you're a Dwarf Eileza and your home is here with us." She replied, "No Toggy, it isn't. Methinks that my home is with Sigmund the Volsung. You promised that I could marry him and so, whenever will that time come? I know that Baron Althjolf is leaving in two days for his new post and I want to go with him." King Togrobeg replied, "Aye Eileza you're right. I know that ye love him and you've been a good sport these last few years. Mum would've hated the idea but I'm letting you go as part of my embassy to the Tervingians. I remember that you and Sigmund are pledged and I bless it. A marriage between the House of Andavar and the House of Volsung will seal our alliance. With all of the fighting these last four years, heaven knows we need all the positivity that we can get now."

The look on the Dwarf King's face grew long and forlorn and said he, "These past battles are only a foretaste of things to come. The final battle is yet to be fought. Scouts from the west tell of great swarms of Ogres gathering and in our old home range at Stansberg the Goblins prepare in hordes. Gargoyles have been seen flying in great formations to Kol Oba. Yes my dear heart, you must be with your Siggy before the final blow falls, whether we live or die." She was fearful and said, "Is it that bad Toggy? Let them come at us with all they have then. Keep a good heart dear brother, for I know that we shall all gain the final triumph." She embraced him warmly and said, "I just know it will be so Toggy Woggy."

When they had let go their embrace he said, "I know that the weather is still cold. Winter is still in its throes but we're dwarves and are used to it. You can handle it Eileza. Prepare well and go on the morrow with the Baron, and have a blessed reunion with your Siggy Wiggy. But however I'm sending Austri and Vestri along with you as body guards. Where you go they go! Agreed little sister?" Eileza was filled with joy, so much so that she broke down into tears of happiness, laughing and hugging her beloved brother. "Agreed Toggy Woggy, agreed!" she replied.

CHAPTER IV

Eileza Comes Home

From the Skald's Tale

We all here at this tale fire, at least those of us who are come to age, have known the joys of romance and love and see the results in the forms of all these strong and handsome Visigothic children about us in Roderick's halls. We have known the sadness of being parted from our lovers, and if we are counted as blessed by the Lord of Asgard, we experience the joy of reunion and of homecoming. Here now I tell thee of the parting away of sadness and the arrival of joy for young Lord Sigmund the Volsung and Princess Eileza Andavarsdottir.

And so it came to pass that Eileza packed her things and set out with Austri and Vestri in the company of Baron Althjolf, and planned to arrive in Thorstadt (unknown as yet to Sigmund) on *the 1ˢᵗ day of Gói and Ein-mánuðr, in the five hundred and ninety eighth year of the first age of Midgard.* The weather was still cold and there was much snow about but the pathways into south were clear. Three days down the Yural River Eileza and her company met a large group of Elves riding north on reindeer. The sky was overcast and there was a light snow falling and the river to their left was frozen in many places, yet there was a current of swift running water swirling in torrents around a jumble of rocks and boulders and fallen logs.

Eileza was pleased to see that it was the company of King Yoshael, the White Wizard of the North. He had with him the Celtic Girl Giorsal Rhydderch, she who had been resurrected from the curse of the Draugr. Eileza saw that she was riding behind Yoshael on the same reindeer, and that she had indeed grown tall since she had last seen her. The girl was now fourteen years old with long blond hair which flowed over her thin shoulders in glorious waves of beauty. Giorsal was dressed the same as female elf youth wearing a gray sleeveless dress which came down to just above her knees. Her arms were covered by a long sleeved green shirt worn under her dress, and her legs were covered by full length olive drab leggings, also worn under the dress. She had on a pair of lace up shoes which came to an inch above her ankles that were light green.

Baron Althjolf was informed by his men that the King of the Elves was approaching and so he went forward to meet him as did Eileza followed close on by Austri and Vestri, while the other hundred or so dwarves remained behind. Shlomael rode up and took his place beside his father as the Dwarves approached on their shaggy ponies. The Baron and Eileza stopped short and he said, "Hail Yoshael King. I greet thee in the name of King Togrobeg. He will be pleased to see you at the mountain." The Elf King and Shlomael rode forward to give greetings. Yoshael steered the large reindeer with one hand on the reins while carrying his staff in the other, dressed as always in his white wizard's attire and tall pointed white hat and long white beard. Shlomael smiled when he saw Eileza and she returned the gesture. Yoshael smiled as well and said, "Greetings Baron, tis good to see you again. Oh look at you Princess Eileza. You've become a most beautiful young woman since last we saw you." Shlomael said, "I heartily agree. You have indeed become remarkably beautiful. I should think that young Sigmund will say the same and much more when at long last he sees you again.

Eileza blushed with a smile and said, "Thank you King Yoshael. I miss Lord Sigmund so much. Has he grown since last we parted sire?" Yoshael replied, "Ah yes indeed he has. He is quite tall now, six feet I would say. I know that he longs for you Eileza. Go to him even as you have determined to do so. There will soon be dark days coming Eileza, and without each other, the two of you shan't survive. I have seen visions of what is to befall the two of you. Don't fear the fiery mountain Eileza, for with Sigmund shall ye come unto it in the midst of a sea. With Sigmund shall ye be, he who will hold you through the shadow of death, in his arms shall ye be. He shall shed tears and from his tears come new life, and behold I shall come from out of the vortex and send thee both away safe, for she who will die must be raised again to life—but only with Sigmund shall it be."

This was a rather strange and cryptic way of prophesying and Eileza didn't know how to respond at first. It sounded like she was going to die somehow and yet still having a life to live beyond that with her Siggy. "I'm not sure what all of that means majesty," she answered in a shaky voice. Eileza saw that Giorsal was holding her adoptive father around the waist and leaning her head against him, yet keenly watching Eileza with her big blue eyes in respectful silence. Yoshael said, "Just remember that when all seems lost at the mountain of doom fear not, for I shall be coming to thee from out of the clouds. Ponder what I have said Eileza. Keep it close and in remembrance in the days ahead." "Yes master wizard," she replied. She wanted to change the subject now for this was making her nervous and so she asked, "Is this Giorsal?" Giorsal herself answered saying, "I am Giorsal Rhydderch, Princess Eileza. Pappa Elf is taking me all around Midgard now. I can hardly wait to see the Mountain Kingdom." Eileza replied, "May your Pappa Elf show you all the glories of it and more Giorsal—I know he will."

The Baron saw that now was a good time to enter the conversation and said, "We're on our way to Thorstadt majesty. I regret that we cannot chat a bit longer but we must be away. Welcome to the Mountain Kingdom and may *Dan Ene Gud* keep you safe, for there is danger in the land." "Danger?" asked Shlomael. The Baron replied, "Huge white monsters M'Lord. The Abomdible Snow Monster of the North inhabits these lands—more than one I dare say, and they'll eat you alive." "Speakest thou of the Yetis my good Baron?" asked Shlomael. "Yes indeed my good prince. But if you stay together in a large body they'll like as not leave thee alone, so farewell and Godspeed my good Elves." "Farewell and Godspeed to thee also my good baron," replied Yoshael. "And to you as well Eileza, he said with a smile." Giorsal simply waved and smiled, and as they passed each other by, riding in opposite directions, Eileza noticed that there were no fangs of the draugr in the girl's mouth anymore and for that she was greatly relieved—for even she had some uneasiness regarding Giorsal.

Many more snowy days past as Eileza and her party made their way down the Yural river and down out of the Stonebelt Fells. Once out of the high country and although it was still cold there was much less snow on the ground, and so the horses were able to feed off of the dry grass by pawing in the snow. Now at long last they were down on the great and dry sage prairies and grasslands of the Hyrcannian steppes, and they made their way west—following the trek of the east-west road across lands still covered in a thin layer of snow. It wasn't really a developed road, but rather a trail over which much commerce and other traffic passed. At long last after many more days, some of which were spent leaning into the bitter cold winds the weather began to warm a bit and through a grove of leafless trees, the trail led down through the broken ridges. There it was, the Thorstadt Stonehenge and now at last they could see chunks of broken ice traveling down the wide flowing River of Rha and Thorstadt by its side on the western bank.

As the city came into view there was nothing stopping Eileza. As the cold air bit her face she rode out ahead of the party. With Austri and Vestri close behind and coming to the river they took the first available ferry and were soon across the wide flowing current. Upon disembarking,

Eileza and her guards climbed back into the saddle and rode the hundred two hundred yards or so up the hill to the eastern gate which was open for business. The soldiers recognized her and letting her pass, Eileza rode for the mead hall as fast as she could.

They came to the main entrance of Sigurd's mead hall and as she and her guards dismounted, they were greeted by two of the King's Thanes, the Knights Sir Arnlaugr and Sir Arnthor. They immediately recognized these Dwarves and Sir Arnlaugr said, "Greeting Princess Eileza of Ariemel. We were told that you were coming, and Lord Sigmund will be most anxious to see thee m'lady." She replied, "He hasn't been told I was coming has he? It was to be a surprise." Sir Arnthor replied, "No m'lady, to our knowledge he hasn't, just as your messages requested. The young Lord was convinced to go on a hunt today by Gustav and Lars, and so he shall return tonight— to a great amount of joy when he seeth thee m'lady. In the meanwhile, come inside for rest and refreshment and a warm hearth. Their majesties await thee with food and drink m'lady." "Both of thee have my thanks oh Thanes of Sigurd," she replied.

When she entered Sigurd's halls and had stomped the snow and mud off of her boots, Eileza felt a rush of emotion for everywhere she looked there were dear memories of those days when she was but a lass and with her Siggy, life had been grand in spite of all that had happened. Lord Gauron appeared and he taking a bow said, "Greetings Princess Eileza. The King and Queen have been told of your arrival ahead of the ambassador and will receive you in the private dining hall." Looking at the two Thanes he said, "I'll take it from here lads. Back to your posts and inform me as soon as Ambassador Althjolf arrives." "Yes Captain," was their reply and the knights returned to the front door.

Just at that moment, a four year old boy with very long red raven hair came running through with a tiny leprechaun boy of the same age running behind him. The boy spun around to meet the leprechaun boy, who leaped upon him, knocking him back against the legs of Princess Eileza. Just then Lilia now aged ten and much larger ran in shouting after the boys, "Enough of this! I'm supposed to be watching the two of you and you shan't get away from me!" When Lilia saw Eileza she stopped dead in her tracks and her entire face lit up with joy like the rising sun itself. "Leeza!" she shouted as she ran to her and grabbed her around the shoulders with the mightiest bear hug that Eileza had had in quite some time. "Oh Leeza; oh Leeza you came home! You really came home to us!" Lila couldn't help but kiss Eileza on both cheeks and Eileza did the same and marveled at how much Lilia had grown these last four years.

The two little boys were at a loss, not knowing who Eileza was and Eileza knew in her heart that the larger of the two boys was Prince Ronan. When Lilia had let her go Eileza gazed at him and made eye contact. The boy was shy and looked down and Eileza said, *"Guten tag."* The boy replied, *"Guten tag."* The leprechaun boy said nothing and Eileza asked, "What are your names?" The taller boy replied, "I'm *Pwence Wonan Sigurdsson."* Eileza was humored by the child's inability to pronounce his R's and smiled and the Leprechaun boy said, "I'm Liam O'Hurleyhune, Son of Shamus and Molly O'Hurleyhune." Liam's face was full of freckles and his hair was rusty red and the boy was no more than a knee height to a standard size human—in fact when Molly bore him he was the size of King Sigurd's hand.

Eileza knelt down and extended her arms out but the children wouldn't come to her. And so she said, "I saw you Ronan when you were born. I was there." Looking at Liam she said, "And you hadn't yet been born when I had to leave. I'm Princess Eileza Andavarsdottir of the Dwarves of Ariemel." Rony's eyes grew big and wide and a smile came across his face and he asked, "Weally? You're my Aunty Weeza that Uncle Siggy always talks about; for weal?" Rony looked down at Liam and said, "She really is beautiful just like Uncle Siggy says." Liam nodded and Eileza blushed. Rony and Liam then took her by her hands and began pulling her along behind them to the dining hall shouting, "Hear ye! Hear ye! It's Pwencess Weeza!"

The lads pulled her into the dining room at a full run and there at the table sat the king and queen and the entire family for something to eat along with Shamus and Molly O'Hurleyhune and all of the Leprechauns along with the Lady Elf Galorfilinde. Ronan and Liam presented their find to the family and Ronan said, "My father my King, its Pwencess

Weeza. We found her we did, Liam and I on our quest." King Sigurd replied, "Now there's a good lad—the king thanks you for your service of bringing home our lost daughter. Here now everyone, give the lads a praise—don't be stoddy." Lord Volsung led everyone there in three cheers saying, "Hip-hip-hurrah! Hip-hip-hurrah! Hip-hip-hurrah!" The boys stood to attention, saluted the king, took a bow, and then doing an about face, the two of them marched out of the room like soldiers as Lila was counting cadence, "Forward, march—up two three four, up two three four, up two three four!"

Gauron smiled and followed the three children out of the room and Eileza and her guards bowed their knees and said loudly and respectfully, "Hail Sigurd King! Hail Gwynnalyn Queen!" King Sigurd replied, "Rise and be seated. We've saved your places. When Ambassador Althjolf arrives as well as the Magyar delegation from Ullich Khan, we shall hold court. In the meanwhile eat and drink Eileza. Austri and Vestri, famous brother of east and west and Thanes of the mighty King Togrobeg, we've ale aplenty for the two of you and skause as well." When they were seated Queen Gwynnalyn said with a happy smile, "Welcome home Eileza. When we got word that you would be coming and saw the post that you sent by the army scouts, we honored thy wish that thy homecoming be a surprise for Sigmund. He's gone for the day on a hunt with the sons of Thonan." She replied, "Thanks majesty. It is good to be home." The queen replied, "We heard the news of the passing of your mother the Dowager Queen. Any day is hard to lose a parent, especially after a holiday and thou havest our sincere condolences." "Thanks my Queen," replied Eileza.

The sand in the hour glass ran down and word was brought to the King by Scap Rolf and Captain Gauron that the Dwarf ambassador had arrived as well as the Magyars and were all assembled in the great hall, awaiting the entrance of their majesties. All were gathering out in the great hall now and Eileza had come out to take her place in the delegation with Ambassador Althjolf when that handsome little boy with long red raven hair ran through the mead hall and behind him was the Wish Maiden, Princess Lila. His ten year old aunt ran behind him trying to catch him. "Ronan, you stop now and wait!" The laughing little freckle faced Prince ran out into the great hall through the door behind the throne and ran headlong into Eileza. Ronan bounced off of her and fell backwards onto the wooden planked floor. He looked sheepishly at Eileza and said, "Swowwy (Sorry) Pwencess Weeza." Lilia pulled Ronan up and dusted him off and said, "Rony, your mum and dah are getting ready to hold court. The Magyars are here; the Dwarves are here and we just really need their help cause of the pikey's so you must calm it down Rony!" Ronan replied, "But what pikey's Aunty Lily?"

Before Lilia could answer, Eileza picked him up and said, "No, not now Rony. You have no need to worry about bad'uns. They're far, far away." She shot Lilia a withering look over Ronan's shoulder as she embraced him and Lilia started to reply, "But…" Eileza cut her off with another withering look and Lilia quickly backed down. They turned to walk back through to the dining hall and Ronan asked, "What's a Slaughter Wolf? Everyone talks about them." Lila started to reply but the Dwarf Princess said sternly, "Lila no!" Eileza replied to Ronan saying, "Just some far away bad'uns that hasn't been here since before you were born."

It was then that the three and half, almost four year old Liam came up and grabbed Ronan by the toe as he was still in Eileza's arms and said, "What're ye doing Rony?" Ronan, looking down at Liam replied, "I dunna know. I been caught that's all." "Oh, ye don't say," replied Liam. Eileza and Lilia took them all back into the dining hall and said, "As soon as court secession is over we got to make plans for Uncle Siggy's birthday party. The children shouted for joy as Eileza led them to the table. Princess Greta rose from the table and said, "I've got these two in hand Eileza. You can go back out to the great hall now.

Molly was wroth at Liam and said, "Oh ye little bucko! Ye're running about like a stampede of prairie cattle ye are!" She looked at Shamus and said, "Well there Mister O'Hurleyhune! What're ye going to do about ye son?" Shamus looked at her in amazement and replied, "Tell me now me darling? Why is it that when the wee lad is in trouble, or back when he was in nappies and the nappies were soiled, was he just, 'my son?'" She replied, "Aye, ye might as well face up to the facts of life Shamus me darling. That's just the way the ball bounces don't ye know." Molly looked over at Greta who was grinning from ear to ear and Greta said, "I'll keep him here with me Molly." Shamus grabbed his son gently by the shirt with one hand and with the index finger of his right hand he lectured Liam saying, "Listen now to ye pappy ye little renegade! If ye don't settle it down I'll be tanning ye hide! If ye as, so much as think about running out of this dining hall and away from Princess Greta, it'll be life on a lee shore for ye Liam! Ye'll ne'er do anything for the rest of ye life than shovel manure in the stables with the servants and ye'll ne'er know the taste of Tanman's sweet cakes and pies! But before that I'll tan ye hide with me strap and ye'll not ever play with Rony again! Now enough is enough! It's time for the king to hold his court and when we're finished, ye better be right here!" Liam replied with his head looking down, "Aye pappy." Shamus replied, "Oh no lad! Look up in me eyes boy!" Liam looked up and his father's gaze bore through him like a hand drill and he said, "Aye pappy. I'll settle down and stay here." Everyone departed as the trumpet fanfare announced the arrival of the king and queen on the Eagle Throne and the start of court. Molly went up the steps to the second floor and then on up the tower stairs where she joined the company of the wizards and the spirit maidens.

CHAPTER V

The Sail Dragon

From the Skald's Tale

Indeed Hister had waited but the Slaughter Wolves were impatient. But in his holding off a massive eastern offensive, in exchange for minor campaigns, Hister allowed Sigurd and his people no true rest of lasting peace and twas during this four year period that little Prince Ronan was weaned and grew in the favor of all who knew him yet in due course he would rise up as a terrible new menace against the dark powers. But for now, there came the green great dragon.

I t was in the spring, on *the 1ˢᵗ day of Gói and Ein-mánuðr, in the five hundred and ninety eighth year of the first age of Midgard on a Þórsdag (Thorsdag [Thursday])*, a group of wide eyed and laughing young Tervingian horsemen were riding across the steppes at full gallop. The young man leading them wore a chain mail armor hauberk as did the other young men with him. "These new horses are the best Gustav!" Gustav replied, "Aye Lord Sigmund! They are indeed!" Behind them rode Lars, Gustav's twin brother as well as fourteen year old Raugust son of Lord Snaevar, along with Gustav and Lars' younger brother Rexor also fourteen years old.

Just then another horseman approached riding as fast as he could towards young Lord Sigmund and his friends. Lars said, "Hey, it's our brother Wenaslaz! I wonder what is wrong." Wenaslaz was one of their older brothers, a young man age twenty two. "Turn around Siggy! Turn around! Get going before it eats us all!" They all met and reined their horses to a stop and soon it was apparent what Wenaslaz was all in fear of. There came a terrible roar and moments later an enormous reptile came over the ridge. Sigmund shrieked, "Oh crikey it's a sail dragon! Let's get the bloody hell out of here!" Gustav was amazed and so he exclaimed, "It's still cold as Hel out here—a sail dragon; all of them are supposed to be in hibernation right now!" "Apparently not this one!" shouted Wenaslaz as he rode by. Come on lads—on the double!"

This kind of dragon ran on four feet but in battle it could stand up like a bear! Its head resembled that of a huge crocodile with an enlarged rounded nose like a knobby ball on the end of his snout. It had rows of teeth just like a crocodile. Behind its head it had very large and muscular shoulders which led into a humped back—and on this humped back there was a massive structure that resembled a ship's sail—a sail with boney spikes protruding from the top of it at one foot intervals. The shape of the sail was thus. It started low in the front going several yards high before lowering once more in the rear at the dragon's tail which was a further ten feet long. This made the sail dragon a total of five fathoms (thirty feet) long. Its legs were five feet tall and from the tip of its savage toe nails to the very tip-top of the highest spines in his sail, this massive beast was two and a half fathoms (thirteen feet) tall.

As they fled in terror from the approach of the charging sail dragon Gustav scowled and looked over at Sigmund saying, "Well Mammoth Rider! What do we do now? What is it with you Siggy? We go out for a ride and there be dragons yonder! How many times does this have to happen?" "What do you mean Gustav? It's not like I plan these things out!" replied Sigmund. Raugust, who was on the horse to the right of Sigmund said, "Why pray tell me is it that every time we have gone out on one of your hunts Siggy do we run into a dragon or a saber toothed tiger?" Sigmund replied, "Give me grief lads! Now's the time to get out whilst we still can! Honest mates I never plan to run into the bloody things—and besides, twas your own brother Wenaslaz that bated the beast in not I, m'lads—really."

As they passed the fields where early springs grasses were beginning show around the melting snow drifts o'er the moist muddy earth the lads could hear the alarm horns of the city bellowing as loud as Wotan's *Gjaller Horn* and could see that the people were fleeing toward the city gates. "We can't let it get to the people before they're all inside the city!" declared Sigmund to all who rode with him. "Good thinking Lord Sigmund," declared Wenaslaz. "We should try and distract the brute long enough for the ballista crews on the wall to get off some shots at it! The only weapon we have that can kill a sail dragon is the ballista. Not even a wind lance will take it out!"

Meanwhile in the city, as the king and queen had officially welcomed ambassador Althjolf and now were discussing an alliance with the Ambassador from the Magyar ruler Ullich Khan, court was interrupted by the blaring of horn blasts. The queen was very glad, for the Magyar ambassador had just made King Sigurd an offer which greatly distressed the queen. It was an offer that would seal the alliance between the Magyars and the Tervingians, but one which would destroy the harmony of the Tervingian royal household.

"What in bloody hel is going on out there?" asked King Sigurd in a loud voice. Gauron ran in saying, "Sire the scouts have spotted a sail dragon on the hunt! He's already at the first ridge and charging in fast!" Queen Gwynnalyn jumped up from her throne and said, "What, in bloody Hel—this time of year, a sail dragon? How odd is that one now. Siggy and the boys were out on a hunt today!" Sigurd cried, "Everyone who can weild a sword or shoot an arrow, follow the queen and I!" The whole assembly rose up at once including the dark haired Magyars. Ambassador Ila-gan smiled and said to Lord Volsung, "Very good of you Tervingians. You welcome us and feed us well, provide good ale—and then arrange a nice fight for my warriors and me." "Twas our pleasure Ambassador," replied Volsung.

The king and queen, along with Lord Gedron and Princess Greta exited the throne room through the rear door behind the throne and headed for the armory. Little Ronan had managed to slip away from Eileza, Lilia and Greta and upon seeing his parents, the child ran to them shouting, "Mum, Dah, wait for me!" Queen Gwynnalyn swept her child into her arms and said, "Rony, now mum and dah have to go run the dragon away from the city. So you need to go back with Aunty Greta to see Grandma." "But I want to see the dwagon mommy!" retorted Ronan. His father brushed little Ronan's long, shoulder length hair out of the child's eyes and said; "One day thou shalt see many dragons my son. But thou must first learn how to fight." "But Dah, Grandpa teaches me and so do uncle Siggy and even mum—but when are you going to teach me?"

Rony was reaching for his father now and the question pierced into the King's heart like an ogre's dagger. The queen turned and looked at the king with the same question in her eyes. The king had been spending so much time conducting the affairs of state that he was beginning to neglect Ronan and so he reached out and took his boy into his arms. "When I return from slaying this dragon, I will take thee to the bear pit and there teach thee the way of valor. That way when I go to Valhalla I know that the son I have will have become a mighty King. "Yes Dahhy King. I'll just wait here then." He planted a kiss on his father's cheek and the queen had a tear in her eye over it all. Just at that moment Greta walked up in search of Rony after having discovered his absence. "Ah there you are you little gazelle," she said to Rony.

The king handed Ronan to Greta who took him with her to the chambers of the Queen Mother. Hearing all the commotion outside and the horns, Princess Eileza handed Liam off to Lilia and rushed out of the dining room, down the hallway and then through the door behind the throne dais. She arrived in time to hear the conversation between Ronan and his father. "A dragon is out there my queen?" she asked. Queen Gwynnalyn answered, "Yes, some sort of sail dragon they say. Siggy is out there somewhere in danger Eileza. Come while the king and I suit up in the Armory in chain mail. There are plenty your size left behind when your tribe went east." Eileza smiled and said, "Thanks but I have my own my queen. I might have known my Siggy Wiggy would get into trouble without me—time to save him." They all marched down the corridor and suited up in the royal armory and were soon met by Galorfilinde the Elf. She said, "There be dragons outside but Sigmund will be safe. He must fulfill his destiny." There was a look of relief on the face of Lord Volsung and everyone there and Eileza said, "Him and me together m'lady Galorfilinde."

At that very moment up in the tower atop the mead hall, the wizards and spirit maidens were observing it all calmly. "When will King Yoshael return Matrona?" asked Min-Tze. Zakarah replied, "He is gone east with Shlomael, but he will return in due course of time when we need him. The Dwarves were in need of his council at Ariemel and also he is taking Giorsal on her long awaited father-daughter journey." Byock and Dithranti sat dinking hot tea. Lady Gladvynn said, "Come Molly, let us go down and find Shamus and Liam." "Aye it sounds like a very good idea. Little Liam will be with Ronan like as not—at least that was where I left him. He's a scamper that one and hard to control when he gets the rabbit in his feet," answered Molly.

At that very same moment all of them felt the presence of an evil force—so much so that they were started. Dithranti said grimly and through narrowed eyes, "There's more to this dragon attack than meets the eye. I feel the presence of a dark force, possessing the dragon, just as happened four years ago at Gergovia." Byock answered, "This lizard should be sleeping for the winter and yet has been awakened by the spirit of Hister. His armies are weak and so he uses this method." Yonas replied, "We must exorcise Hister from the dragon so that the men can either slay it or drive it off before a lot of people die."

The White Wizard of the Centre Midgard, the Faun Lord High Elder Aesop was there with his wife the Spirit Maiden Vulcrus and he said, "We can best rid ourselves of this blackheart from the Thorstadt Stonehenge." Molly said, "Aye but there's no time from the sound of it all." Gladvynn agreed saying, "Molly is right. We can do this from the city gate just as you did in Gergovia my father." The old Celtic Wizard replied, "And so shall it be. We can do this from the eastern gatehouse atop the battlements. Let's go." They all ran down the steps following Dithranti and once down on the ground floor of the great hall, Molly and Gladvynn broke off and went to the dining hall to see about Liam for they knew that there mustn't be any fear, trepidation or worry concerning her small child when it came time for Molly to excercise her power with the Heart of the Sea.

Two huge birds flew past the city. They were great white eagles and when Dithranti saw them he smiled. "Not to worry folks. Clovis and Merovinge are on the job." Merovinge said to Clovis, "Oh love here we go again. Another beastie on the hunt like as not." At that moment the dragon came over the ridge! Clovis replied, "Would you look at the size of that thing! It seems we're batting a sticky wicket today darling." She replied, "Not so much as us love but poor Sigmund down there!" He answered, "Right you are darling. We better fly on down there and lend a hand. Jolly good show. There's something a bit odd about this dragon. It's rare for them to be out of hibernation this time of year or to come so close to a city like this unless the beasty is starved; or manipulated by sorcerery. We've seen a lot of mastodon bones around that must have been dragon slain so I'd say that some other motive is driving the old fellow forward."

People were crowding through the gates as fast as they could. However there was another, strictly military gate that King Sigurd had ordered constructed four years ago just after the great battle. It was through this gate that King Sigurd and his queen led an army of four hundred horsemen as well as Ila-gan and his fifty Magyar Horse Archers. "Look my King! It is Sigmund and the boys!" cried the queen. He replied, "Yes my heart! And look at them. They're with Wenaslaz trying to lure the beast away and save those wagons trying to get into the main gate! Let's go help!" Eileza was going as well and she rode her pony Silvertopp, for nothing was going to keep her from being away from Sigmund any longer especially in a moment of danger.

Far away in his forbidding fortress of doom Adawulf Hister Carpathia was in deep concentration—alone in the chamber which housed his mysterious new orb and the Scyring Chalice. His power had grown again since his stinging defeat four years ago and the stalemate and see-saw, back and forth horse archer battles of the last four years and so now the *Ruler of the Dark North*, or so he styled himself was back up to his old and more serious tricks—not only plotting against King Sigurd, but against the wizards, the spirit maidens and the druids for whom his hatred knew no bounds. Through the eyes of his Huggin spies Hister had discovered a sleeping sail dragon, a mere dumb beast. And so with malice of heart he extended his spirit into the beast in order to possess it as if he were a jötunn and easily took control of its body in order to use it as if it were his own. "Today I shall strike a blow at my enemies!" quoth he in a mood of dark but evilly happy madness—as his spirit projected through the Scyring Chalice and enhanced by the strange new crystal orb. This orb was the pupil of the All Seeing Eye and it began glowing reddish flame and orange like the setting sun—yet having a black slit up and down the middle. This frightening feature made the entire object appear like the eye of a dragon or a serpent.

With the spirit of Hister burning in its eyes the sail dragon came in hot pursuit Sigmund and the boys who were riding around it in circles! Hister saw that it was Sigmund and said to himself, "So it's the Volsung whelp! We meet again at last, guardian of the man child!" The sail dragon struck at them trying to get one or more into its mouth. It was dinner time for him and Siggy seemed like a nice crunchy morsel to snack on! He just barely missed Sigmund but it was due to the fact that Merovinge and Clovis flew in and attacked the dragon's head with their talons that saved Siggy and when they'd turned the beast away from Siggy they twain flew up and out of its reach as quickly as possible. The dragon jumped up to bite at them as would a fish going after a mosquito but the changelings were much too quick for him, and when the massive reptile landed on his hind legs the ground shook beneath him.

Lord Gedron got the last of the wagons through the main gate and then ran up the stairs to the top of the fortifications to be with the ballista crews! Seeing Sir Horsa and Sir Anton he said, "Shouldn't you boys be with the scouts?" Horsa replied, "We needed training on the ballista and today was our turn." "Well it looks like today we all get some real training. It seems like my little brother has stirred up the beast today!" Anton laughed and replied, "He grows more like you every day Lord Gedron." There was a round of affectionate laughter. Down at the next tower to their right they could see Lord Raedwald commanding a crew, and in the other direction, the ballista crew on the tower was commanded by Sir Radau, who'd once been a Royal Thane and a great knight of the late King Osrik of the Gepids.

Twas then that the massive sail dragon stood up on its hind legs, and let out a mighty roar! Sigmund and the young warriors began a hasty retreat toward the king and his cavalry with whom they soon joined forces. However Sigmund had not as yet noticed that Eileza was there in all the swirl and rush of horsemen and fleeing peasants. Queen Gwynnalyn was fully dressed in her armor and helm and ready for a fight. She said, "Ok Siggy. Who's the new friend you brought home? Don't you think that he's a bit big for a pet?" She was smiling and the king said, "Here it comes on its hind legs! We have to lure it in close so that the ballista's can fire as many bolts into the monster as possible! Let's go!" Lord Volsung saw the eyes of the dragon, and they appeared not as the eyes of a serpent, but red balls of burning flame with no pupils. "There's an evil spirit in the beast!" cried Volsung. "See ye the eyes?"

At that moment Sigmund saw Eileza as she moved from behind Queen Gwynnalyn and as their eyes met both of their hearts fluttered and their stomachs were instantly filled with the collywobbles. A rush of joy filled the young man's heart as he saw for the first time in four long years the beloved girl of his dreams and the love of his life. She hadn't grown any taller since he last saw her but she was much more physically mature and shapely and that fact wasn't lost on Sigmund even in the midst of these dragon troubles. She was even more beautiful than he remembered. Her blue-black hair was longer, thicker and darker than before, but her skin was still swarthy brown and smooth, and her eyes still as dark and piercing as they were on the day that he had first saw her five years ago. He thought to himself, "Four years ago my girl went away and look, she's come back a woman—indeed a very beautiful and woman." His heart melted in love as he gazed upon the most magnificent creature he'd ever seen. They say that 'absence makes the heart grow fonder' and for Sigmund the Volsung that was an understatement when it came to his beloved Eileza.

Eileza saw how much more Siggy had grown and how he, from the size of his shoulders, appeared much more muscular with a light, thin coating of a moustache. "Siggy Wiggy, Siggy Wiggy!" she cried out in joy. Sigmund cried out in equal joy as they rode at full gallop towards each other, "Leeza, you're here!" "You're bloody right Siggy. I wouldn't miss a good dragon fight. You ought to know that by now Siggy, and I say when you stir up a lizard you do it all in double sizes! Where'd you find old teethy face at anyway?" In spite of the sail dragon, Sigmund was weeping for joy to see his long lost love after four long years.

As they rode back towards the menace side by side and now well out in front of the king and queen and the knights he replied, "Well you know me Leeza, if you're going to get into trouble, make it big. At least it's not an Ogre pack this time." She smiled back and standing up in the stirrups of her saddle she reached up and over from the back of Silvertopp and she softly punched him on the shoulder and replied sheepishly as she batted her eyes at him, "Oh Siggy, Ogres schmoegers!"

Being unable to help themselves they reached for each other from across their horses. But it was awkward since she was on a shaggy steppe pony and as she stood up in the stirrups, Sigmund pulled her from her pony with a burst of strength and onto his own horse. She felt the welcome embrace of his strong arms and as their lips met, the sounds of the dragon and the commotion made by all of the men at arms seemed to go almost silent as tears of joy filled their young eyes as they passionately kissed each other. "I've waited so long for thee Siggy Wiggy," she sobbed in joy. "He replied both sobbing and laughing at the same time, "Where hast thou been all my life Leezee Weezee Sneezy Deezy. Every day I've missed thee my beautiful dear heart!" The young woman answered passionately, "We shan't ever be apart again my Siggy Wiggy Miggy Diggy." Both star crossed lovers were feeling such emotion for one another till they were having sobs of happiness and joyful reunion. Their tears of joy mingled on their touching cheeks but the roar of the dragon brought them back into this world and they made ready for the fight. Eileza pushed away and leaped like a hart onto the back of her pony *Silfrtopp* (Silvertopp).

King Sigurd and Queen Gwynnalyn who were riding side by side, him on his white war horse Yggdrasil and her on her golden mare Gullfaxi saw the romantic reunion taking place up in front of them some distance away in spite of the chaos of the dragon fight and they looked at one another. Their eyes met and both felt the same emotion towards one another that the young people out ahead were feeling and the king said, "Grim would be the day that I would be forced to part with thee My Heart." She replied, "I belong only in thy arms My Hunter—forever and always."

Lord Gedron saw the reunion of Sigmund and Eileza from the top of the tower and smiled in happiness for he knew that his little brother would have died every day of a broken heart had Eileza not come home. Sir Horsa and the knights saw it as well and he said, "Shouldn't you be seeking a bride M'Lord? You deserve to be as happy as the young lad out there and his betrothed." Gedron replied with a huge smile, "I've a good prospect mates but methinks my lips are sealed for the moment."

Shamus O'Hurleyhune had been in the court meeting the Magyars when all this fuss arose and he and the laddies, Aonghus Killian, Fearghal Bronach and Ruairi O'Flannin headed to the palace dining hall and found Liam there with Lilia. Shamus and the laddies went to the table and sat down. Liam climbed onto his father's lap and it wasn't long before Molly and Lady Gladvynn joined them. "There's quite a beastie outside the city," said Shamus. "I want to go up on the wall and have a look see." "Aye go then me husband. But ye'll ne'er take Liam with ye!" "No, no me darling Molly, I would not dare take him up there."

She continued to retort him but with a smile and in jest, "And did ye think ye were going to leave me behind with Liam? I want to see the beastie as well and Dithranti says that Hister possesses the thing!" Shamus replied, "Oh now it's just like he tried to do with Llygaid Coch! He's a bloody egit this Hister and he deserves a baytin he does! Well Princess Lilia is doing a fine job sitting with Liam and he'll not give her the slip." Lila relied, "Right you are Herr Shamus. I know all the tricks because I used to pull all of the tricks when I was a little kid too." Liam slipped from his father's lap and sat up on the table facing Shamus.

Lady Gladvynn spoke up saying, "I want to stay here as well but we've got to get to the gatehouse. I've seen enough dragons in my lifetime laddies and if Hister is in this one he must be stopped." Fearghal, with his ever present stalk of barley in his mouth said, "Aye I've seen dragons before. If ye seen one sail dragon ye seen 'em all. If ye'er going out there so am I." Everyone knew that Fearghal loved Gladvynn and that was why he wanted to go with her to the wall. It would be quite a match if those two were ever to be married, Gladvynn being so tall and he being a wee little Leprechaun—but stranger things had happened before in Midgard.

Greta was there with Rony in her arms and Molly placed a gentle hand on Liam's shoulder. "Come Liam. Come to Mummy now darling." The little Leprechaun child jumped down and came to his mother and Molly kissed him and said, "Now I want ye to stay here with Aunty Lilia and Aunty Greta and little Rony. You'll stay here with Rony and not run away—there's a dragon outside and ye must stay put." "Aye Mummy," Liam replied. Shamus leaned forward and looked Liam right in the eye saying, "And let me be telling ye Liam. If ye get the rabbit in ye feet and gives'em the slip it'll be ye who gets the baytin. Ye stay put lad and obey Lilia or it'll be life on a lee shore for ye me bucko! Understand boy?" The tiny leprechaun child replied, "Aye pappy. I promise to stay put with Lilia, no matter where she goes."

Shamus began to turn away with a smile saying, "Aye then—all's well me son." Just then a thought crossed Shamus' mind and pulling off his derby hat he jerked back around and looking at Liam and pointing an index finger of suspicion he saith, "Oh know ye don't." "What meaneth ye pappy?" begged Liam in frustration, "I promised to stay with Lilia." Shamus replied, "And that don't mean ye go and talk her into to taking ye out into danger. There'll be none of that! Understand ye me?" Liam knew that his father had caught on to his plan and so with a sigh of defeat he said, "Aye pappy. I shan't a do it." "There now," replied Shamus as he hugged his child warmly. Molly was smiling and said, "Liam ye father knows all the mischief ye can ere do because he did it all the same to his mammy and pappy back home! Shamus, our Liam is a chip off the old block as me pappy Connor used to say. Never tell the lad about the *Shamus Rampage* or it's off to the peat bogs with ye." As they were departing Liam asked anxiously, "What was the Shamus rampage pappy?" whereupon Molly kissed Liam on the check and said, "Ne're ye mind son," as Molly picked him up and placed him into the waiting arms of Lilia and Rony said, "Well Liam it looks like we're stuck here again holding down the castle."

With Liam secured, Shamus led the way and the Leprechauns and Gladvynn left the Mead Hall heading out to the main western gate— where they took their places—well out of the way of Lord Gedron and his ballista crew. The other wizards and spirit maidens were there ahead of them and Gladvynn said to Molly, "It's time. Take out the Heart of the Sea." They heard the roar of the giant reptile and Molly said, "I don't believe me eyes! That's the strangest dragon in Midgard!" She was terrified by the sight of it and Gladvynn said, "Have no fear my spirit learner. Take the Heart of the Sea into your hands and let it be our Dolman."

Molly reached into her dress into took the magnificent and magical gemstone from underneath her garments and holding it high above her head it began to glow as she faced the direction of the dragon. Dithranti held his staff in the air beside her and as the others gathered around them in a circle and locking hands the wind began to blow. In the meanwhile on the other side of the river, the power of the Dolman in the Thorstadt Stonehenge was awakened as well and quite suddenly a great and towering black thunder cloud appeared over the city. Lightening flashed and thunder crashed as the power of the earth was harnessed and channeled yet again. This was true magic, powered by love and the natural power of the earth, as opposed to witchcraft and sorcery—which was the art of power for power's sake in order to control and dominate others against their will.

Seeing through the eyes of the dragon, Hister saw Molly holding up the Heart of the Sea with Dithranti by her side as well as Byock and the others in a circle of power around them. "There it is! There it is! It's the Heart of the Sea!" he snarled. Now everyone heard the voice of Hister speaking through the beast and knew that once more, the Kingdom was being assailed by the dark powers. Hister's demonic possession forced the great reptile up and now the beast was running at them on its hind legs and from out of its mouth went the sorcerer's evil laugh echoing through the wind and the storm. Dithranti was shouting, "Hister! Thou shall not pass, thou wicked servant of Loki! You have no power here! Thou art nameless here! In the name of *Dan Ene Gud*, thou art cast out from the dragon!"

The wind took Dithranti's hat off of him and blew it into the street behind the gate as King Sigurd and his warriors rode in circles around the beast, firing arrows which would not penetrate the scaly armor of the sail dragon. Sigurd looked and saw Dithranti and Molly up on the gatehouse and shouted, "The wizards are out! This dragon must be possessed of a jötunn!" "It has to be Hister again!" shouted Queen Gwynnalyn, "He's back!" The voice of Hister roared as the sound of many waters from the mouth of the dragon and said, "Yes wench queen I am! And today Sigmund dies—for he shan't guard the man child nor mentor the whelp!" She shouted back in defiance, "Not today or ever thou son of a pig dog! Before long thy kingdom shall be gone and I'll stand over thy broken corpse and drink to the victory of the Mighty Griffin!"

The dragon was now within fifty yards of the wall when suddenly the Heart of the Sea seemed to expand into a big ball of blue light. Dithranti extended the end of his staff towards the dragon and everyone in the circle including Molly said, "Be gone servant of Loki, back into the darkness of thy abode!" The light was like the sun shining in its strength and the spirit of Hister could no longer stand in the presence of the Holy Lamp and so was forced from the body of the dragon.

Back at Kol Oba Hister fell backwards from the Scyring Chalice and onto the floor with his right arm over his eyes, for indeed the light had momentarily blinded him. The power drained from both the stone chalice and the pupil of the All Seeing Eye as Hister lay panting on the floor trying to catch his breath. Once he had regained himself Hister stood up and noticed that Argob and Throostra had at last arrived. In a calm tone he said, "Our setback is due to the combined strength of the enemy." Throostra asked, "Then we too must gain more allies, just as they have gained druids and others." "What do you propose my young apprentice?"

asked a sly sounding Hister. The Gnome replied, "It is time to call upon the help of the Witch King Thrain. He's a demigod and my sister Volva has influence with him—surely we need him now."

Hister was angered by the suggestion and said, "Never! I have been promised the rule of Midgard by Loki and Thrain would disadvantage me and usurp my rights! Only when Ragnarok comes shall our Lord Loki call upon Thrain. And besides all of that, not even Loki can trust Thrain—how much the less can we trust him? Let him be Dark Lord in Valland, for I'm Dark Lord here! Do not speak to me of Thrain. Let the witches worship him, for I will not." "But is he not of your blood?" asked Argob. Hister grew angry and said, "Only in the remote past and that only by a fluke! Speak to me not of Thrain for there cannot be two kings here! When this is over I shall have the power to vanquish Thrain as well and so Valland is of no consequence!"

The sail dragon came out of his trance and was very confused as to how it was that he'd come to be in this predicament. The last thing that he knew, he'd been safe in a nice warm cave and now here he was, out here in the winter and freezing cold. This would have put any fellow into a foul mood and this sail dragon was no exception. He shook his head violently back and forth trying to regain his senses, and twas then that he saw all of the men around him. The beast began to give chase. "His eyes have changed back to normal—the jötunn is gone! Now Horsa, fire the bolt! The king and Sigmund are leading him to us!" cried Lord Gedron.

The great weapon swacked and the bolt swished as it flew and embedded itself into the chest of the beast! Two more bolts from Raedwald's crew and from Radau's crew found their mark. As the energy from exorcism died off and the winds began to calm down, the dragon let loose from its nose a flow of near liquid flames that struck Radau and his men! The top of the tower and the ballista itself caught fire killing the warriors. Radau had given his life defending the city.

The wizards, spirit maidens and the leprechauns ran down the back stairs and out through the gate. The dragon turned away with blood gushing from its wounds. It stumbled over the ridge and died. The King and his troops followed slowly behind it and watched it fall. "We should bring a ballista out and make sure it is dead, "declared Ila-gan. The King answered, "No Ambassador. We have done enough. This beast will be allowed to die in honor. Unlike the Scythians, this sail dragon had no personal vendetta to service—and he himself has become a victim of Hister. Ila-gan replied, "You are most noble and mighty my Lord King. Now I see why you are called the Mighty Griffin." Sigurd replied, "I am not the griffin Ila-gan. Not I but the men, the knights and the shield maidens who give their all for their families. They are the mighty griffins not I."

The King saw that the sail dragon had breathed its last and said, "We will carve this body and then burn the rest in a pyre. There is enough meat for the whole city if any choose to consume. A cheer went up from the warriors but Eileza had a look of yuck on her face. She said, "Nope! Not I Siggy. I don't eat sail dragon or any other kind of lizard bake." He replied, "It probably tastes like chicken." "You eat it Siggy! I'm not touching it. Oh that nasty smell, can't you smell that smell Siggy? Nope. I'll pass."

The two of them looked over at Queen Gwynnalyn to see what her reaction was. She proclaimed aloud, "There is meat for all—for those who want to chance it, thanks to Prince Sigmund who stirred the beast up for whoever wants to eat it. All hail the Mammoth rider!" Sigmund looked at Gwynnalyn in desperation and cried, "But I didn't stir it up this time!" King Sigurd changed the entire subject and said to the people, "On the fourteenth of the month, young Lord Sigmund will be seventeen years old. We have much to prepare for and to all of our joy, Princess Eileza Andavarsdottir has returned to us, and to Sigmund. There shall be a gala celebration in the mead hall in honor of the Mammoth Rider! All cheer for Sigmund, who has not received a gift, but has given his hungry people a great feast—for those who relish such meat at any rate! I shan't partake myself but leave it all to those with less refined tastes than myself. "The warriors began chanting, "Sigmund! Sigmund! Sigmund!" Eileza was cheering at the top of her lungs. Gustav looked at Lars and Raugust and said, "I'd like to know what lucky charm he has." "Well it covers you Wenaslaz. You were the one who went down and shot at it!" stated Lars. The older brother replied, "It was on me before I ever shot at it lads. Twas the sorcerer's doing and not mine."

Sir Arnlaugr rode up and delivered a message to the king and then rode away and the countenance of the king fell. The Queen came up close beside King Sigurd and said, "That was a good thing you did for Siggy. Otherwise people would have blamed him for stirring up the sail dragon and being reckless, in spite of Hister's involvement in all of this. But you turned it into a triumph for him. But as far as eating lizard My Hunter; I shan't be touching it. Besides have we not learned from the Elves what is proper to eat My Hunter? Reptile meat is wont to make one sick—but many of our people have yet to take up the elvish diet in spite of our encouragement." Sigurd replied in jest, "But it tastes like chicken My Heart." She replied," You eat it darling! I'm sticking to skause with normal meat—elk lamb or beef—since I've started eating meat again. No lizard and no swine."

She could see that the Mighty Griffin was sad and so removing her helm she asked, "What is wrong My Hunter? I can see from the look on thy face that sad news has come to thee. What did Sir Arnlaugr say to thee that thy crest is so fallen?" He replied, "Yes My Heart. Once more I have received word that my mother Aslaug and brother Rognir are nowhere to be found; even after the word we received all those years ago—four years and nothing!" Gwynnalyn looked into his eyes and placing her arms on his shoulders said, "I haven't given up and neither wilt thou My Hunter. There're still ten search parties out investigating and tracking down all leads. They'll return to us Sigurd—and when they do, we shall celebrate the reunion of our family. I love thee so much My Hunter."

CHAPTER VI

Love's flickering Fireside

From the Skald's Tale

By the light of a flickering fire was a proposal made—one of a gallant young knight to his lady fair. To her was his heart pledged and the sweet flame of romance energized the beating hearts of Sigmund the Volsung and Princess Eileza Andavarsdottir.

T wo weeks of joyful days did Sigmund and Eileza spend together, spending private moments in loves embrace and trying to make up for the last four years. She told Sigmund about the passing of Rutia but went into few details, promising to tell him the entire story after they were married. They were seen out and about by the townsfolk, riding their horses or spending a bit of time in the Crow's Beak Tavern over a few drinks, listening to the minstrels and watching the *Schuhplatter dancers*.

On one day Molly and the Leprechauns leaned over the wall waving to them above the gate, and as soon as the royal couple had passed under them and were exiting the fortress gate into the city they ran over to watch them going up the main street towards the Mead Hall. Lord Gedron remained on the gate supervising the crew as it worked on the ballista, for who knew if Hister would send yet another dragon.

The king and queen went out with the family and their Magyar guests one day for a ride and a hunt in the cold air, but finding no game about they had all returned to the Mead Hall. The king and queen, along with Sigmund, Eileza and Galorfilinde Elf returned to the royal armory and removed their chain mail. It was then that little Prince Rony ran through the door with Liam on his tails and not far behind was Lady Gladvynn and Fearghal Bronach. Fearghal was saying, "Aye now boys ye canno run away from us like this!" He said, "Sorry my queen, but ye mum had some business and brought little Rony back to us and now he and Liam up and scampered away when he heard you all were back." Queen Gwynnalyn held out her arms and Rony jumped into them and hugged her. "It's quite alright Herr Bronach. Rony and Liam are a handful," replied the queen with a smile.

As the day grew late, the king and queen had a final session with the Magyars, and then took a private meal in their chambers with little Rony. The Royal Chef Master and Brewer, Tanman and his wife Lady Sandilin brought in a hot meal and fresh ale for the king and his family. It was good Skause, a soup made of hot brisket, barley and vegetables for them all, with fresh bread. There was a plate of fried fish for the king but the queen did not savor fish unless she was starving. Rony loved both skause and fish and for him Tanman had made a sweet desert of strawberry preserves. When

Rony saw it his eyes lit up and a huge smile crossed his small face and he exclaimed, *"Danke Herr Tanman!"* (Thank you Mister Tanman) The queen gave her boy a stern look and using formal language in order to get her point across saith, "Oh no little prince. Thou shalt only eat that after thou hast finished the rest of thy food!" Rony dropped his eyes down to the table and replied in a defeated voice, "Yes Mum."

When Tanman and Sandilin had left they ate and had a nice family evening there in the lamp light of their private chambers. The queen held Rony in her arms and rocked the child to sleep in their large rocking chair and then when he was fast asleep and the queen saw that his eyes were moving rapidly back and forth beneath his closed lids, she laid him in his bed and tucked him in. Sigurd and Gwynnalyn kissed their son and themselves retired to their bed.

Once they were snuggled in Sigurd said, "I am quite disturbed over the news that came in from the west my Heart." "You mean about the Centaurs My Hunter?" "Yes my heart. Remember we had only thought them to be legendary. How can there be a beast which is half man and half horse? It just seems to go against the natural order." She replied, "Indeed it does My Hunter, but if this report be true, that these Centaurs are real, and have aligned with the Slaughter Wolves, then it stands to reason that the legends we have heard out of Hellas about the Minotaurs must be true. The body of a man with the head of a bull is also unnatural! Hister has to be behind this and through him Loki!"

Sigurd sighed and held Gwynnalyn in his arms with her head resting on his chest with her hair loose and undone for the night. He replied, "This has been rather a phony war since the great battle at Rony's birth. Hister really wanted Rony dead and all of us remember that Lilith, the Huldra would have killed both of thee and even stole Giorsal back—had it not been for the Sons and Daughters of Light. I fear that war will soon come to us again My Heart."

She could hear in his voice a slight tremble and knew that he needed to be supported and encouraged. She rose up and crossed both of her arms over his chest and rested her head thereon and when she did, their eyes locked gaze and it seemed as if they were looking into one another's soul, so very close were they. "She gave him a soft and warm kiss and then said, "To Halja with the Centaurs and Minotaurs My Hunter! We're a strong and brave people and thou art a great and mighty king who loves us all. We shall triumph over all of them My Hunter. Goblins or Gargoyles, human or not so human! We shall win and Rony will grow into the future King that he was prophesied to be by the Elves." She smiled and gave him another kiss and said, "I'm on thy side My Hunter and not even death can separate me from thee! I love thee—so much so that thou canst not even imagine how deep it is and together we shall win the ultimate victory, so help us God!"

He knew that Gwynnalyn his soul mate was indeed a gift from Asgard and his greatest ally. He replied, "Thou havest all my love my queen and I shan't ever forsake thee and Rony. Some kings take many wives and this makes for evil in the household—the children of one wife conspiring against those of another and thus civil war happens. King Yoshael once said that in the beginning, *The One God* created one man for one woman. He called that man Adam, and the woman he called Havah. Therefore I will refuse the offer of the Magyar Khan to send his sister here as a second wife to seal our alliance. I shall not break my vow to you as a husband My Heart nor ever shall I seek the chambers of another woman such as most kings eventually do. How dare Ullich Khan even purpose such a thing for all the kings of the steppes no My Heart in this matter! This is the kind of thing that Idanthrsus and the Scythians and his Serpent Maidens do and it isn't my way." She replied with a very happy look and said, "I am glad My Hunter; for I could not bear the thought of another woman sharing your embrace." Sigurd reached over and trimmed the lamp for the night and shared loving romance the night long with her for whom all his attentions were made manifest.

The Circle of the Spirit Maidens and the Sons of Light gathered out in the Thorstadt Stonehenge that evening. King Yoshael and Prince Shlomael were still away on his mission to the Dwarves. Zakarah said, "Galorfilinde my daughter, thou hast done well over the years as has Shlomael. Now we must prepare your daughter Aubriel for her mission here." Galorfilinde replied, "She will make a good Norn. The Dwarf King will soon remarry and in due course of time an heir to the throne of Ariemel will be born. When thou said unto me that I should choose a Norn from among my children I chose Aubriel. She is young and spirited; barely one hundred yet some in the world of men will mistake her for being the same age as a human girl in her teens. Of course Mother, thou knowest all of this. Thou art her grandmother and were Midwife when she was born. Mishael and I feel she is ready and the Dvärg child will need a Norn. "Zakarah replied, "Good choice. She stands out among my many grandchildren. Is she on her way?" Galorfilinde replied, "Even now, though the late winter and early spring throes are still across the land, she's made the decent off of the pack ice. Many soldiers are with her and methinks she'll arrive here in Thorstadt in a week or so—depending on the weather." Zakarah then said, "Mishael misses thee so very much. This knoweth me—but I also know that he's acting very well as thy father's *Prince Regent* in Alfheim. The daily day to day affairs of our kingdom must be attended to and Mishael has distinguished himself."

Dithranti said, "This phony war phase will soon come to an end and what the visions have told me are portends most ill, at least in the short term." Yonas replied, "I have foreseen it as well brother Dithranti, as has Byock and Aesop. The black tower Hister is building continues to rise to fulfill his evil purpose—a new *Tower of Babel*." Byock said, "Hister continues to obtain the pieces of the All Seeing Eye for the temple that he intends to build atop that profane monument—the power of Babel must not raise again in Midgard." Aesop responded saying, "Yes, but as long as Molly has the Heart of the Sea, the Holy Lamp, the Eye will not function as it was designed and the gateway shall remain sealed." Vulcrus then said, "Hister will soon try to possess the Holy Lamp." She looked at Molly and said, "Hister will attack you, but we here, though we be few, are one."

Min Tze came into the conversation and said, "Molly you have grown over these last four years in knowledge and power of holiness. Soon you will be the *Spirit Maiden of Erin.*" Lady Boudicca smiled and took Molly by the hand saying, "Gladvynn, Spirit Maiden of Brython has trained you well and you have been one of the best Spirit Learners I've ever seen. *Dan*

Ene Gud has called you from birth for this task and you will soon have the honor to join the Circle of the Spirit Maidens. Also, I see in my Spirit that you and Shamus have conceived. In eight months you will give birth to a girl." Molly was not surprised that the Spirit Maidens already knew even though she hadn't said a word. They could see the fire of the soul of the unborn child, glowing like a bright and holy fire torch within her womb. "Have you told Shamus yet?" asked Gleadra. "No, not as yet M'lady but I soon will. Me little Liam is going to have a sister."

Sigmund with Eileza sitting pressed against his side ate supper with other the Leprechauns in the private royal dining hall, for Tanman's servants had served up racks of Elk ribs from a fresh kill. Across the table from Sigmund and Eileza sat young Lilia. Their Sister Greta soon joined them as well as their father Volsung and Mother Gerda. With them was the powerful warrior of the Tervingian Thyssagetae, the Reik *Radagaisus*. Since the entire royal family of this tribe had been killed four years ago in the war, this man, now age twenty six, had risen up and became the leader of these people within the United Kingdom of Tervingia. Yet he secretly desired the old order and had become fast friends with Lord Hodbrodd. The queen had no trust in him whatsoever and hated the fact that Greta was in love with him. But many others also called into question his true character, for he was a man of the taverns and hemp lodges and frequented the Crow's Beak Tavern and other pubs throughout the realm on his business. At other times Lord Radagaisus went away on long hunting trips in the Jarlstan area with Hodbrodd.

Somehow during all this and he'd managed to lure Lady Greta into a relationship with him. Greta had promised herself to Sigurd's brother Rognir—but alas with his disappearance five years ago and no word since—she'd given Rogy up for dead and fallen in love with Radagaisus, the second most detested man in the court after Hodbrodd. And yet Lord Volsung allowed it, for he refused to entangle himself in Greta's heart matters—unless her intended began abusing Greta in any way.

Radagaisus took his seat next to Greta and all eyes were on them now in anticipation of some announcement, and the younger Volsung daughter looked back at everyone and the room fell into a dead silence. Greta said, "Father I've thought long and hard and yes, I want to marry Lord

Radagaisus. We love each other so very much and this will bring the one I love home to me and the loyally of the Thyssagetae to King Sigurd and this house—to which they pledged four years ago at the coronation." Lila mumbled to Eileza under her breath, "So that's why Greta doesn't have tea parties with me and Briggy anymore!" Queen Gwynnalyn put her forehead into the palm of her hand in utter shock and Greta flashed an ugly look at her elder sister. But Gwynnalyn wouldn't dare usurp their father the Lord Volsung in this matter even though she was the Queen of Tervingia and most certainly Sigurd wouldn't either—even though he was concerned about what would happen should Rognir return home.

The marriage question had been asked of her a year ago and when Greta had informed her sister a violent argument had broken out—one that nearly come to blows and was only silenced by the thundering intervention of Volsung. And now Greta had given her answer. Volsung replied, "Very well Greta. I will let thy mother take charge from here on and you can let us know when the wedding will take place. Come now Radagaisus; let us go to the bear pit and have a talk—about taverns and hemp lodges." He looked back at Sigmund and said, "Son, if thou doest what thou hast told me you were going to do, follow all that I have told thee and everything will work out." Sigmund replied, "Yes father I will." Eileza looked at Siggy with a knowing glance over her elk ribs.

Volsung left with Radagaisus and immediately the room was full of chatter. Eileza jumped up with a huge smile and ran to Greta and hugged her. The Queen mother was one huge smile (ignoring Gwynnalyn's scowling anger) and Sigmund went to his sister and hugged her saying, "Congratulations on thy dream coming true Sis." The Leprechauns were thrilled and joined the circle around Greta and Shamus had little Liam on his shoulders. "Aye laddies, this calls for a round of ale!" exclaimed Ruairi. Aonghus said, "Aye so where's the Royal Butler Mister Tanman? Someone go fetch the lad and have him serve up a round of ale for us all and a dram of Red McTavish." Fearghal smiled a teethy smile with his barley stalk gripped in them tightly and said, "Well me boys, it looks like we get two celebrations for the price of one." "I shall take my leave of this party," stated the queen and so taking her ladies in waiting she departed without speaking to either Greta or Radagaisus.

Molly, who was wearing her long emerald green dress, with her long red hair hanging loose and tumbling about her shoulders soon joined them from upstairs and when Shamus informed her of the joyful news, she jumped up on the table and went to Greta to congratulate her with a hug. Liam jumped from his father's shoulders and onto the table and was soon by his mother's side, laughing and carrying on in joy even though he had no clue as to why all of this was happening. He only knew that everyone was happy and Greta was more than happy to take the little child into her arms in a group hug with Molly and Shamus, both of whom were now standing on the table as well. Tanman was soon there with the ale and even Greta swigged down a mug or two once she had sat Liam down to play with Rony.

Soon it was time to leave for the night. Gerda said, "Come Lilia, time to get ready for bed. Greta, let's get back to chambers and get started with wedding plans, and finish up with plans for Siggy's birthday tomorrow. Greta sighed and said in a bit of anger, "I can see that Gwynnalyn approves not of my happy state. When she gets an idea into her head about someone she can't get it out no matter how wrong she is mum and I'm tired of it!" Greta now whispered sarcastically," But what can I do? She's the Queen of Midgard. But I've trained as a shield maiden in the bear pits as much or more than she and when the tournaments come I'll challenge her. What else can I do?"

Gerda wanted to maintain peace and harmony between her children and said, "I've always hated the tourneys, especially now that women are allowed to join in that madness Greta. It's bad enough that I have to see my boys out in the joust—but my daughters as well! Really Greta, that isn't the way. She'll come round my dearest—you'll see." Greta whispered her angry reply, "I should think she'd already have come around! It's been a year." Gerda put an arm around her youngest daughter and said, "I think that she's upset, hoping that Rognir would return and you could still marry him—the king's brother as had been planned." Greta said, "Mum, I loved Rognir but it's been four years now since the flood which took him and Aslaug over the falls in the Fells of Ararat and I don't think he's ever coming home. He's dead and I've accepted that, even though no one else has." She and Gerda left the room.

Molly looked worriedly at Shamus after over hearing all of that and said, "We better go ourselves. We need to get Liam tucked in for the night and as well I have a wee spot of good news for you." She smiled and squeezed Shamus' hand. Then with Liam on her shoulders, Molly, hand in hand with Shamus they leaped down to the floor and Liam giggled with joy as the family ran out of the dining hall.

As the excitement began to die down, Eileza headed to the door, and then turned to see Sigmund watching her. She gave him a sideways motion with her head to follow her and the two of them swiftly exited the dining hall. Lilia started to follow but they rudely turned her back. "Oh alright Siggy, have it your way Leeza! Maybe Briggy will want to do something before she has to go to bed!" Lilia stomped off very offended.

Sigmund and Eileza went into King Osrik's old chamber and then with a lamp in hand went into the tunnel, checking to make sure Lila wasn't sneaking along behind them. It was damp and musty and and a bit cold and yet for these two it was warm—for it held memories dear and most precious to them. There were cob webs to bust through but this didn't bother the princess. "We're not running away again are we Leeza?" asked Sigmund in in jest. "I mean, there's Ogres out there!" She laughed and replied, "Oh Siggy Wiggy, Ogres schmoegers." Sigmund remarked in his own mind how much more mature and woman-like her voice had become since all those years ago when he and her had first walked through Osrik's tunnel in their attempt to run away—and at that sad day when they'd been forced to part ways. Both of them remembered that twas in here where he and Eileza had said goodbye to each other and had wept in each other's arms. The place was nearly a sacred shrine to them of their love.

They saw a fire glowing red and orange at the end of the tunnel, and emerged outside near the river. There was a platoon of Gepid pole axmen sitting guard duty at the mouth of the tunnel and when Sigmund emerged with Eileza one shouted, "Halt! Who goes there?" "Tis I, Lord Sigmund with Princess Eileza, *Wachtmeister (Sergeant) Hardrada*," he replied. "All well and good M'Lord," came the reply. Sigmund and Eileza walked passed the warriors and stood in the bright moonlight, overlooking the great River Rha.

Sigmund was now quite a bit taller than Eileza. He was nearly six feet tall and towered over her. She was five feet and two inches tall and was fully grown. She looked up at him and smiled and his heart melted. "Happy birthday Siggy Wiggy," she said all the while looking closely up at him. "Sit down on the ground crossed legged." When he'd done so Eileza reached into her leather shoulder bag she took out the beautiful polished gold coin, the diamond-set medallion that she'd made for him back at Ariemel. It had a hole on the edge through which a beautifully woven beaded leather cord ran with the two ends tied off. Standing behind him she placed the treasure of her love around his neck and pulled his long hair over it. And then leaning around his right shoulders she kissed his neck and he turned his head into hers and their lips met in passion. Now looking down at her gift he took the medallion into his hands and saw every intricate design that she'd crafted into it. Sigmund said, "This is just wonderful Eileza. It is beautiful and the workmanship is just so fine that even in the lamp light I can tell that that is you on the coin."

She replied, "I made it myself for you Siggy. When we left here you remember how sad I was. Especially when I told thee how mother had a terminal disease—being away from you was so hard. After all we'd been through together in the war; your family was more of a family to me than mine own. Togrobeg has always been good to me but when he remarries to Lady Araelia things will grow distant between us I fear. And when our mother died three years ago—after we had worked so hard at being a mother and daughter—well it's been a hard road Siggy and it is my entire fault Mother died." Sigmund couldn't stand to see her so sad and as shed rested on his shoulders with both arms around his neck and her mouth at his ear he pulled her around and took her into his arms in a tight embrace. "Siggy I'll tell thee how mother died another time. I just can't right now. I told thee some bit about her illness it before I left but not all." She began sobbing and Sigmund held her strong but gentle as she let out four years of pain and frustration.

In the firelight Sigmund could see that her face was wet with tears and after she had brought herself under control she said, "We came to our new land, and oh my, it was so beautiful. Under a mountain we found gold and silver and in another place diamonds. We gave the land itself the name Yurallia, for our people. We began building the city of Ariemel, named after my great grandmother, and a Kingdom in a promised land. From the first ore that we mined and smelted, I fashioned this for you—from mine own hands. I always knew that I would come back."

Looking into his eyes in deep love as she lay in his lap she said,. "You've grown so much taller than you were four years ago and even more handsome and strong I might add." In her mind she remarked how muscular he had become and how deep his voice was, and how full and manly were the features of his face. She was glad that he (excepting for that very thin dark red wisp of a moustache) was still clean shaven—for in this way she could remember the youthful Tervingian boy she had fallen in love with nearly five years ago.

Sigmund continued to hold her as she lay in his lap. He sat cross legged facing the river and their lamp beside him. The camp fire of the soldiers burned brightly behind them through the trees and the salt cedar casting dark shadows into the night there near the banks of the mighty River Rha. Once again their lips met softly in a long passionate kisses and in between the lovers then watched the bright shining spring moon and it's reflection off of the cold river water.

Sigmund thought of something. "Eileza, will your brother remarry and have a child as an heir to the throne?" She replied, "Yes, Araelia will marry Toggy and have a child—that gets me off the hook from having to be the Dwarf Queen—if Asgard forbid something happens to Togrobeg." She grinned up at him happily and asked, "Why?" Sigmund replied, "Well, that means Togrobeg wouldn't have any more objections about who you marry. I mean, you would now be free to choose?" Eileza began to smile and replied, "Did we not pledge our troths Siggy Wiggy? King Togrobeg approves it my lover—told me so himself and that's why I'm back home in thy arms Siggy Wiggy."

Sigmund took a deep breath and then turned around on the ground to face Eileza. She stood up and he took her by the hand and slowly asked, "All those years ago we pledged our troth and so let's reaffirm it. Eileza Andavarsdottir, will you marry me? Wilt thou be my one and only wife for forever?" She began crying again, this time for joy and she quickly dropped down on both knees in front of him and taking his face into her hands she planted kisses all over his face and said, "Absobloodylutly right I will Siggy Wiggy Miggy Diggy!" She forcefully pulled his head to hers and gave him a kiss of legend.

But suddenly she stood up and Sigmund knew what was coming next. How could he forget that when Eileza was happy she would wrestle with him and give him a right hard body-slam? She let him stand up and then quicker than he could bat an eye the small stocky young woman was under him, flipping him over onto his back and pinning his shoulders to the ground—he grunted as he impacted the hard ground. She looked down at him and in the background they could hear the axemen laughing about it. He asked, "Is this how our wedding night is going to be Leeza?" Pulling his head up to hers by his ears she said, "Thou hast no idea the passion of Dwarrow women darling and thou art surly going to find out soon." She kissed him again and then easing his head back to the ground she said, "Well looks like we have an announcement of our own to make at your birthday bash Siggy Wiggy Miggy Diggy."

A familiar voice came from up in a tree. Looking up Eileza and Sigmund saw two great horned owls. Clovis was saying, "Jolly good show kiddos. The wife and I wish you both all the best you know, right Merovinge?" She replied, "Oh right you are love. But darlings now always remember that marriage can be a bit like thunder and lightning at times, and other days quite a thrill. You'll be a team, right Clovis?" "Ah yes indeed Merovinge and I might add Sigmund, that there will be days when you come home and will find yourself batting quite a sticky wicket and not have the faintest idea why?"

Siggy and Leeza didn't quite know what to say at first but soon Leeza chimed in and asked, "Were you two up there the whole time listening to us?" Merovinge replied, "Of course not love. We were just out of earshot until now, until the actual wedding proposal?" Clovis new of Eileza's famous temper and said, "Sigmund old chap, your mother Gerda asked us to come along as chaperon you see. We saw you leave by the tunnel and so flew over and kept our beaks out of your private conversation until

Merovinge deemed it proper we fly over." Merovinge looked at Clovis and said, "Blame it all on me now will you Clovis Changeling and you truly shall be batting a sticky wicket!" He replied, "Oh my dear, go ahead and get cross with me will you? See if I give a hoot!" Siggy and Leeza broke out laughing and she said, "I hope our marriage is happy as yours is." Clovis looked at Siggy and said, "There's a good lad now. Come now, rendezvous' over, time to go home." Siggy and Leeza got up off of the ground and dusted each other off. The Changelings jumped off of the thick tree branch and on the way down transformed into White Wolves. "Come now kiddos, time to go home," said Merovinge as she and Clovis walked with them past Sergeant Hardrada and the warriors, and back down the tunnel.

CHAPTER VII

The Grand Duke of Wodenburg

From The Skald's Tale

It came to pass at this time that the King would show his trust for Sigmund by giving him a great task. It was a grand festival for a noble young warrior of the great Tervingian nation, the great day on which Sigmund the Mammoth Rider had been born to Volsung and Gerda of the Getic. And with Eileza Dwarf once more at his side, life now seemed so very good. And that day of Sigmund's Blot was just propitious for the king to bestow on him a title and grant him lands.

igmund's seventeenth birthday was on the festival of *Valisblot the fourteenth day of, Gói and Ein-mánuðr in the five hundred and ninety eighth year of the first age of Midgard,* and the celebration was grand. It was almost as great as his rites of passage celebration had been four years ago for young Sigmund and in front of the entire court his father dubbed him a knight with his sword," and then presented him to the court saying, "I declared four years ago that this my son, Sigmund, twas a man! But I told him that when I knew he was ready to take a wife I would announce when that time had come. Sigmund has been faithful in all things and to the troth that he pledged with the Princess Eileza four years ago in these very halls as has she been as well. Twas announced to us yester eve that the troths were confirmed and so for thee my son, Sigmund the Volsung that day has arrived and thou mayest now chose a bride and enter into marriage and to the raising of children. Sigmund has proven his honor in battles and slain the enemies of his people in combat. He shall take his place as an *Ealdorman* in the *Witena Gemot.*"

Sigmund went forward unto the throne and kneeled before the king and queen who were sitting proudly on the Eagle Throne. The king stood and, taking out the Sword Tyrfingr, dubbed Sigmund saying, "I hereby dub thee Sigmund the Volsung to be the first Grand Duke of Wodenburg. Those lands, their wealth and the Getic tribe shall be yours to build upon and to cultivate. Rise Sigmund, Grand Duke of Wodenburg. Let all of us drink and be merry and celebrate the birthday of the Grand Duke of Wodenburg."

Across the court Eileza was there with Austri and Vestri and she looked upon her Grand Duke through the shining eyes of young love. Now there were other young ladies in the court who had a keen interest in Sigmund such as the nineteen year old Lady Borghild, sister of Aestrith and youngest daughter of the Steward Tanman and Lady Sandilin—and the second of Queen Gwynnalyn's Ladies in waiting. Now that Prince Sigmund was able to choose a bride, he was going to become an even greater draw to the various young women who desired the hand of a Duke. These women were very jealous of Princess Eileza, thinking of her as an unfit bride due to the fact that she was a dwarf. These ladies who were batting eyes at Sigmund when Eileza was away knew that he was already betrothed to Eileza. Now they were hearing it straight from the lips Lord Volsung himself just now but still they thought that if they could turn on their charms they could steal him away from Eileza—for they (especially Borghild) wanted the title that Eileza would have as soon as she and the Grand Duke were married. But they stood no chance at becoming the *Grand Duchess of Wodenburg* for Eileza had won his heart years ago—and for her and her Siggy Wiggy it had always been about the true magic of real love and not of land or titles or court status.

None of these women of the court had the sense to think about the violent response that Eileza was likely to give if she thought any of these 'courtly women' were trying to steal her mate! For women among the Dwarves were known for their violent defense of their marital prerogatives—a famous case being when Thorhild the Shield Maiden Berserker killed Óðalfríðr (Othalfrithr) Alfriggsdottir in the bear pits of Ariemel for attempting to steal her husband *Norðri* (Northri). Thorhild defended her marital rites in combat under Dwarvish Law and slew the usurper—who was also a highly skilled and aggressive shield maiden. For the dwarvish women are the guardians of the sanctity of hearth and home and can kill another invading female under sanction of law—if it be proven true in a court of law first. Dwarrow women defend their rights even more aggressively than they love their men and thus Dwarvish men rarely are involved in polygamy or adultery—for she has the right also to have the man made into an eunuch for such offense if proven in court; unless she chooses to divorce him—however she may do both and Eileza had just the temperament to defend her conjugal bliss in such manner as her friend Thorhild had done—for there is no wrath in Midgard as furious as a Dvärg woman scorned!

As for the lands he had received Sigmund was pleased. Wodenburg, the old Getic home fortress was a rocky mountain south in the Getic tribal area, and Sigurd had reconstructed the fortified city on it with its Mead Hall to guard the area from the Goblins and the Scythians. The garrison there allowed the Getic people in the area to tend their crops and have a measure of safety from Goblin Storm Trooper raids. Indeed Wodenburg had once been the seat of the Getic Nation on the southern steppes, in the days of King Rothgar, Sigurd's father but at the start of the Scythian conquest it had been sacked and burned by the Slaughter Wolves. But Sigurd had successfully reconstructed it during the last four years on a grand scale—by the standards of the peoples of the steppes.

Eileza was quite happy with a beautiful smile on her swarthy dark, smooth skinned face and dark piercing eyes when King Sigurd now said, "Rise and come forth Princess Eileza Andavarsdottir of Ariemel." She got up when called and came forth to the throne wearing a beautiful blue and white dress with silver leggings and black shoes. At that moment as well the Priestess Byrnhilda came before the throne from out of the door behind the throne. When Eileza was there, she took her place in front of the king and queen and Sigmund took her by both hands and the two of them looked into each other's eyes. The queen's mother and her entire family were sitting close by to witness it all. Today was a big day. "Let the witnesses come forth!" declared the king. Clovis and Merovinge walked forward in their human shapes and took their places.

The queen said with happiness and enthusiasm, "Today, my brother the Duke of Wodenburg and the Princess Eileza Andavarsdottir are to, for the first time in public, pledge their troths to one another for one year; at which time they shall return here and be wed." A wave of murmuring, some unhappy but most happy swept through the assembled guests and all those young ladies, (especially Borghild) those with the unhappy murmuring ceased to bat their eyes at Sigmund. Sigmund's friends were not in the least bit shocked by this turn of events but the look on Lady Borghild's face was very broken and sad and angry—not to mention extremely jealous. Perhaps one of the sons of Thonan would be a better and safer choice for her to woo with her charms.

The priestess took a cord of sheep skin and tied Sigmund's left hand to Eileza's right hand and said, "Let Asgard witness today this betrothal. It is as binding as marriage except for the sharing of chambers. Whoever breaks the betrothal thus commits adultery. Sigmund Grand Duke of Wodenburg; do you betroth thyself unto this maiden, not only by our laws but the laws of the Dwarves and give unto Eileza the only conjugal right unto thyself, and recognize her right as matron to defend her bliss?" Sigmund replied, "I Sigmund, Duke of Wodenburg do betroth myself unto this maiden under the laws of the Dwarves and of the Tervingians and do grant her exclusive marital bliss to myself, rejecting all others."

The priestess then asked, "Princess Eileza Andavarsdottir of Ariemel. Have you received the blessing of your family and your king?" She replied, "I am allowed my free choice in matters of matrimony, and now do claim my rights to Sigmund the Volsung as mine under your law and the laws of the Dwarves—and claim my right of matron of the home to defend my rights against all females who challenge my rights to Sigmund the Volsung, in the arena of combat to the death. And I do freely grant Sigmund the Volsung exclusive right to his marital bliss with me and I do reject all others." The pledges of the dwarvish marriage rite shocked those courtly young ladies and so Borghild knew that Eileza would kill her if she tried to entice Sigmund and her face was downcast—she hadn't any reason to hope that Sigmund would have chosen her anyway, for the entire time Eileza was away she'd tried to charm the young Volsung and he'd spurned her for the promise of his true love Eileza.

"Very good then," replied the priestess. "Princess Eileza Andavarsdottir, do thou betroth thyself unto this man?" She replied, "Yes, I do. I Princess Eileza Andavarsdottir do betroth myself to this man and claim my marital rights to him." The priestess asked, "Who then witnesses this betrothal?" Clovis with one blue eye and one green eye this time, for he never had been able to get his eye colors right during a changeover replied, "We, Clovis and Merovinge of the Changelings declare that we have witnessed the betrothal of this man and this maiden." He winked at Siggy and said, "Jolly good show old chap." The priestess declared in a loud voice, "So let it be written, so let it be done. I declare them to be betrothed unto one another! And according to the laws of the Dwarves, are there any ladies who would challenge her right to this man in combat? If so let them say so now." Aestrith looked at Borghild and said quietly, "If you want Sigmund, now the chance." Borghild quickly turned and looked at her sister with wide eyes of fear and shaking her head said, "Entirely too dangerous Aestrith." "Wise choice," replied Aestrith. No young lady dare do so, least of all Borghild and so when no challenge was given the priestess said, "Then by the laws of the Dwarves betrothal is sealed and unbreakable except by death or eunuchdom!" The crowd let out wild cheering as joy filled the mead hall and as Siggy and Eileza left the throne, Lord Radagaisus came forward."

The queen with her chin held high and her nose in the air said rather coldly (and that fact was noticed by everyone especially Greta and Gerda whilst the king and Lord Volsung looked at one another with raised eyebrows), "Today Lord Radagaisus and my sister the Princess Greta are to betroth themselves to one another for one year, at which time they shall return here and be wed." The king then said, "Come forth Princess Greta Volsungsdottir to the throne. Greta was wearing a beautiful white dress with blue sleeves and a crown of flowers was woven on her head. She took the hands of her knight and the two of them faced the High Priestess Byrnhilda.

The priestess took a cord of sheep skin and tied Lord Radagaisus' left hand to Greta's right hand and said, "Let Asgard witness today this betrothal. It is as binding as marriage except for the sharing of chambers. Whoever breaks the betrothal thus commits adultery. Lord Radagaisus, Reik of the Thyssagetae do you betroth thyself unto this maiden?" Radagaisus replied, "I Lord Radagaisus, Reik of the Thyssagetae do betroth me unto this maiden." The priestess then asked, "Princess Greta. Hast thou received the blessing of thy father?" She replied, "I have." "All well and good then," replied the Priestess. "Princess Greta Volsungsdottir, do thou betroth thyself unto this man?" She replied, Yes, I do. I Princess Greta Volsungsdottir do betroth myself to this man." The priestess asked, "Who then witnesses this betrothal?" Clovis replied, "We, Clovis and Meroving of the Changelings declare that we have witnessed the betrothal of this man and this maiden." The priestess declared in a loud voice, "So let it be written, so let it be done. I declare them to be betrothed unto one another!" The crowd let out low key cheering this time and Greta took note of it and in her heart blamed her sister as the two of them left the throne, for Radagaisus was unpopular among the people and the queen especially.

Later that evening the wizards and the spirit maidens gathered in their circle of meditation in the Thorstadt Stonehenge and Byock said, "A great test is soon to come for this house." "Indeed it is so," answered Aesop.

Yonas said, "We are here to help but they must pass through the ordeal by their own strength." Dithranti said, "We can help them do the work, but they must be willing to do it whether the supernatural is there or not. We cannot do all of the work for them." Gladvynn asked, "It involves Molly doesn't it?" Boudicca replied, "Aye, indeed it does." Vulcrus was nodding in agreement as was Gleadra and Zakarah said, "Yes and that is why she could not be here this evening. This is going to be a traumatic time for her especially. But also the time has come for my Grandchild Aubriel to face tests as well. Shlomael and many of our troops are in Ariemel with Yoshael. I have sent for Aubriel, and even now she journeys from Alfheim. She has descended the Ice Pack shelf and will be here within days. She is a Holy Woman and a brilliant Spirit Learner. She must pass her testing as well before she can join our circle. She is destined to marry Shlomael and when the time comes for Yoshael and I to ascend, they twain shall take our place in this circle." Boudicca replied, "Then they will face the test with Molly? Zakarah nodded in reply as all of them quieted into their prayers and meditations.

CHAPTER VIII

The Smithy of Nineveh

From the Skald's Tale

And now oh King Roderick, I shall tell thee and these people more of the saga of Teobalf! It was he who brought us the secret of steel, having obtained it in Assyria. Know that he stayed for four years in that cruel city of legend, where it's Kings were bitter tyrants, even as ruthless as the Slaughter Wolves. He suffered much at their hands, but stayed the course. But he became like a son to the Forge Master and adored by his children. In time he then came home with a gift for King Sigurd, even greater than that of steel.

The great city of Nineveh sat alongside the eastern banks of the River Tigris in the land of Assyria. It was a vast city surrounded by rings of high stone walls. So large was this city, that it was actually a complex of three cities enclosed within the same fortifications. The walls were so wide that one could race three chariots abreast and still have room for bystanders on the side. It was to Nineveh, four years and six months previous, that King Sigurd and his people had come to obtain steel. They had to have weapons which would make them the equals of King Idanthrsus and his allies.

Now in those days, the Assyrian Empire ruled in the lands of the Tigris and Euphrates Rivers and beyond, and was known as a vicious and dangerous, aggressive nation. Yet in spite of the Assyrians around him, the Sword maker Shalmaeser was a kindly gentleman, well known for his deep knowledge of the Secret of Steel. He had swarthy dark skin and curly black hair, and weighed about one hundred and thirty five pounds. His beard was thick but short and he wore a round conical shaped hat with a flat top that was woven of sheep skin and embroidered with threads of silver and gold. Four years ago something deep within him, like a voice, told him that he should honor the requests of this barbarian king and his warrior queen from the north who had come to him requesting to purchase weapons of steel; for it was not Assyrian practice to arm barbarians with weapons of steel, lest those barbarians shift from friend to foe. And then when the mighty beings from the sky appeared who many in Midgard thought were gods and had blessed both the weapons and the king and queen of this far off northern tribe, he knew that it was appointed as his destiny that he train Teobalf in the intricacies of the Secret of Steel. Making steel was much more than simply adding charcoal to molten iron. It was a precise art and those unfamiliar with the smithing process would produce inferior weapons, or even plows that were too brittle and thus would break or even shatter when put to the test. The art of the smithy in Midgard was consider holy by many people and a smithy in steel most especially so. In this art, the blacksmith was known as a smithy; however his workshop was also sometimes called a smithy as well, so one had to know the context in which the word was being used.

So it came to pass that Teobalf stayed there in Nineveh for four years at first in the guise of a servant to the Smithy of Nineveh, and later as a known student, who it was assumed would someday enter into the service of the Assyrian Empire. So trusted was *Shalmaeser Smithy* that the presence of this big, blond white skinned barbarian from the far north was never questioned. In fact the Forge Master had given silver coins, about twenty Assyrian Shekels' worth, to King Sigurd, in order that it might be the truth, when he told the Assyrians that Teobalf had been purchased from Norse barbarians as a slave. During his stay there in the land of the Tigris, Teobalf had learned to speak fluent Aramaic, which was the language of not only the Assyrians, but several major nations in this region.

It came to pass in the *five hundred and ninety eighth year after the great deluge, on the 1ˢᵗ day of the month of Gói and Ein-mánuðr* in the late winter, at the dusk, Shalmaeser Smithy summoned Teobalf to the evening meal of lamb and lentil soup and flat bread. There in Shalmaeser's cozy home above the shop, and there with his wife Bashemath and their fourteen year old son Peleg and twelve year old daughter Aisha, Teobalf was welcomed once more into their home. Teobalf had trimmed his hair and beard, both of which were Nordic blond. His eyes were sea blue and his nose slim and thin. He was dressed in a baggy brown over shirt and trousers with Assyrian sandals.

The home of Shalmaeser was a rather typical one story structure made of stones and bricks with floors of red brick cobblestones. The walls of the home, both inside and out and as well the outer wall along the front facing east was plastered over with white stucco and was sitting at a street intersection which was paved with rough rocky cobblestones. The house was approximately fifteen feet high, forming a rectangle fifty feet long on the north-south and thirty feet wide on the east to western ends. Blocking the house from the street, there was an outer wall which had a large cedar door for foot traffic which faced the eastern street. This wall was twelve feet high and in between it and the front part of the home there was a space of about eight feet which ran from the south corner to the north corner. At the corners the outer wall turned and was attached to the house itself and there was no outer wall on any other side of the home. However there was a family outhouse built in a tiny courtyard off of the north end of the insula which was curtained off for privacy, with a small clay bell hanging with which one would ring before entering, making sure to avoid any embarrassing situations.

From the outer door a short walkway of cobblestones led to the front door of the house, which was built in the style of that region, an insula surrounding an interior courtyard. There was a flight of steps which led to the top of the house which was a flat roofed structure, and here in the evenings of the long hot days of summer the family would find relief as they relaxed, unwinding from their long day of work. There was a door blocked by a simple multi colored curtain, which exited from the dining room out into the courtyard where there was an outdoor kitchen having a hearth and a bake oven. They also had their own well there in the courtyard, and just across the rectangular area were the smithy shop and work areas as well as the servant's quarters and a stable.

On the south side of the courtyard there was a large doorway, rather like a hallway gated by two double doors of cedar at the outer edge. This led to the street on the south side of the stone and brick home which allowed the access of carts and horses and twas through this gate that the master's clients and customers would enter and exit during the six working days. One thing that was noticeable was that up in the main house and unlike the other homes in Nineveh, Shalmaeser's had no closet or niche for the idols of household gods—for as Teobalf learned, the master and his family worshipped only one God; who as he also discovered was *El Shaddai* the God of the Elves and the *All Father God* of his own people—the God who was called by the Northmen *Dan Ene Gud,* meaning, *The One God.* For at this time during the first age of Midgard, the northern people had not yet come to worship, nor did they treat Thor and Wotan and the other Aesir as gods or Loki and his Vanier as gods. This corruption came later, but had its small beginnings with the Vandals of King Genseric.

There was a stone trough out in the servant's quarters which was used for bathing and there was another such tub inside of the main house on the north end for the family to use. They would heat water in great iron pots on the hearth out in the courtyard, and then bucket it in to whatever bath tub was being used. All in all this was quite a handsome home and the living quite comfortable. Very few homes of the rich, other than the royal palace here in Nineveh offered a bath tub and hot water for their slaves or thralls as they were known among the Gomerians of the north.

Teobalf was welcomed at the door by Aisha. The child was five feet tall had very long curly black hair like that of her mother, eyes as brown as an acorn and a skin tone of swarthy brown just like her parents and brother. She wore a long tan dress which fell around her ankles and bare feet, identical to that of her mother. She smiled up at the tall and powerful Teobalf and jumped for joy and in her excitement said, "Uncle Teo, welcome to supper! I made the bread myself today and Mum made the stew." She smiled a beautiful smile and in her young eyes, everyone could see how much she adored the big Tervingian Barbarian. "I made sure she put radishes into it just as you like. Come on over here in your place. I've even put an extra big cushion for you to recline on!" He bowed to her with a smile and said, "M'lady and fair young damsel, I thank thee for thy most kind consideration." The girl blushed with a smile and took him by the hand. The child loved him very much.

The people down in this region of Midgard do not sit at high tables in tall chairs as do the people in the north and west, rather the tables are no more than two feet off of the floor. They recline on big cushions and ornate pillows while eating and one could easily shift around and stretch their legs.

Peleg was a tall thin boy with hair just like that of his father. He wore cloths identical to those of Teobalf and his father and his voice was in the process of changing from that of a boy to one of a young man. He said with a smile on his face and in a tone of delighted excitement, "Uncle Teo, after supper, will you tell us more stories of the far north? I want to hear more about Sigmund! Tell us about the Ogres and Goblins and the Gargoyles again and that Sorcerer from Dakkia!" Aisha, having Teobalf by the hand said, "Come and sit uncle Teo. Ignore my brother, he's an oaf. But if you do tell us more stories, I should like to hear about the Getic Queen and how beautiful she is. How do the young girls such as I dress up there?" She sneered at Peleg and led the Barbarian to his chair.

The voice of Bashemath came from the kitchen saying, "Come now children, let Teo sit and talk with your father. Aisha, come in here and get bowls and spoons and set the table. Teo is hungry and wants to taste your pita bread." Teobalf sat down and Aisha filled a cup of wine for him and sat it in front of him, and as she was leaving for the kitchen he said, "I thank thee M'lady for your kindness. Thou art a princess most noble Aisha. My Queen would be honored to know you." Aisha beamed a smile back to him, took a bow, and stepped through the curtained doorway into the kitchen.

Twas at that moment that a servant, a young man of sixteen by the name of Calah, dressed much as was Peleg only in cloths of a much poorer quality (but without a hat) came into the room from the outside. He had with a basin of water along with his twenty year old sister Borsippah who carried a towel. She was Bashemath's maid servant and Calah was her brother. They knelt down and starting with Teobalf, who was being given hospitality as a guest, washed everyone's feet, and then departed. Borsippah, was in a servants dress with her long dense black hair tied into a pony tail, looked back at Teobalf with a slight smile and he was quick to return it.

Master Shalmaeser sat at the end of the table as father of the house, which was lit by several large olive oil lamps. The walls were covered with fine tapestry rugs of yellow and orange zig-zag stripes and the floor was of fine cedar wood, brought to Nineveh from Phoenicia.

Peleg took his place at his father's right hand and removed his conical hat, one which was nearly identical to that of his father. "Welcome once more to my table Teobalf," said the Forge Master with a smile. He lifted his glass of wine as did Peleg and said, "I propose a toast. Let us drink to home and hearth, family and friends." The three of them raised their fired and polished clay cups, which were the color of a blood moon and touched them, and then drank down the white wine—which was made from the finest grapes the Tigris Valley had to offer.

Shalmaeser then remarked with a laugh, "Men we must be careful and avoid too much of this good wine—twas just this same sort of wine that got our ancestor Noach into trouble. I know we've all heard this story many times, but in the telling and the retelling there is remembrance. Peleg also knoweth the entire Epic of Gilgamesh by heart. But rather than that legend, Peleg, after the blessing for the wine and bread do tell us once more the true story of father Noach and the wine—for in the story there is a point that I wish to share with Teobalf." Teobalf said, "Ah yes, we too have stories of Lord Noach. Our people are descendants of his son Yapet through his son Ashkenaz and Ashkenaz's son Tervinge, also called Tyrfingr Ashkenazsson." Everyone nodded in reply and Shalmaeser said, "The sword that I forged for Sigurd was in fact the reforged sword of Tyrfingr Ashkenazsson. Sigurd knows this for I told him and it was for this reason that Wotan inspired Sigurd to come here. The Gwynnian Scythe however is altogether different—a new creation forged from the iron of a falling star. It has powerful magic Teobalf and you shouldn't forget that."

The boy was happy to comply in the retelling of Noach's wine story and just at that moment, Aisha returned with a tray full of bowls and spoons and set them at each place around the table. Bashemath came in with a big clay pot of hearty lentil and lamb stew, cooked with big red radishes. Normally this would have been the task of the servants but not today. The smell filled the room as Aisha took a dipper and filled, first the bowl of uncle Teo and then her father's, her brother's, then that of her mother and finally her own. She then returned out to the kitchen and brought out a large platter of steaming hot flatbread covered over by a white cloth. She sat it down in front of her father, and then refilled everyone's cups of wine. First uncle Teo, then her father's and brother's, followed by those of her mother and herself.

As Borsippah and Calah exited they closed the curtain behind them and quickly made their way past the oven and hearth where the fire was going very good and the hot water in the great iron cauldron was steaming up and getting near to boil. Calah, wash basin in hand went north across the little courtyard and into the toilet down which he poured the dirty water onto the ground. Afterwards he took a scoop of some sort of scented white powder from a large clay vase, and dumped serval heaping scoops down through the toilet seat before closing down the lid. After making sure that everything was tidy, he left the toilet facility and returned the basin to the table by the well where his sister had hung up the damp wash cloths and towel upon a rack at the end of the table to dry. Afterwards, he and his sister went across the courtyard and through the smithy shop and into their quarters.

The door to the servant's quarters was oval shaped on the top and six feet tall, and across it hung an orange curtain which reach down to within two inches of the cobblestone floor. The quarters consisted of one large outer room and three separate rooms on each side of the common room, and the entire place was floored with red brick cobblestones. On the western side of the common room was a hearth and in it burned a small low heating and cooking fire.

Once they were inside he said, "Borsippah. When Teobalf leaves someday, he's going to go back to that barbarian kingdom and shall leave you here! He's a barbarian of Midgard and when he has fully learned the Secret of Steel, he'll leave forever and go home! How can you believe his exaggerated promises?" She retorted, "What business is it of yours little brother? Teobalf loves me and will never leave me behind! If I go with him, I can be someone! I have the chance to have children that shan't grow up as Assyrian slaves!" Calah replied, "Ok sister, but you can't just go off and leave me here. We have always been together ever since the Assyrian Army burned our village in Akkad and slaughtered our parents when I was six! Are you just going to get rescued by some Gomerian and leave me here in Nineveh?"

She took him into her arms and replied, "Where I go, you go Calah, just as I promised you when our parents died. We were lucky that Master Shalmaeser found us both together in the slave market and bought us, else we would have been parted forever. He is a good man Calah, but we were not born to be his slave or anyone else's. We will be free someday baby-brother. Besides, you're just jealous that I have someone else who loves me as much but in a different way as you do Calah!" They both grinned at each other and embraced and prepared to eat their meal.

The servant's quarters were chambers that were warm and comfortable just off of the side of the shop. Noises outside drew their attention. There was a platoon of heavily armed soldiers marching outside in the street and turning the corner going west towards the Tigris River which they could clearly hear as they shut the doors behind them. The thud of their marching boots could be heard and as well the servants and even the family reclining to dine could hear the clatter of the horse's hooves on the cobblestone pavement. They could hear the rumble of the chariot outside on the street pulled by two mighty war horses which was traveling just behind the Assyrian Army platoon.

Borsippah and Calah reclined on cushions at the low table and ate their supper of bread from a clay plate and stew dipped from their own pot by Borsippah into their bowels at their own little table in the midst of which sat a flickering oil lamp. Each had a glass of red wine as well and a small flagon of it sat on the table next to the large clay stew pot. She remarked, "Teobalf told me that where he comes from in the north, soup like this is called skause and that there is always a pot of it on the hearth in every mead hall for anyone who comes in hungry. I wonder what a mead hall looks like. I've never heard of one until Teobalf spoke of them-but he said they are the great halls, the palaces as it were of his peoples lords and kings. They seem much more welcoming than the palaces around here—for no Assyrian king would have soup on the hearth for any guest who might come in. It sounds of—well it sounds of freedom Calah."

Teobalf, although not a slave or a servant, shared a room out here as well. His room, as was Borsippah's and Calah's were separate from each other, something again unique for in most places thralls had no private rooms at all, being required to sleep together on the floor in some large open room. Not so here but they all shared the same common dining area—each door having a curtain for privacy, a table, reclining cushions, lamps and a bed with a straw mattress. When they were finished she said, "It's time now. The hour glass had run down. Back to work, it's time to go gather the dirty crockery and get it washed."

Meanwhile Aisha sat down to the right side of her beloved uncle Teo, and to her right sat her mother, who was on the left side of her husband. Master Shalmaeser took up his cup of wine and lifted it saying, "Blessed is the God of Noach, who creates the fruit of the vine." They all joined him in raising their glasses and touched them saying, "To life." After everyone had drunk, Shalmaeser removed the white cloth from the bread. Teobalf looked at the fine loaf and said, "Ah, this is wonderful looking bread. But not as beautiful as she who made it." He looked at Aisha and smiled and she blushed. Then Shalmaeser blessed God for the bread saying, "Blessed are you God of Noach, who brings forth bread from the earth, and has blessed the hands of she who made it." He looked at Aisha with the deep love that a father has for his daughter and she said, "Thank you Abba." He then broke the bread and passed it around to everyone who reclined at the table. And so now, Peleg told the story of Noach and the wine as they ate:

> "It is written in the scroll of the beginnings saying that God blessed Noach and his sons and ordered them, "Be productive, multiply, and fill Midgard. All the living creatures of Midgard will be filled with fear and terror of you from now on, including all the birds of the sky and dragons, everything that crawls on the ground, and all the fish of the ocean. They've been assigned to live under your stewardship. El Shaddai said 'Every living, moving creature will be food for you. Just as I gave you green plants before, so now you have everything. However, you are not to eat meat with its life—that is, its blood—in it! Also, I will certainly demand an accounting regarding bloodshed, from every animal and from every human and all the speaking creatures of Midgard either in the air or on land or in the sea. I'll demand an accounting from every human being for the life of another human being and from the life of a speaking creature from another speaking creature. Whoever sheds human blood, by a human his own blood is to be shed; and whatever speaking creature either on land, in the air or in the seas sheds the blood of another speaking creature, by either human or speaking creature his own blood is to be shed—because El Shaddai made human beings in his own image and gave souls into the bodies of the speaking creatures. Now as for you, be productive and multiply; spread out over the land and multiply throughout it.' Later, El Shaddai told Noach and his sons, 'Pay attention! I'm establishing my covenant with you and with your descendants after you, and with every living creature that is with you—the birds, the livestock, and all the wildlife of the earth that are with you—all Midgard's animals that came out of the ark. I

will establish my covenant with you: No living beings will ever be cut off again by flood waters, and there will never again be a flood that destroys the earth. God also said, "here's the symbol that represents the covenant that I'm making between me and you and every living being with you, for all future generations.'"

"'I've set my rainbow in the sky to symbolize the covenant between me and this Midgard, and whenever I bring clouds over Midgard, I'll remember my covenant between me and you and all the speaking creatures either on land, in the air or within the seas and every other living creature, so that water will never again become a flood to destroy all living beings. When the rainbow is in the clouds, I will observe it and remember the everlasting covenant between God and all living beings on Midgard" "God also told Noach, 'This is the symbol of the covenant that I've established between me and everything that lives on the earth.'"

Noach's sons who came out of the ark were Shem, Ham, and Yapet, and Ham later fathered Canaan. These three were Noach's sons, and from these men the whole of Midgard was re-populated. It was in this time that El Shaddai created the Elves, and coming from the Ark, Lord Noach was greeted by them and all worshiped El Shaddai

Father Noach was a man of the soil and was the first to plant and farm a vineyard. He drank some of the wine, got drunk, and lay down unclothed right in the middle of his tent. Ham and his son Canaan saw father Noach this way and told his two brothers outside, mocking their father! Then Shem and Yapheth took their father's cloak, laid it across both their shoulders, and walking backwards, they both covered their father's body. Their faces were turned away, and they did not see their father like this, so humiliated. When Noach sobered up and learned what his youngest son had done to him, he said, "Canaan is cursed! He will be the lowest of slaves to his relatives." He also said, 'Blessed is *Dan Ene Gud* of Shem, and may Canaan be his slave. May God make room for Yapheth; may God live in Shem's tents, and may Canaan serve him.' Noach lived three hundred and fifty years after the flood. After Noach had lived a total of nine hundred and fifty years, he died."

When Peleg had finished his father put an arm around his boy and hugged him saying, "Well done my good and faithful son." Then he said, "While we consume this wine, we must be its master, and not let it become the master over us. The drunkard can be compared to a lamb, a lion, a pig and a monkey. When he takes his first few sips, he is like a lamb, quiet and unassuming, maybe passive. This is until he takes a few more drinks, at which time he becomes a man of decision, not to be trifled with! He is a great warrior and a conqueror! But alas, because the wine is an elixir to him, the drunkard cannot stop but continues to drink more and more wine, until he is like a pig wallowing in the mire of his slop. On and on he continues throughout the night, until he is like a monkey that is screaming, leaping from tree to tree until in a stupor he crashes to the ground. Let us as a people make sure that we are none of these. Let us not be found without raiment because of strong drink. For even a holy prophet like father Noach can allow himself to fall to the enchantments of too much wine or other intoxicating beverages and substances. And Teobalf, we who know the secret of steel must be especially vigilant, for with intoxication cometh imperfection in a smithy. That imperfection will seep into our craft and the things that we produce will be inferior—thus our names will become mud in the eyes of those who once trusted us to make, not only their swords and axes, arrowheads and other weapons, but the farmer for whom we've made a plow—and the horsemen who shod their mounts with that which we make in our smithies. Keep this all in mind Teobalf, and when thou hast returned to the steppes King Sigurd will find in thee the vindication of his trust."

Teobalf replied, "I must agree with this Master Shalmaeser. In my own land, we produce an abundance of mead and ale. Wine is a luxury we don't have a chance to taste too often—unless the Hellene traders bring it up from the coast. But I've seen drunkenness at times in the mead halls of our kingdoms and in the taverns, and the results are similar to the example thou have given. I've heard a similar story before of Noach, father of all men here in the first age. My people are sons of Gomer, father of Ashkenaz, father of Tyrfingr. They are of the blood of Yapheth, son of Noach. It is amazing that Noach only died two hundred and fifty years ago. The ancient fathers were blessed with lives like those of Yoshael and the Elves of which Peleg spoke."

Twas then that the servants returned to clean up the table and wash the crockery as was their duty and as they did so the Forge Master said to Peleg, "Son, go now and get the bundle." "Yes Abba," was the boy's reply. Peleg got up and went into a bedroom and soon returned with something long wrapped in a fancy blue and white and silver woven blanket. As Calah and Borsippah removed the dishes from the table, Teobalf was very curious as to what this was all about.

With the entire family looking on Master Shalmaeser said, "Teobalf, thou may have noticed that we're somewhat different than the other Assyrians around us. We don't eat swine's flesh or shellfish, or horse meat or certain kinds of birds like they do. This is because in my younger days, we crossed over and lived for a short time in Gobekli Tepe amongst the Dwarves of Tubal. And a few years later at Salem in the land of Canaan at the school of the Melchizedek where we were taught the ways of Noach and also the Elves—first from Master Yonas the Dwarf who is as you've heard, the White Wizard of the South. Yonas himself was learned student of the Wizard King Yoshael in the days when the Elf Lord dwelt as the Melchizideck of Salem. They are the Sons of Light called to be holy wizards by El Shaddai. Before the Melchizedek and his people departed for the land of Forever Ice as I said, I went to his school—a school which the Elves call a *Yeshiva;* which was later given over to our own still living ancestor, Shem the son of Noach. Afterward he too was called Melchizedek and is there unto this day. And we are not Assyrians, but sons of Evri, who was a descendent of Noach's son Shem. We are of the Evrim, and we are not Assyrians."

Teobalf asked, "And yet thou art a smithy M'Lord. Who taught thee the secret of steel and by whose hand did the craft come?" The master replied, "I was taught by the Elves, by Yoshael himself, for twas the Elves alone who knew the secret of steel after receiving a revelation from Weylandr himself—and gave it to the world of men through my hand. He said that the time was coming when a great war would come to Midgard between the Sons of Light and the Sons of Darkness, and that my swords would be the first given into the hands of the Barbarians of Midgard in order to combat the tyranny of an evil sorcerer. I knew that when King Sigurd dared come all the way here from the steppes to have swords made by my hand, and when they were blessed by Wotan and Thor, that that time prophesied by the Melchizedek had come and days before that I had a vision, and I saw you in it, coming to me to learn the secret of steel."

Teobalf replied, "I find that to be incredible Master. So I really do have a powerful purpose to help my people. Hister of Dakkia is that evil sorcerer that you were told of Master, and his threat is beyond measure. I always knew that you and your family were very much different than the people of this city, whom I've noticed are of a very base sort. Their army is every bit as cruel as the Scythians in my country. Even the way you treat Borsippah and Calah is so much different than the way other slaves, thralls as we call them in the north, are treated in Nineveh." Shalmaeser replied, "Yes, we have learned a better way from the God of Noach and Yoshael, El Shaddai. There are no other gods save he. All others are unreal, or parts of him. Your All Father God, *Dan Ene Gud* is the same God as mine Teobalf."

Shalmaeser changed the subject saying, "Ah now about Borsippah. Thou have, as we've all noticed, taken quite a keen interest in her over the last two years." Teobalf replied, "Yes Master Shalmaeser. I truly, deeply love her. I've been intending to ask you for permission to have her hand in marriage. Thou art more to her than just a master, but a father. Her father and mother have gone either to Valhalla or Freya's Hall and so, if thou art not her father then who is?"

Bashemath was saying, "Come now children. You must help clean the dishes. Borsippah will be doing other things this evening and so it is our task this night. Come, come now." The younglings didn't move and she became stern and forceful saying, "Aisha I said now! Peleg, I said to get moving this instant young man!" The kinderlings replied nearly in unison and with much disappointment, "Yes Emma."

Master Shalmaeser spoke with a pleasant voice saying, "Teobalf, of a truth, Borsippah is a fine girl and will make you a beautiful wife. She is loyal and faithful and above all, honest. Truth is the grandest of all creations, and she is truthful. Her village, as thou knowest was sacked and burned and her and Calah's family killed by the army. I found them both miserable and terrified in the slave market by the Tigris. I bought them both for sixty shekels of silver and brought them here. The boy will not want to part with his sister though, I can tell you that for sure. But she needs to be away from this cruel place, wed to a man that will protect her, and I knowest that thou art that man Teobalf. I'll have my scribe draw up the marriage contract tomorrow. There shan't be time for the usual one year of betrothal though Teobalf." He replied, "And why is that Master Shalmaeser?" The Forge Master replied, "Because as of today, thy training is complete my young apprentice. Already know you that which thou needeth to know. Thou hast learned well the secret of steel, as well as of tin and all metals. Thou hast learned what it takes to make the best swords in Midgard Teobalf and the spiritual ways behind our craft. And so there cannot be the year of betrothal. We will do the marriage ceremony and the betrothal at the same time in seven days hence, for afterward thou shalt return to thine own land. And as a gift I will give you Calah—for now thou art ready to take on an apprentice."

Teobalf replied, "My father Haldorr as thou knowest was our Getic Smithy. He was killed when I was six by the Scythians leaving me without a trade or a father. My Mother Svanhildr remarried soon afterwards to Eyvender the Falconer—but I never fancied hunting with birds, although he taught me well. It will be good to return home to my people and see my family, especialy my little sister Nessa

Teobalf was moved with happiness and continued to speak saying, "Master, what thou hast done for Borsippah and her brother, and for my people and me, there is no sufficient reward. I thank thee Master Shalmaeser." The Forge Master replied, "Every time that thou tellest the truth and liveth by the truth, that will be my reward. The God of Noach will see it himself. Live by his laws, which I have taught thee these past four years, and the blessings of which I spoke of in the past four years will be manifest in thy life Teobalf. Any greater instruction in these matters thou must seek out from the Elves, for they too are of the children of God as well as mankind."

Master Shalmaeser opened up the ties on the cloth bundle and unrolled it. He removed from a black ornate scabbard, the most beautiful sword that Teobalf had ever seen before. It was a double edged hand and a half sword about two cubits in length from pommel to tip. It was engraved up and down the length of each side of the blade on both sides from the edge to the fuller with flames. The fuller gave way to the central ridge four inches from the tip, and past this point there were no engravings of flame. On both sides of the blade along the fuller, Master Shalmaeser had engraved three rising griffins, which he knew to be the emblem of all the Tervingian tribes. There was one on each side below the rain guard, one on each side at the midpoint, and one on each side of the blade where the fuller gives way to the centre ridge. The cross guard was one inch wide, half and inch thick and six inches long. The grip was made of mammoth tusk ivory and the pommel was a two inch eagle head made of polished steel, into which amethyst stones had been set for its eyes.

Teobalf's eyes glistened as he saw it and Master Shalmaeser said, "Receive this sword as your reward for your success here as my apprentice. This sword is, the *Griffin Edge*. Just as the Griffin has the body of a lion and its strength, so does the one who wields it, and the sword itself, have the strength of the Lion. Just as the Griffin has the head of an Eagle, and is keen witted and sharp, seeing afar from high above, so does the wielder of this blade—and the tip of the blade is like the piercing tip of an eagle's beak. Unsheathe the Griffin Edge only in honor, and put it not away in dishonor. I chose the symbol of the Griffin as it came to me in the visions of the night—the symbol of King Tyrfingr. Twas later that word came to me from the Hellene merchants that some years ago all of your tribes of Tervingia had formed a new Steppe Confederation. That your king and queen of the Getic now lead a united Tervingia—and that the Griffin of King Tyrfingr is the seal of your nation and tis said that King Sigurd has been called the Mighty Griffin. Fitting since he is the direct descendent of that warrior king. If all this be true then Sigurd is the first king of a united Tervingian kingdom since the heady days of Tyrfingr." Teobalf was struck with awe and had no words at the moment to reply except, "I thank thee for honoring me so Master. The sword is a blade of magic."

The Master stood up now and summoned his family back into the main room. He sent Peleg to summon Borsippah and Calah, and they were all soon back to witness what was about to take place. Then he said, "Kneel Teobalf Haldorrson to receive your honors." Teobalf knelt down and as he did, he could see Aisha smiling so very brightly and then he saw the gaze of Borsippah fixed upon him with, not a smile, but never the less a happy look. Master Shalmaeser touched Teobalf's two shoulders and then the top of his head with the Griffin Edge and said, "I have done this according to the custom of thy people. Thou art a *Master Smithy of the order of the Evri*. Rise Master Teobalf—and now you come to his side Borsippah my daughter." She quickly came to Teobalf's side and the Forge Master placed their hands together and said, "Borsippah, I have consented to your marriage to Master Teobalf, which shall be in seven days hence. Calah, it is my wish that thou go with Master Teobalf back to Tervingia, and be his apprentice. Thou will not be separated from Borsippah by all of this. So let it be written and so let it be done."

CHAPTER IX

Svetlana

From the Skald's Tale

We know of Hister and all of his plotting with Loki to conquer and rule Midgard. Now hear of his mother, the Carpathian Cave Witch and the Thrall of the Witch King Thrain! She too had evil plans and schemes and would not be left without power in the New Order of Midgard!

Once upon a time in the middle of things, in the faraway crags and recesses of the Carpathian Mountains, there lived an evil hexe (witch). She was the mother of Hister and had taken a keen interest in her growing Grandchild, Eblilis. The boy was now nearly five and spent his time between the fortress of Kul Oba and the home of his Grandmother Svetlana. She dwelt in a cottage made of wood and thorns, which sat over the mouth of the cave where she conducted foul rituals and along with her coven of six witches, one of which was her daughter Angrboda of Myrkvidr, serving the evil purposes of the Witch King Thrain. Hister, Svetlana and thirty five old Angrboda together formed what was known as the trinity of evil, although these witches were enthralled by their true master, the Witch King Thrain. Thrain watched Hister and all of his doings from afar; waiting for his time to rule had not yet come and Hister for his part, in spite of the fact that his mother and sister were servants of Thrain, had no desire to share the glory promised to him by Loki or anyone else including the detestable Thrain—in fact he hated Thrain. Hister hoped, through his mother and sister to spy on Thrain and know the intentions of his rival on the dark side of the spirit realm.

Svetlana was sixty six years old now. King Radu of Dakkia was Hister's father, for she had born Hister on the day of *Samhain* in the five hundred and fifty fifth year of the first age of Midgard, making Hister forty five years old that year. She gave birth to Angrboda ten years later once again on *Samhain*, but whose daughter was she, that of Radu or that of Thrain— for there was much gossip in Dakkia in those days. Of a truth Angrboda wasn't the daughter of Thrain but gossiping tongues always like to wag. Svetlana was the third wife of the King who ruled his kingdom of Dakkia from the ring fortress city of Abrud. Radu knew that his son would never be King of Dakkia—that would be the honor of Prince Draco and so Hister was given the title of *Count of Azetbur* for he being the son of a lesser wife would never reign as King of Dakkia. But indeed the witch had known this all along. Svetlana sought to make her son a sorcerer and her daughter a witch and indoctrinated them into witchcraft. Therefore for both Hister and Angrboda Svetlana guided their education for she sought for them, to rise to power by the means of sorcerery and this wicked woman knew very well that for the sake of hate she had unleashed monstrosities into Midgard.

She no longer shared the embraces of Radu nor had she any desire to do so, for once she had birthed Hister and Angrboda, her need of him was fulfilled. She had two brothers, Kain the elder and Dax the younger, the first age sixty and the second age fifty five, both of whom were estranged from her and her children and dwelled in Abrud. Kain was a cloth merchant and Dax was his partner and were quite wealthy. Neither brother ever mentioned Hister in the presence of anyone for they wished not to be associated with him or Angrboda and neither did they wish to be known as the brothers of Svetlana the Cave Witch. Even though she was still considered a concubine-wife of King Radu this brought the brothers no glory—they feared her witchcraft as did King Radu.

Svetlana stood five feet ten inches tall and weighed one hundred and seventy five pounds, and consumed a diet of swine's blood and raw pig meat to her was a delicacy. In fact it was a wonder that she hadn't died of the terrible illnesses brought on by such a despicable diet. Her hair was shorn off and her head was shaved bald and she had a silver coated bone in her nose. On her forehead, a pentangle was tattooed in black. She wrapped her head in a thick green scarf. She wore large pentangle ear rings, had a long black dress whose collar extended far out from the back like some sort of half clamshell. Her face and head were colored white with makeup and her lips and eye sockets, as well as her finger nails were painted black. Her eyebrows were decorated by a touch of leafy green and between her eyes was a red dot of paint, as well as one on the tip of her nose. She cut a rather strange and comic sort of character and all who saw knew that she had quite taken leave of her senses.

In the forty five years that had passed, King Radu Carpathia had come to fear the growing power of his estranged son Adawulf Hister Carpathia, especially when armies of thralls were seen constructing the massive black fortress of Castle Kol Oba in a place that was well outside of Hister's shire down in Azetbur—for he'd usurped the lands of another noble, the Count of Bârgău of whom it was said that Hister had turned into a tree, and was seemingly unstoppable.

King Radu was taken aback by Hister's usurpation of the mountain pass to construct this daunting fortress, for Hister was the Count of Azetbur, and his county or shire if you will, was in the regions where Fulcrum of Azetbur had once ruled, well south into the Dakkian fells where that great Carpathian Mountain range turns from its southerly direction and goes west, finally entering the black land of Morag where Ogres do dwell in numbers most fearful. Bârgău Pass (also called Tihuţa Pass) was a very strategic location in those parts of the Carpathian Fells by that same name, and was the gateway to both the steppes and to the interior of Dakkia and Radu knew that but was much to terrified to stop Hister—and in fact was a mere puppet of his own evil spawn—for his small mountain kingdom had been swallowed up inti Hister's Empire.

The Castle of Kol Oba was a foreboding structure of black basalt rock and was well beyond anything Radu Carpathia's engineers were able to construct and the old king dare not risk the wrath of his own son and lesser wife, and so his small regional kingdom was swallowed up into Hister's Empire, the pawn of his own wicked son who styled himself as *Ruler of the Dark North*. And there was Hister's mother there all the while, goading him on to darker and greater evils than had ever been imagined in Midgard.

Angrboda Carpathia, ten years the younger of Hister, became the Witch of Myrkvidr and was a concubine of the Witch King Thrain whenever he bid her come west to Erdemorden. This woman was very evil and was also known as *Frau Eisenwald*; for at a time in her youth she had been given in marriage by her father King Radu Carpathia (at the behest of her mother Svetlana) to a Burgundian Necromancer of that name. For twas to his cottage in the Iron Woods of Myrkvidr that Eisenwald brought her—but little did this conjurer realize that she was already enthralled by the lure of the Witch King Thrain. She knew herself to be fertile and when she was unable to conceive by her new husband, she slew Eisenwald with a dagger in the back as she lay in passion with this evil necromancer—in order to absorb his powers. Angrboda then offered up his body as a burned sacrifice on an altar of black stone to her lover, the demigod Thrain. Each time she traveled to Erdemorden unto Thrain he became her foul Incubus and fathered her children the twins Fenrisulfr and Mánagarmr, the *Varulvers* (Werewolves) of Myrkvidr—known also as *Månenhundene* who were the horrific Moonhounds spoken of as terrorizing all lands around dark Myrkvidr on the full moon nights. Some say that Lothar the Defiler was the sire of the Moonhounds but twas more likely to have been Thrain. Thus the tangled web of Thrain was even then being woven in which he hoped one day to ensnare the peoples of Midgard.

On the same day that Sigmund was being rewarded with the title of Grand Duke of Wodenburg, Svetlana's grandson, the young Eblilis who was tall for his age and thin with an olive skin complexion and dark brown hair sat in the dining hall at the Castle of Kol Oba. His eyes were blue, a trait he had inherited from his mother Heike. He was dressed in black and was barefoot as Svetlana held him on her lap in the dining hall while she shaved his head and painted the boy with white make up. "Yes my little precious. You shall rise and be a great King. The blood of kings flows through your veins, both of Helmgard and Dakkia. You shall learn my sorcery, and the sorcery of your Father you shall weild, my precious Eblilis. Here, have some more meat." She fed him some chopped pieces raw slugs and leeches and Heike said, "Yes, you shall indeed little son. You are my beautiful boy."

Although silent for now, Heike hated Svetlana and cringed each time that foul woman held her son. Today she had bruises, for when Hister had begun to beat the child; Heike came to her son's defense and had broken a flagon over Hister's head. Hister went down and she fled to her chambers with Eblilis, and this morning the evil monster had exacted his revenge. For all that Heike may or may not have been she truly loved her son and planned that he be the utter ruin of this entire wicked family—through him she would be avenged.

Eblilis reluctantly ate the slugs and leeches from Svetlana's fingers (for she treated as if he were a pet Yorki) and just said, "When Grandmother?" She kissed him on his forehead and replied, "When you are well grown Eblilis. But beware and do not anger your father. He has grown more powerful than I anticipated and soon will be beyond my control" Eblilis replied, "Yes Grammy I know because da beats me and kicks me! Mum saved me and he beat her up! One of these days Grammy, I'll be big enough to beat him up!" She replied, I know dar (darling) but you must endure." Heike replied, "Matrona, how dare thee say unto my son that he 'must endure' his father's abuse! He shan't have to endure it matron and it will not be allowed to continue!"

Svetlana replied, "Yes, Hister has grown beyond what I anticipated and I shall intervene on behalf of Eblilis today. But thou oh Heike must tread lightly so that my son still has use of thee—for I need you with me. Thou shalt soon be ready to join my coven and become a Witch of Carpathia, pledged to the service of the Witch King Thrain. Then I will secure your leave and that of the lad here of this place and bring you both to Erdemorden, the halls of the Witch King Thrain of Valland. But we have bigger fish to fry than your problems with my son. Beware of the power of the Circle of the Spirit Maidens. They are powerful Heike and before this is over we must face them down and destroy them. I leave it to my son, your husband Hister to deal with the Sons of Light and the Druids! It is for us as brides of Thrain to deal with the Circle of the Spirit Maidens! That Zakarah will soon learn to her chagrin that hell has come to breakfast literally! Come, everyone eat quickly, it is time for the evening sacrifice to Loki. The sow is ready to be tied upon the altar. You look so handsome my little Eblilis. Come with us to the Black Ziggurat.

Svetlana led the way to the Ziggurat, across the massive stone causeway that connected it to the fortress. They were joined by Hister and Throostra and a group of Gnomes in black robes and hoods, as well as the Gargoyle King Dragos the Green and several of his advisors. There were groups of thralls coming down the ramp, which wrapped around the tower and led to the top. The tower was only half way complete, and yet it was rising like a terrible scar on the otherwise beautiful landscape, and was at this phase a good two hundred feet tall. The plan was for it to rise to a height of six hundred and sixty six feet. A shrine in the shape of pentangle was to be constructed there and into it would be placed the *All Seeing Eye*, at least when Hister had located all of it.

The thralls bowed low to the ground as the entourage of evil began their ascent up to the top, where there was an altar where this evil troop sacrificed a pig to Loki three times a day. Hister and his mother walked together at the head of this group with Dragos not far behind, followed by everyone else. Heike, whose face was painted with green make up, around which flowed her long locks of red hair, had the frightened little Eblilis by the hand as they made their way up and the little boy complained, "Mum, why do we have to go up there all the time? This place is dank and my legs hurt! Please let's go back Mum and get some real food! Grandmother's food is grotesque!" Heike put him up on her shoulders and said, "We go by order of your father my son but I've saved you some good venison for later lamb."

The wind was blowing and a storm was moving in as they continued to climb. The moon was showing through a hole in the clouds which looked like the mouth of a dragon. Heike had on a dress identical to that of Svetlana and her lips and eye sockets were painted red, with a black dot on her nose and between her eyes and her hair was dyed green as Hister had ordered.

On Hister's shoulder sat Argob, the sorcerer's Huggin and Svetlana said to her son, "Hister, must you keep that ugly fowl? Honestly son I never understood your infatuation with Huginn's Folk. Send it back to Ravenswood, please? For I tell you that King Svart of the Huggins is the very face of treachery. His daughter Morgana, which also comes and goes as she pleases around here, is wily and unpredictable and by keeping them in your service, our entire purpose is put into danger and another thing Hister! You will no longer strike Eblilis!"

He snarled back, "Dear Mother, this is my fortress and the servants I choose are my choice and mine alone and the boy is mine as well! The King of Huginn's Folk is my ally in that war mum and that is something that you must accept!" She replied, "You should take care to spend more time with your son and not to turn him against you by this treatment! He is your heir Hister and I cherish him! Listen to me lest my anger strike thee a blow even worse. He must see you for the powerful sorcerer that you have become by the hands of the Vanier and want to carry on what we have started and if he grows up hating you everything that you have built, he will tear down!

Hister replied, "What do you mean, 'carry on' what I started? Soon we will have immortality Mum and I'll not have need of a replacement. My agents are out searching Midgard and soon we will have the final pieces of the All Seeing Eye. Ragnarok as we desire it will come and I will rule all of Midgard for eternity. You dear Mumsy will sit a Queen and ride your beast across the length and breadth of the empire and our New World Order!"

She retorted, "Ragnarok! Immortality and a New World Order you say my son? You have not even succeeded in these last four years to crush the Tervingian Rebellion! Now Sigurd is more powerful than ever and rules all the tribes of Tervingia as a single, United Kingdom—and what of the All Seeing Eye? We have the pupil and three sides only! It will not function yet Hister and even when we find where Yoshael the Elf hid the other pieces that Leprechaun girl has the Heart of the Sea, and without it the device cannot be activated."

Hister laughed and Argob swalked. Hister replied with a laugh, "I have set in motion a plan to secure the Heart of the Sea, without inviting an invasion of this fortress before the completion of the Black Ziggurat! The fighting must remain away from this place in other lands and soon the rebellion will be crushed and the Heart of the Sea will be mine. I will rid the world of all Leprechauns in our new order! There is no place for such a race of deformed animals and I will not allow them to pollute the races of Midgard with their blood any longer Mother. And for thy sake, I shall be kinder to my son."

She replied, "Keep your eye on the goal son! Don't let your hate for the Leprechauns depath us from the goal of winning this war. Four years ago we could have destroyed them, but you forced Idanthrsus to send troops east in the winter where they were annihilated, more by the severe cold than the rebels themselves Adawulf. It was your reliance on the Scythian King that has gone on to cost us lots of time, endless back and forth battles from one end of the steppes to the other, and continuation of this fruitless policy will force us to expend even more treasure. The battle must be waged by sorcery Adawulf."

Hister replied, "Indeed Mum but have you not said that patience is a virtue? What is four years to people like us? But you are right concerning sorcery. Forget you not that we are up against the wizards and the mages of Midgard? Sorcery thus cannot be the only weapon. And so I will not send an army, yet to Thorstadt or Ariemel any more until we have the Heart of the Sea." Svetlana replied sarcastically, "And just how do you expect then to get the gem when it is around the neck of Molly O'Hurleyhune who is in Thorstadt?"

He wagged his head and replied, "Down in Byzantium there are shops which sell vessels made from a commodity brought from Cathay called porcelain. Now let us say that there is a thief who wishes to seize one unique vase. Will he go in broad daylight and stampede a Taurine Bull into the shop or send forth a Minotaur? Never for he knoweth that on the day he does this, the bull or the Minotaur will smash not only the other vessels in the shop, but the one he desires for himself. Or worse for him, the shopkeeper will know why the bull has been sent and then hide the priceless vase away when he sees the attackers coming. Though the shop will be destroyed and all within, yet the shopkeeper will escape with the vase. Now the thief has tried to break in during the night to steal the vase, but has found it guarded so securely that he dare not make the attempt. So, by and by he found the shopkeeper's child unguarded and playing freely in the open, and seized the boy for ransom till the shopkeeper should deliver up the vase to him in a secret place. A place far away from where the thief actually lived. And when the shopkeeper had brought the vase, and it had been delivered up to him, the thief's gang set upon the shopkeeper, slaying both him and his child. If we are to obtain the Heart of the Sea, this is how it must be done."

Svetlana replied, "And barring that, what is the plan?" He replied, "Then we will be forced to march against Sigurd without it." Throostra said, "And all the armies of the Gnomes shall gather with you oh dark, evil master." Hister said in reply to the groveling little Gnome, "They do better to keep the Fauns at bay. Your father understands this even if you do not—right Argob?" The Huggin bowed his great raven's head from his perch across the room and said, "By your command master."

They made their way to the top and performed their sacrifice as usual. The lightening flashed and the thunder peeled but Loki didn't appear to them as he had done in times past. All around them though, there were the Jotnar moving as black shadows of the night. Eblilis was terrified of all of this and Hister came up and seized him from his mother's arms and stood him on the ground!" Svetlana glared in anger at Hister and said firmly, "Remember our talk about the lad!" He saw the look of hatred in the eyes of Heike and so he suddenly became nice and soft spoken. "There, there now Eblilis my son come with me unto the sacrifice and savor the power of the dark side." He took the confused little boy to the altar and then he said, "Eblilis my son look out over the world here from this tower. See all of it? All of it is mine, and I will give you a share of it as long as you bow down and worship me, for I am the image of the beast. I am the Son of Loki. You will grow up and take your place beside me here and then destroy Ronan when he comes against us for the final battle for Midgard."

Eblilis replied, "Dah, who is Ronan?" Hister answered in an emotionless, unfeeling tone saying, "He is the Son of Sigurd the Tervingian. He was sent into the world as a warrior of the Sons of Light, their so-called *Anointed One* in order to kill us all and take my throne. You were sent into this world by Loki to destroy him before he destroys us." Eblilis understood none of it but in the child's terror of his father, he dared not ask any more questions but he knew that he was always safe in the arms of his mother. And so he took comfort in this and from that day forward he grew in strength. Eblilis replied, "By your Command Da." From that day forward Hister dare not strike his son anymore, for the power of his mother as the most powerful witch in Midgard was legendary and he owed all of this to her.

Loki watched all of them from the top of one of the pinnacles of the castle, in the human shape of a barbarian warrior with long black hair, silver plate armor, gray trousers and black boots. He had two swords in sheaths on his back and was having a good laugh at the sight of Hister and his troop, so comical looking were they. "Human fools!" quoth he in a sarcastic laugh as a storm began to blow generating thunder and lightning which struck the castle's highest tower.

CHAPTER X

The Dark Elf

From the Skald's Tale

"Oh Skald Lothar, wise story teller, tell us more of the elves?" "I shall indeed little young Ragnar. I have told thee from whence they come so that all who sit here in Roderick's Mead Hall may know. But thou art wise for such a small child to ask such questions of so noble as race as far yonder elves. Thou hast heard all that is good and noble of Yoshael's kin, but now let me tell thee of one elf, Samael the Prodigal, the famous Dark Elf of Midgard.

Our epic saga must now turn back the pages of time a century before the days of which I'm telling thee of, to the *four hundred and ninetieth year of the first age of Midgard*—when Galorfilinde gave birth to the twins, Aubriel and Samael by her husband Mishael. The children were the glory of their father and mother and the delight of their Grandparents. The Crystal Star Palace in Alfheim was their home and the pitter patter of tiny elven feet was heard. And as they grew and became strong, many more Elves were born` from Galorfilinde and still yet a great many more from Yoshael and Zakarah, for *El Shaddai* had sanctified their marriages and commanded them to be fruitful and to multiply—and his gift to elvish women was pain free child birth.

What is one hundred years in the life of an Elf? Their children mature slowly, and so even after twenty years Aubriel and Samael appeared like human kinderlings of ten. The twins in the decades to come grew to be very tall and slim with long white-blond hair and sleek pointed ears and eyes of emerald green and slender aquiline noses. The minds of Elves mature well beyond their physical bodies and at an early age, Samael became ill at ease, wanting more than what he was ready for. He became a restless prodigal and a trouble maker. He was disruptive and a puller of pranks. Therefore his father Mishael sent him out to work in the quarries for white granite so that he would know the life of hard work that his many, many cousins were laboring at, building their new city which thrived with thousands of children—a great many more children than there were adults. Aubriel too was sent, only she absorbed the lessons that her Grandfather intended for her, and in due course returned to the palace and was betrothed to Shlomael in a courtship to last one hundred and twenty years.

Samael, while being rather a black sheep of the Elvish kind, absorbed exceptionally fast all of the knowledge of spiritual powers and customs for which the Elves are famous, and even learned to counsel others in their hours of need or depression. He learned as well the martial skills of a warrior, and no one was his equal in Alfheim. But because of his less than serious attitude and his reckless desires he wasn't trusted fully by either his parents or grandparents—and thus was soon out of the inner circle.

Many, many years now passed and one day, King Yoshael sent for his dear grandchild Aubriel. She had grown into a tall and slender elf mate and was no longer a child and as she came in to the study where her grandfather had taught her so much and there he sat at a small wooden table with Zakarah at his side. Aubriel was their delight and the jealous Samael knew it, for it had been many years since his grandparents had trusted him with anything other than small, trivial matters as he saw it. More's the pity because his father Mishael and Mother Galorfilinde were very proud of Samael on the day when King Yoshael appointed him as *Royal Chief Architect*—for Samael had a gift of alchemy and mathematics that it would take the world of men thousands of years to develop.

But Samael wanted less responsibility and more fun and he perceived that, far to the south in the land of Hellas (for he'd ruled out Phoenicia as being less civilized and Egypt because of the Evrim and the power of Pharaoh) he could find all of the worldly pleasures he so desired. Yet he was not allowed to leave the Kingdom of Alfheim, even on an out of body night flight. For Zakarah feared that, seeing the unholy images and the licentious lives of the mortals would be a hook in Samael's jaw, and that wishing not to return home his soul would linger there, and back home his body would die. No one had ever died in Alfheim and the parents and grandparents were not willing to take the chance that Samael would be the first. But Samael chaffed under these restrictions and would soon rebel.

Aubriel came in to her Grandfather and Grandmother and said with a bright, happy face. "Hello Grand Father. Grandmother, the day is so grand. You two should really come outside and enjoy the grass and the green trees. The waters are flowing through the gazebo dome and down the side of the hill over thick moss and the flowers smell grand." "Come to me my child," replied Yoshael. "Come to us and have tea little one. Give your Grandfather a hug." She came to him and embraced him, and Zakarah handed her hot tea and sweet Elf Bread." Aubriel said the sacred prayer, "Blessed are you Shaddai, King of the Universe who brings forth bread from the earth. Amen." Her grandparents were very pleased with Aubriel and let her know it.

"Aubriel, I have a very important mission for you. You must take a journey into Midgard, said Yoshael. "Aubriel's eyes light up even more and she replied, "Then I get to go through the orb again on a night journey?" Yoshael replied, "No not this time. For this journey you must go with both body and soul, to a place called Manching. I will tell you how to get there. Once there you will locate two children who have been called by *Dan Ene Gud* to be both a wizard and spirit maiden. Their names are Dithranti and Boudicca. They are to come here and I shall instruct Dithranti while your beautiful Grandmother instructs Boudicca. There will be other journeys for you Aubriel if you are successful with this one."

The young she elf replied, "Grandfather, I am very honored by your love and trust and will do all that you ask of me. I will ask one thing though. Can my brother go with me on this quest?" Zakarah had a grave look on her face and said, "Aubriel, I fear for your brother out there in the world. He is weak and will succumb to temptation. He must be protected from himself and cannot ever leave the Kingdom. You know this little one so why do you ask?" She replied, "You both have taught us well, how God gave the world a second chance after the age of Adam. He created both of you and through you all of us. Can we not give Samael the same chance?"

Zakarah the Lady of Urðarbrunnr (Urtharbrunnr) wore her beautiful white dress and glowed with light, as did Aubriel. The Spirit Maiden arose and stepped over to the window. Long ago the elves had discovered the secret of glass, and all of their windows were made of it and they had passed this knowledge on to many in the world of men. She looked down and saw Samael sitting below with a book of drawings. Next to him were several cousins. They seemed to be working on city planning and building. She could hear their thoughts Samael was talking about the foundations for the new amphitheater and then he said, "This is an important project Yoavael but I must do something greater." Yoavael replied, "Is their nothing greater than being trusted by Grandfather to build all of our cities?" He replied, "They no longer trust me with anything greater than physical building and I want to see the world Yoavael. I feel that I was meant for something greater than just bossing around stone cutters and building streets! I want a taste of the life out there in Midgard. I want a life of commerce." "Where will you go Samael?" asked Yoavael.

Samael stood up and began pacing back and forth saying, "I've thought of many places Yoav and weighed the merits of each place; I've visited the world on my night journeys and narrowed it down to three places;

Mizraim, Hellas or Phoenicia. I had to rule out Mizraim." "And why so Sam?" asked Yoav. "For are there not Evrites living there who believe as we do—in the same God?" Samael replied, "And that's why I shan't go there Yoav! Those Evrim were taught by grandfather before they left Canaan to live in Goshen, because of a drought if memory serves and I want away from all things elvish—they're too much like us in too many ways and besides it has to do with our grandfather's prophecy."

Yoavael smiled and asked, "And which one might that be Sam—there are many." "I know," answered Samael. "He says that our God is going to send a *Law Speaker* to them from among their own—as if he hadn't made enough Law Speakers when he created the Elves; and that our God is actually going to meet that man on a mountain somewhere in that region and give written laws called a *Torah* to them. I've heard enough law around here for a lifetime and methinks I shan't go to a place where I'm going to get a double dose of it from God and then from a mortal—and besides he says that plagues are coming to that land in a mere four hundred years. I'll have only just started when I'd be forced to upsticks and run! And besides the ruler of that country is called a Pharaoh and the bloke is a bleeding tyrant who'll tax me out of hearth and home! And besides all of that if those Evrites see that there's an Elf mucking about the blighters might ask me to help them in some way or to teach a religious class or some such nonsense. If *El Shaddai* is going to come down from Asgard—something that as far as I know he hasn't done for his own Elf children—and that he's preparing the chaps their own Law Speaker who knows his onions; then they sure don't need me."

"Then what about the other places," asked Yoav. Sam replied, "While the Phoenicians are master mariners and have a right healthy trade network they're much too primitive and besides all of that, that part of Midgard is always torn apart by wars! No, I want to go to Hellas—the quietest and most advanced civilization in Midgard outside of the Far East. There I can establish free commerce and live life on the wild side—and be free of lawgivers—Elvish or Evrite. But who am I kidding! Grandfather shan't ever let me leave and if I ran away they'd track me down! I'm doomed to boredom Yoav!" Samael slammed the plans down on the table and headed inside the palace.

Zakarah returned from the window and spoke private telepathic thoughts to Yoshael. "Melchizideck let us speak of Samael." "I am listening Enkelien," replied Yoshael. She said, "Our first Grandson is not happy in his work. He longs for the world of men." He replied, "It may be that we have to let him taste the sweetness, and allow it to turn to vinegar in his mouth." They opened their thoughts back to Aubriel and they began speaking in the natural. Yoshael said, "Maybe you are right Aubriel."

At that moment Samael came in. He was very tall and thin and his hair was white-blonde. His eyes were emerald green and he was nearly the image of Aubriel. He unlike the other Elves had chosen to wear black trousers. His shirt was black as well as his cape and hood. "I heard your voice calling to me Grandfather. Am I in trouble once more sir?" Yoshael replied, "You are not in trouble Samael and I haven't called thee for a report on the construction. No Grandson I've something greater for you to do."

Samael looked skeptical but he replied, "I will do anything you ask of me Grandfather." "Good," replied Yoshael. "Both thee and thy sister are to leave the city on a quest. The both of thee shall traverse the forever ice south into Midgard to a place called Manching. Once there you will find two kinderlings, young ones of tender age named Dithranti and Boudicca. They're mortals and have been chosen by *El Shaddai* to be educated here in the Yeshiva. Speak to their parents before you ask that the children be sent—and the parents will send them. For the Æs (Ayşe) [Angel] Gabriel has spoken to them in this regard. Assemble a troop of Reindeer Cavalry and outfit them for a journey of two months."

Samael was overjoyed and replied, "Aubriel and I shall do so at once Grandfather." Zakarah said, "Beware Samael of the wiles of the world of men, lest that which is sweet turn to vinegar in your mouth. Commerce for commerce sake as practiced by most men and speaking creatures has become a perversion—for it is the greed of them all and not of the pure and uncorrupted trade of we Elves dearest heart. And remember that no matter where thou goest, God always has been there first and shall not leave Midgard bereft of a Law Speaker." Samael thought that this was a very strange, cryptic statement from his grandmother, but it left his mind very soon in his rush of excitement to leave.

When the grandchildren had departed the study Zakarah said, "You know that he shan't return, don't you Melchizideck?" He stood up from his chair and had a tear in his eye as he placed his tall white, pointed hat on his head. He took his beloved by the hand and as they walked out of the study he replied, "Yes Enkelien, I know. We can only pray that when he reaches rock bottom and the world of men turns on him, that he'll come to his senses and return home." She replied, "I dreaded this day would come Melchizideck but thou art right. We cannot hold him back any longer. He must indeed become the *Dark Elf* after all, our prodigal grandson."

Two days later before it was time to leave, Samael came in once more to see his grandfather and said, "As your grandson, I know that I have wealth which is due me. I ask that it be given to me in gold and jewels grandfather, that I may have a means to engage in commerce among men along my journey." Yoshael acted surprised (although he wasn't) and replied, "Commerce? "You are an Elf Samael. What need have thee of commerce as it relates to men? True there is commerce among we Elves—but here there is no greed and covetousness to make it evil. But for mankind and most other speaking creatures except the Merwif to a much lesser extent this is not so—for in their pursuit of wealth they use commerce to enrich themselves at the expense of others—for example food. Though their brothers starve they will not give them food unless there is gold or thralldom in return and those who steal a morsel of bread in a famine to feed a starving child are damned into the dungeon."

"Those who build houses expel those who cannot pay up in gold or silver—and even their doctors are tainted by the greed of avarice and the times are coming in the world of men in a yonder age to come, when those who cannot pay for the healers craft shall be hauled into houses of judgement by agents of the crown and then left to the cold wrath of a debt collector—and shall even deny people lifesaving elixirs to those who cannot pay. And that age to come shall be an age of machines of seeming magic, but with more sorcery than magic—and many shall die of dreaded diseases—for those who make the elixirs shall wallow in beds of avarice and greed and they shall say, 'We have to recover the cost of the elixir by commerce and those who cannot pay must suffer.' Woe unto the doctors and the lawyers in those times and it shall only end in their perdition when the Son of Heaven has come to rule all of Midgard with his Torah." "He asked, "A Torah? Like the one thou sayest *El Shaddai* will give to the Evrite Law Speaker?" Yoshael replied, "Yes indeed and when the second age nears its end, he shall send from among that same people and even greater Law Speaker from out of Asgard. You may even see him Samael—assuming that your ascension time hasn't come yet."

"Those times have not yet come Samael, but the knowledge that you pass on to the world of men shall hasten the day. So beware of the commerce of greed dear grandson. Keep it pure and free of greed and for those who cannot pay, gift it unto them—for we are the Holy Elves of El Shaddai and our task is to be a light unto mankind to show him that there is a far, far better way to build a society." Samael was quite amazed at his grandfather's prophecy concerning the age of magical machines and simply said, "I shall indeed remember all that thou hast spoken of my grandfather." Yoshael replied, "See that you do Samael and you will be the first Elf to have the opportunity to teach this to the greedy and avarice men—wherever thou goest."

But then Samael thought on the prophecy and asked, "When shall these things come to pass grandfather?" Yoshael replied, "No one knows the day exactly of the comings of the *One Messiah*—but only our Father *El Shaddai*. I do know that he shall come twice, once at some point near the end of the second age to come; and again well after that when the time of the machines have come once more—as they were before the great floods then know that it is time and his second coming draweth nigh. These things are spoken of in the *Scroll of Hanokh* for all to know my dear grandson so teach all who will listen and fall not into the commerce of men." "It sounds as if thou art sending me forth on a mission other than just finding two human children Grandfather." Yoshael replied, "The life of every Elf is a mission Samael. But in any case your grandmother and I will have long since ascended in Ljosalfheim before he comes—and tis just as well for I've seen in visions what shall be done unto him by the world of men."

The twin's mother was there and Galorfilinde said, "What Thou art asking revealeth thy intentions son. Thou intend to abandon Aubriel down in Midgard and run away! Father, I shan't let him go!" Samael acted surprised and said, "No, no really mother. I just want a little spending gold!

The world of men works on spending and commerce, and even greed—not like ours and I will return mother." Galorfilinde's eyes filled with tears and she was comforted when her father put a gentle arm around her shoulder and drew her into him in a loving paternal embrace. "Very well Samael, thou shalt have thine inheritance." "I Thank thee Grandfather. This means a very lot to me. And I shall remember our laws grandfather. I will always be an Elf."

When Samael had left Galorfilinde said, "Father, thou art enabling him to carry out his defection!" "Maybe so Galorfilinde," he replied, "but until he descends down this dark path he is choosing, he'll never be able to ascend to any higher level than what he is now. He shall return after a long harsh road of trials and tribulations—and indeed live past the second age—undetermined is his time of ascension. Trust me special one, it must be so." "I shall miss my boy Father, and I want to fly to him on night journeys when thou sayest that the time is right. Wherefore shall he go?" Yoshael replied, "He wants to avoid the coming of the Evrite Law Speaker and avoid meeting our God when he comes to Sinai should he stay four hundred years so he definatly isn't going to Mizraim. I've foreseen that he will go to Hellas and there set up his, 'commerce,' in Delphi. But he's unleashing forces in human economy that he little understands and those upon whom those forces are unleashed have no understanding. Samael won't go unto Mizraim for fear of the coming plagues of judgment against that kingdom and the Vanier whom it's people worship—yet where he goes there shall be unleashed a plaque of Black Death."

Galorfilinde's eyes widened in wonder and fear at this talk of plagues and she replied, "Delphi? Indeed Father, Delphi is one of the places where you hid a part of the All Seeing Eye. We Elves are immune to all diseases which afflict Midgard. Please tell me that this will be so for Samael." He put an arm around her should and as they walked to the window to look down below and seeing Samael dashing across the courtyard Yoshael replied, "Yes Galorfilinde his body is immune but his soul shan't be—for he shall be tormented in his dreams by the suffering that he's unleashed. He will be needed there as well for a good purpose and everything is proceeding as it should child. Let's go and have tea and crumpets shall we?"

CHAPTER XI

Farewell to Samael

From the Skald's Tale

More things than should have been known in Midgard
except by Elves were brought to the world of men by
Samael for too much food to soon sourest the stomach and
so the stomach of the kingdoms in Hellas were soured by
the knowledge that was brought unto them to soon by the
Dark Elf of Midgard.

So it was that Samael departed his grandfather's Kingdom, and when they had located young Dithranti and Boudicca in the forests around Manching gathering firewood, they went into town with the kinderlings and spoke to the parents. Now Dithranti's father Argyle had been killed by a cave in down south in the salt mines. But the Æs (Ayşe) Gabriel had rescued the children—this tale has been told already at another tale fire. And so when the saddened mothers had given consent for the younglings to go north to Alfheim and they were a mile north of Manching, Samael set his plan into action. He sent Aubriel to bid them go north to Alfheim, while he took his money and his reindeer and abandoned the Elves. He traded in the reindeer for a horse in Manching, intending never again to return to the house of his grandfather. Aubriel was deeply hurt by this and feeling very betrayed—for she felt that she had gone out on a limb for her brother and that he had cruelly snapped it away from her out of the infection of greed—which an Elf wasn't supposed to have. She carried with her deep resentment for Samael from then on in the coming century. The younglings were bewildered by it all.

O'er hills and rivers, mountains and dales, Samael found his way south into Hellas where he took up residence in the city of Delphi, taking up a life a riotous living. He was now the *Dark Elf.* As long as his great fortune held out his friends were many. He even learned commerce and greed, to cheat and to swindle better than the best and with his superior knowledge of mathematics, which in a small measure he shared with *Mnesarchus the Ancient* who was the Hellene ancestor of the great *Pythagoras*, he managed to keep up his life of sin and debauchery. He began dealing in cloth, metals, spices and olive oil.

Samael established a fleet of merchant vessels which sailed through the *Pillars of Hercules*, into the Celtic Sea to Brython where they traded their wares for tin ore. He made three voyages himself. By the time of his third voyage to Brython (there were many others elsewhere) Dithranti had grown to full manhood, married Boudicca and traveled home. There Dithranti established the *Order of the Druids*. While in Brython Samael carefully avoided the Druids, for they were to him, Law Speakers and too religious for his comfort—for the Elves were indirectly responsible for their foundation and Samael wanted nothing to do with them.

Far away back home though, his grandfather used the power of the great *Dolman of the Crystal Star Palace* (the orb) to keep an eye on Samael, and even came to his beloved grandson on the night journeys, careful never to waken the lad—yet wanting more than ever to embrace him and welcome him home. Samael had felt drawn to Delphi for some reason, and he wasn't sure if it was because he knew that his grandfather had placed a portion of the All Seeing Eye under the temple, or for commercial reasons. Maybe it was the presence of different Hellene women over the years who was deeply in love with him that made him always return to Delphi from the sea voyages or from chariot races, keeping it as his centre of business— yet he was a heart breaker, leaving those poor women when they grew too old—also being careful not to father any half-elven children with any of them; for he feared the consequences of this—a race of immortal half elves which would grow beyond his control and usurp the land and his commerce. But once thing that he thought he was sure of was that he would stay there indefinitely. The humans no longer feared him as an Elf and in fact, as long as his money and fortunes held out were his friends and colleagues. But in this environment he lost his way and his compassion and even turned away widows and orphans and those with illnesses he charged in gold for his gift of Elf Medicine. Many poor blighters turned away and the anger of Asgard was kindled against this unfaithful and ungrateful Elf.

A century passed and just after Samael's third voyage to Brython ended the hand of *Dan Ene Gud* struck Hellas because of Samael and the Dark Elf was thrown down from his ivory tower. There was a collapse of all commerce in Hellas as plague ravaged the land and for Samael everything went all to pot. He thought he might earn a bit through his healing arts but immediately found that his God had taken it from him. Though he was immune to this Black Death, all those around him save a very few died and many Hellenes turned upon the Dark Elf, for twas easy to blame him for the raging death which scourged the land from Sparta to Thessalonika. The currency of all Hellas was coins called Drachmas and these was worthless due to hyperinflation and in this Samael was guilty for he'd persuaded the kings of that land to devalue the coinage with base medals. He'd introduced the concept of loans with usury and soon all the poor souls of the land were indebted to the money lenders of the land—and when no one could pay because of absurd usury rates, the poor were cast out! Farmers lost their lands and a rebellion started in Corinth by landless peasants flying red flags whose goal was to rid the entire land of kings, money houses and most of all Samael! Civil wars and revolutions raged and many kings of Achaea were beheaded and the money lenders burned at the stake. A new form of government was thought of during those evil years called *Republic*.

There was war with the Dorians and the Mycenaean's and with Troy. The city of the Minoans on the islands was destroyed by a volcano! The people of Hellas heard of the rise of a terrible new empire on the steppes above the dark sea and famine gripped the land. All that Samael had built collapsed into ruin, and with his money and ships gone and his clothing in rags, he was forced to hire himself out to a pig farmer! But one thing he had going for him though, was that fact that he had found true love very recently—a woman whom he would have taken home had desired to return there.

CHAPTER XII

Powers of the All Seeing Eye

From the Skald's Tale

In our age it's never been seen and not one trace of such a thing shall ever any man find. The All Seeing Eye is that talisman of which I speak. Power of stars and powers of wind, earth and fire were gathered say the legends within the heart of the Eye. Was it talisman or amulet—who can say for it has vanished into the mythology of the past and though many seek its power for power's sake—woe to him that findeth it!

The All Seeing Eye and the thought of the power that it would unleash drove Hister ever onward. He would not be dissuaded from his scheme, so sure was he that Loki was going to keep his promises to him once their version of Ragnarok had come to pass. In sacred sights all over Midgard warriors of the Dark Quest searched for the parts, which the wise Yoshael had hidden. Hister already had the pupil, which had been retrieved from Gobekli Tepe by his ancestor Gigan of Shinar and carried into Dakkia centuries before. The base had been found in the city Jebus in caverns beneath a grain thrashing floor under Mount Moriah in Canaan, which the Elf King had placed there.

This talisman has been explained in other tale fires but it must be told again for remembrance sake. The All Seeing Eye was a pyramid shaped object made of crystal, constructed in the days of King Nimrod by the evil craftsman of the Vanier named Volundr, and was then place into a temple on top of the Tower of Babel. It has many uses but since Loki and his minions had been shut out of Asgard, Volundr thought that this device which harnesses the mystical power of creation to do what it does, thought that the Vanier could pierce the veil of heaven and throw down the gates of Asgard—and thus would come Ragnarok and the Gotterdammerung. Were they foolish enough to think that they could throw down the everlasting doors?

The All Seeing Eye was six feet tall when fully assembled consisted of eight pieces. The centre was an orb called the *Pupil*. It was about four feet around and if used for good, this eyepiece says the legends, would glow in the shape of a human eye. If used for evil, it would glow as a red orange snake eye with a black pupil. It sat on a flat base plate of crystal seated in a rounded basin in order that the orb wouldn't roll. These are the first two pieces, the *pupil* being the first and the *base*, square shaped and flat being the second. Then there are four clear crystalline pieces similar to the base, which form the *sides* of the pyramid and are triangular in shape, also with rounded basins in the centre that allows each piece to fit over and around the pupil as it sits on the base plate. The seventh piece is a white crystal *cap stone*, itself a small pyramid shaped piece one foot tall and on each side, a foot long. On top of this there is a space rounded down into the top of the capstone in which fits the eighth piece, which is a gemstone is known as the *Heart of the Sea*—and why the gemstone? Behold *Dan Ene Gud* saw from Asgard what the Vanier where attempting, and while for some reason known only to him, God allowed the device to be completed.

The Heart of the Sea, which was coming to be called *The Holy Lamp* due to the great light emitted by the gemstone allowed the device to draw in its power from all elements of creation and the natural energy of the earth and the All Seeing Eye, cannot be activated without the Heart of the Sea. Each piece can be used separately as a talisman or amulet, but the separate pieces will not function in the way that Volundr designed the entire device to function when it is put together as a single unit.

Why, if the All Seeing Eye was a thing created by the dark side, could it be used for good and why is a part of it called the *Holy Lamp*? The answer is simple. It's a device and like any device or weapon it depends upon the motives and the heart condition of those who weild it. Thus the weapon that is forged in the smithy of an evil swordsmith can be used if captured by a good person. The Holy Lamp was touched by God, unknown to wicked old Volundr, and so the very thing that allows the device to function, is the very thing that *Dan Ene Gud* controls—thus showing that he is in ultimately the king of his creations.

This is not true of all things created by the dark side, such as the Volundr Rings but it was true with the All Seeing Eye. Why? Because *Dan Ene Gud* allowed this device to be created, and made sure that his own true servants could seize it and use it against those who have betrayed the world; and why not the rings? This is because they are designed to attack and ensnare the souls of men, elves or other speaking creatures, whereas the All Seeing Eye is merely a tool for the physical and pertains not to anyone's soul. Using the All Seeing Eye will not cause a being to lose their immortal soul in and of itself such as do the Volundr Rings—but how they do it is a mystery best left to wizards to explain.

CHAPTER XIII

The Dark Quest

From the Skald's Tale

I must say unto thee, oh my Visigoths that the plots and schemes of Hister began to reach ever more heights of infamy in his mad desire to obtain the pieces of the All Seeing Eye—the Holy Lamp. Svetlana perceived how it might also increase her power and raise Eblilis to power as a King when the time of his father was over, for she perceived that her son was going to be destroyed by his own blind ambitions and that there was no way she could prevent it. And oh, let us in no way forget the boy's mother Heike, for she thought how she might use sorcery to her own advantage, and destroy Hister with it! Did she know that one cannot use Satan to destroy Satan?

I t came to pass in the days of Pharaoh Neferhotep of the first of Egypt (called Mizraim by the elves), that Yosef the Evrite was elevated by the King as Grand Vizier. Having been thrown into a dry cistern in Canaan twenty years before and then sold as a slave by ten of his brothers, Yosef became the chief steward of Potiphar, the Priest of On. Being falsely accused of rape by Madame Potiphar Yosef was cast into prison where he spent the next fourteen years of his life. During this time he became trusted by the warden of the prison, so much so that he was elevated as a chief of the fortress below the warden. He was innocent of all crimes that the woman had accused him of.

Yosef was a good descent man and *Dan Ene Gud* gave him the understanding of dream interpretation—and when the Pharaoh was made aware of this, he took him from the jail to interpret the King's dreams. And so he did, and the Pharaoh's dreams were Prophecies of seven years of plenty and seven years of blight and famine. Yosef was elevated to be the Grand Vizier of the Empire of Egypt and afterward he was called by the Egyptians, Zaphenath-paneah and soon afterwards he was wed to Asenath, daughter of Potiphar. His wise policies saved all Mizraim and the surrounding region from starvation.

Twas in the days of Pharaoh Sobekhotep III, Neferhotep's grandfather, who knew as well Abraham, Zaphenath-paneah's Great-Grandfather that Yoshael brought down the first side piece (the third piece) of the All Seeing Eye, and having gained the full confidence of Sobekhotep, secured it within a secret chamber deep inside the Great Pyramid at Giza. Sobekhotep III had come to know the true God as a result of his dealings with the Evrim and so when Yoshael and Zakarah brought this to him for safe keeping, they knew it would be in good hands. Yoshael, knowing that a Holy Man from among the descendants of Shem would soon rise as the most powerful Grand Vizier in the history of Egypt and that all would go well until the times of the rule of the Holy Man Yosef were fulfilled, departed with his oldest two children by ship for Hellas, where the second side was placed under the Temple of Delphi.

It came to pass when Zaphenath-paneah had been given his office and the nation was secure in his charge, that he was called in the night to a secret meeting by the Pharaoh Khahotepre. With Zaphenath-paneah was Potiphar, who now served him. It was all in the deepest of secrecy and there were guards all around heavily armed and bearing torches. Pharaoh said to Zaphenath-paneah, "Now that you are my Chief Steward I must take and show you something that we've been charged to protect. This must not fall into the hands of anyone from out of the dark north or from anywhere else! There was an Elf Wizard who came here with it many years ago during the days of my grandfather Sobekhotep. You probably know of him as well Zaphenath-paneah." He replied, "Indeed I do my Pharaoh. He was called Melchizedek—but none of us have seen him since I was a small, small child." Pharaoh replied, "Then you know well the story of the All Seeing Eye?" Zaphenath-paneah replied, "Indeed your majesty I do and I also know that Melchizedek dismantled it and hid the pieces all around the world. Did he bring a piece here to Egypt your Majesty?" Pharaoh raised an eyebrow and replied, "Indeed he did. Come, let us go up and enter the pyramid."

Pharaoh led the way and even the guards were among a very select few who knew about this—in all there were a mere six of them who knew, and the rest, numbering about twenty, would stay behind outside of the pyramid. They quickly made their way out of the great palace, whose walls were decorated with ornate hieroglyphs of daily life, commerce, and scenes of worship from the temples. They passed the new Khartoosh containing the name of the very Pharaoh who now was leading the way out on this mysterious quest deep in the night. All of these Egyptians, including now Zaphenath-paneah, had shaven faces and heads and wore white shorts and no shirts. Their eyes were painted with dark makeup making them to resemble the eyes of the cats which these people so adored.

They arrived at the water and quickly entered a boat. This was indeed strange and rather cloak-and-dagger because the royal bark was tethered to the dock nearby. Pharaoh wanted no one to notice who it was that was headed up to the pyramid at such a strange hour of the night. Once in the boat the soldiers paddled upstream and into the waterway beside the Sphinx. The whole area was lit by oil torches and the light flickered off of the Sphinx and reflected off of its fine whitewashed finish. Overhead the stars were bright and full. The boat quickly made its way up to the end of the canal at the foot of the Great Pyramid. Once the guards had tied the boat to the dock, Pharaoh with torch in hand said, "All guards except the chosen six are to stay here and let no one pass. You six are sworn to secrecy on pain of having your tongues cut away."

Three guards led the way and three brought up the rear as Pharaoh, Zaphenath-paneah and Potiphar walked between them. Making their way up to the stone door, they opened it up and entered the massive, smooth sided and white washed man-made mountain of stone. They made their way downward hundreds of feet in a sloping tunnel that was in no way decorated with any of the typical hieroglyphic artwork of this kingdom. They passed by an entrance that led upward into the pyramid structure itself, and on down into the bedrock and a bit later they found themselves at a closed door. "Guards, remain here," ordered Pharaoh. Potiphar opened another door and the three of them entered into a dark unfinished room. The place was musty and smelled of earth and so quiet that Zaphenath-paneah could hear loudly the ringing in his ears and the beating of his heart.

There was a spade leaning in one corner and Potiphar used it to pry open a doorway in the lower right hand side of the back wall of the large room in which they stood. It led into a crawlway, which Potiphar led the way into. The three of them, in spite of painful bare knees, crawled through it approximately twenty five feet where it ended in a small chamber. Once inside it and able to stand, there it was, the first side piece of the All Seeing Eye. It was made of clear crystal about a foot thick and part of the centre of it was round inward so that the pupil or orb would fit nicely and the thing was very heavy.

When Zaphenath-paneah saw it, he never once attempted to touch it but said, "Yes, I feel the power that comes from this piece of the talisman your majesty and I know that this cannot be allowed to fall into anyone's hands, good or evil sire." Pharaoh replied, "You are wise as always Grand Vizier. If the forces of evil find this and it is reunited it with it sisters and the talisman be reassembled, darkness will consume Midgard."

The three of them departed and resealed the chambers and by the rising of the desert sun, everyone was home in the palace. Zaphenath-paneah made sure that the piece was secure and kept it a secret. He was a holy man of *El Shaddai* and knew the God of the Elves and while he lived, no one could hope to get their hands on it and never once did he try to use it for divination. What need had he of divination when the Creator himself spoke to Zaphenath-paneah and revealed to him all manner of sacred and holy knowledge beyond the power of any mere human dabbling in the occult. This incident happened a generation or more after Yoshael had hidden this piece within the pyramid.

And now our tale goeth back to the days when Yoshael was hiding the pieces of the All Seeing Eye and the journey of the Elf King was indeed an epic quest for Yoshael requested the aid of the flying Unicorns Chi-i-Lin and his wife Qi-Lin. Qi-Lin flew Zakarah back to the Elves' land of creation where she hid the capstone (the seventh piece) within the Ark of Noach atop the Mountains of Ararat. Chi-i-Lin flew Yoshael thousands of leagues to the southeast to the part of Midgard known as Hodu, where he placed the third side in a sealed vault within the Temple of Varanabha.

Yoshael and Chi-i-Lin flew the fourth side, (the sixth piece) of the device around the ends of the mountains of Shangra La, the highest of all the fells of Midgard where they secured it in a cave in the cliffs above the small circular rock temple of Ruthok. These things were quite heavy and Yoshael and the flying Unicorn King were glad to be rid of them.

The seventh and smallest piece was placed in the care of the Merwif and became known as "The Heart of the Sea," and also as the "Stone of Nechtan" because it was given into the hands of the first King of the Merwif, Nechtan and much later it became known as the Holy Lamp. It would be safe under the sea with the Merwif for no earth born person or speaking creature could travel beneath the waves of the ocean to steal it. Without it the All Seeing Eye wouldn't function as it was intended. Without this gemstone the talisman simply wouldn't work. It was the smallest piece of the talisman yet indeed it was the most important.

And why didn't Yoshael himself take a piece of the Eye north when he and his family were sent away from Jebus by the Angel of El Shaddai? This was because, even the great Melchizideck, listened to the advice of his soulmate Zakarah who advised against keeping any of part the All Seeing

Eye in their new land. "There should be no reason for hostile nations of treasure hungry beings of any race in Midgard to come trekking across the Land of Forever Ice in a vain attempt to possess the powers which the Eye will unleash. No Melchizedek we should give the last piece away. We are on a higher level of Spirit Realm than anyone except the Angels and we need no such amulet or any talisman in order to commune with our Holy Father El Shaddai." The father of Elves then replied to the mother of Elves saying, "Wise words Enkelien," (Angelic) replied Yoshael.

Their son Shlomael was a tall man as Elves go, with a thin body and slender face. His skin was white and his hair was, like that of his father, long and white blond. His face was smooth shaven and his eyes were a crystal blue. So much different than that of his sister Galorfilinde was he, yet both had come from the same father and mother. Within their blood would be the diversity of all the future elvish people. "To whom shall we trust this gem to then Father?" asked Shlomael. Yoshael didn't answer directly but turned Galorfilinde also saying, "Take this final gem stone to the Celtic Sea where you are to take ship to the Isles of Solorlingues. Take this small staff and dip it into the water facing west on the beach. The Children of Manannan Mac Lir will come to you. You must give this gem to one Merman and one only, King Nechtan. When he sees that you are an Elf, he will know that you are my children. Shlomael, Galorfilinde, go together on this quest and when it is completed you both join us in the new land—for I go to prepare a place for you, that where I am you may also dwell my children."

And so it was that Shlomael and Galorfilinde did as their father Yoshael asked of them and delivered the final piece of the All Seeing Eye safely to the Merwif. In one year they returned, and were led by an Angel to the new land, where they joined with Father Yoshael and Mother Zakarah in the founding of a shining new kingdom in Midgard, the Kingdom of Alfheim. During these years all the families of the Elves continued to be fruitful and to multiply until in short order a whole nation of people developed. Even Zakarah continued to give birth to one child a year, completely free of pain up until her five hundredth birthday when her fertility ceased. Such is the case with all women of the Elvarim, that after five hundred years their child bearing centuries are over and like Zakarah, Elvish women carry and give birth to their children completely free of pain—unlike womankind and the females of the other speaking creatures of Midgard for upon them has fallen the *Curse of Havah* spoken of in the *Scrolls of the Beginnings* and in the *Scrolls of Eden* and in the *Lost Tales of the Midgardsvolk.*

A century passed and Hister sent out dark riders on quests to retrieve the pieces of the All Seeing Eye and unfortunately, they'd been very successful—for the wicked Vani, Volundr had revealed the locations of the pieces to Hister after a sacrifice or two. And now began the Quest of Doom. Ogres, evil men some Gnomes and many Gargoyles went forth in all the directions from Hister's castle and twas the Gargoyles who were to fly back to Kol Oba with each discovered piece. To the faraway places in the east like Varanabha and Ruthok, Gargoyles had been sent and these ugly devils had done their job quite well over the last four years. Rameses himself retrieved the Capstone from the Ark of Noach. Retrieving the final three pieces was going to prove much more difficult, despite the fact that they were much closer.

CHAPTER XIV

Danger in Mizraim

From the Skald's Tale

Far and wide and round is our world of Midgard and on it are many kingdoms, some most strange. One of the most grand and most strange to us was that of Egypt, called Mizraim by the Elves and the Evrites—the kingdom astride the Nile River of Cushan Midgard. The dark quest of Hister's servants had led these knaves most foul down to Mizraim to steal that part of the talisman there and thus disturb the peace of Pharaoh.

I t came to pass in those far off days of the first age of Midgard during the time which King Sigurd journeyed to Assyria on his famous Quest for Steel that a force one hundred Gargoyles and a thousand Gnomes led by the Gargoyle Lord Gorgo who was a cousin to King Dragos the Green, arrived in the city of Gaza in the land of Canaan. Behold the *Philistine Tyrant* in that city who was favorable to the cause of Hister, reinforced this strange looking unit of mercenaries which then marched on the Jebusite Citadel of Zion in chariots. In those days the titles of the Kings of the Philistines was *Tyrant.* The king of Jebus, who was a Canaanite, was unwilling to resist the Philistines and terrified by the Gargoyles, quickly surrendered and the city fell without a fight. The School of the Prophets, guardians of their part of the Talisman fought to defend the hiding place and most died. The survivors were driven away but unfortunately they were unable to secure the base piece of the All Seeing Eye, which by the end of the day was in the hands of Hister's Mercenaries. Gorgo then returned unto Gaza where he paid the Philistine Tyrant two hundred talents of gold. He immediately sent Commander Rameses home carrying the base along with an escort of ten Wing Troopers. Now it was on to Egypt to find the next piece.

The great river Nile flowed wide and deep from a great deep forest and mighty lake thousands of miles to the south in Cushan Midgard. It had two branches, one called the Blue Nile and the other known as the White Nile. It is the life blood of this land, flowing northward to the *Medelhavet* (Great Sea) through the lands of Dongola and Nubia. From out of Sheba it is joined by the Blue Nile which also flows forth from a mighty lake known as Tanis. (Not to be confused with the City in Egypt of the same name.) The waters flow ever northward past the storied lands of forgotten Nubian Kings until it enters the Land of Mizraim, Great Egypt at the Second Cataract. When one has passed this point, he is in the land of the Pharaohs, and subject to their power.

Down flows the Nile most great and wide and during its seasonal floods it washes down alluvial soil which is rich nutrient filled mud and this is life for the crops of the people of Upper and Lower Egypt—the sons and daughters of Mizraim who was the builder of the Great Pyramid. On past the great monuments which during the first age of Midgard were still being built it goes, past Syene, Thebes, Abydos, Siut and Noph—until before thy very amazed eyes there stands before you at Giza, the massive Pyramid of Mizraim and his Sphinx. Long after Mizraim other Pharaohs would try and copy him, building other structures around it and even a Step Pyramid at Saqqara, but none could match the height or genius of mathematics which the Father of Egypt embodied within this, the greatest monument ever constructed in Midgard.

But Hister's Dark Quest Warriors cared nothing for any of this because their main concern was to slip into Egypt and retrieve the piece of the talisman from within the vault of the Great Pyramid. So the Gargoyles took flight and traveled along the coast, westward towards the city called Sin while their Gnome allies boarded their four ships at Raphia, and sailed down the coast and bound for the same destination. With them went a number of Philistines led by an officer named Hector and twas he who'd had been sent out from Gaza at the behest of Tyrant Ackish. The Gnomes feigned that they were nothing but a jolly group of merchants on a grand trade expedition sent out by their leader King Throng and Queen Theresa. Hence it was plausible to the Egyptians that these strange Dwarves would have come out on an expedition as they claimed.

Lord Gorgo and his Wing Troopers kept themselves well hidden in the Reed Marshes of the Nile Delta in the region of Goshen around the area of the city of Tanis, intending to await the arrival of their Gnome and Philistine compatriots. They just couldn't march against the Egyptians and take the prize—for in spite of the chaos in the Egyptian regime since the sad demise of Grand Vizier Zaphenath-paneah, Pharaoh Khahotepre was secure on his throne and the army was strong. His was not merely an army of footmen and cavalry as ones sees back on the Steppes of Midgard, but an army which had perfected the use of the chariot and no force of Gnomes and Gargoyles were going to defeat it. No, lifting the piece of the All Seeing Eye from the Egyptians would have to be done on a secret night raid—by thieves in the night as it were.

The ships of the Gnomes were full of all manner of trade goods, and they put into the harbor of Sin, and faced inspection by the Egyptian Port Authorities. The Philistines, who spoke the same language as their

Hellene cousins but with a different accent as well as Egyptian, interpreted for the Gnome Leader Captain Dunsel. Dunsel was dressed in typical Aegean Sailors garb except that he had a Gnomishr hat; a hat which was made of cloth and covered his head rather like a stocking and had a piece which flopped over to the left ending in a puffy ball. The whole thing was a hideous green as were Dunsel's teeth. He stood about five feet tall from head to toe and sported a chest length rusty red beard and a big nose rather like a knobby round ball.

The Egyptians that boarded the ship were dark sun tanned officers in official white robes with shaved heads and faces and their eyes were painted to resemble cat eyes. There were two officers, one about five feet twelve inches tall, who carried some papyrus scripts and a feather pen. His assistant was half a head taller and carried a jar of ink. With them were six soldiers in typical Egyptian military garb and the cloth Pharaohonic style turbans having flat sections facing forward beside each ear. These ran the length from the temples of their heads down to their shoulders. The rest of the turbans came down around their shoulders and a bit down the backs of their necks and were dyed in a chess board checker pattern. These were dangerous looking men with fierce countenances of dark eyes and shaved faces and heads and looked to the Gnomes as if they meant business and would either kill or arrest anyone making trouble.

The officer looked with distain at Captain Dunsel and asked roughly. "I am Harbor Master Amunsnefru and this is my secretary Tutankhotep! Who are you and what is your nation? On what business come ye down into Egypt?" Hector the Philistine bowed a bit and dutifully interpreted what the officer said, whereupon the Gnome replied, "I am Captain Dunsel, leader of this trade expedition. I am come down from the far north from the Kingdom of the Nibelungen which lies beyond the Dark Sea, from my Lord King Throng. We are sent here to trade for fine papyrus and exotic spices—for our fine fish oils and northern fleeces."

Amunsnefru replied, "Well and good Captain. You must pay the royal tax first in order for the privilege to trade in Egypt, which will amount to one percent of the assessed value of the cargo on all your vessels. Your ships will be searched for weapons. Any weapons you have must be declared before the search and then handed over to the Captain of the Guard—for which you will be given a receipt. Upon your departure they will be returned to you after the payment of a storage fee on five percent of the assessed value of the weapons in question! Failure to declare all such weapons before our inspection will result in your imprisonment in the sea dungeon for a period not less than one year and no more two. Failure to pay the storage fee will result in the confiscation of the said weapons Captain Dunsel. Do I make myself clear shorty?"

Dunsel was clearly upset by the remark and more so by all the rules and he replied, "You have made yourself, abundantly clear My Lord." Amunsnefru replied, "Have ye any weapons to declare shorty?" The Gnome scowled at being called 'shorty' but dare not act angry. Dunsel ran down a short list of the weapons that they carried for self-defense, and seven crewmen from each ship turned in about twenty bronze short swords, ten tridents, one mace and ten spears with bronze points. These were marked and tagged and taken away by the soldiers of Tutonkhoras and then Amunsnefru declared," Then let the search begin Captain Dunsel. Commander Tutankhoras, send your men to search all of the vessels in this convoy."

The soldiers did so but found no weapons for the crafty Gnomes had wrapped all of their hardened steel weapons and slings with rounded steel ball ammunition, an arsenal of bows and crossbows, and thousands of arrows and bolts with steel tips in sacks. These sacks had been hooked to the under sides of the ships at the very centre of their hulls at the keel. After an hour or so and with all fees paid Amunsnefru said, "Ok shorty, you and this crew of runts may trade in the city! Welcome to Egypt!" Dunsel bowed politely but cursed under his breath.

CHAPTER XV

Lord Gorgo

From The Skald's Tale

Come now and let me weave another sad tale! Let me tell you of how the evil Gnomes and their Gargoyle friends, desecrated the monument of Great Egypt, of Mizraim himself!

T he wily little Captain Dunsel and his Gnomes traded some of their wares in the city called Sin but also received permission to go south to the Capitol City of Noph, for which they set out for on the second day of their sojourn in the Land of Egypt. They had retrieved their weapons from their ship hulls in secret deep in the shadows of the night and joined forces with Lord Gorgo and his Gargoyles, who had managed to remain hidden within the saw grasses and papyrus reeds of Goshen.

Dunsel and his Gnomes bought camels for the journey and after an extensive planning session with Lord Gorgo, they continued south, passing through the cities of Pibeseth and On, where they boarded a Nile River transport vessel which took them and their camels the remaining eighteen miles to Noph. Here they took up lodging in the merchant's quarter of the city which was near the Bazaar. In the meanwhile Gorgo and his Gargoyles stayed well hidden in the saw grasses along the Nile. Gargoyles were an almost unheard of being in Egypt and if they were discovered a tumult would result and the mission would fail. He and his Wing Troopers were very impressed to say the least by the massive cities of stone and the towering pyramids which lay before their eyes. After all, they had traveled from the far north where the great cities that they knew of were made of wood and sod. They could not have dreamed that there were places like Egypt in their wildest fantasies, nor could they conceive of as to how it had been built. Dunsel and the Gnomes had the same sort of feelings that night as they took up their lodgings in Noph with their ever present Philistine interpreter Hector with them and his ten men.

Lord Gorgo's men had just slain a crocodile and were slicing it up to eat raw when suddenly a glowing light appeared before him in the night. And now when his black dolman or sorcery began heat up in his pocket, Gorgo removed it and immediately the talisman glowed angry red—Gorgo knew his master would now appear. It was the dark of the moon and in the halo appeared a vision of Hister. Lord Gorgo bowed before the vision as did his men and he said, "What is thy bidding oh Dread Lord Darkness?" Hister replied, "What progresses have ye to report Lord Gorgo?" The Gargoyle Officer replied, "As you know Dread Lord

Darkness, Commander Rameses began making his way north with the base of the Eye from Jebus some days ago. But the stone was unexpectedly heavy Master and it will take him some time to get it to you. He will be required to fly over land and avoid the shorter routes across the Medelhavet and the Dark Sea due to the weight of the object Master—for it cannot be allowed to fall into the abyss if dropped. They must take turns with it and rest every few leagues."

Hister replied, "This was not unexpected Gorgo. What progresses have ye and Dunsel made towards obtaining the next piece?" Gorgo replied, "We are near the Great Pyramid and are well hidden from Pharaoh Khahotepre's troops. Dunsel and his Gnomes as well as Hector and his Philistines are in Noph in the guise of merchants. I have sent out scouts this very night to ascertain how well the entrance is guarded Master and when I am able to meet with Dunsel and Hector we will set our plans in motion Dread Lord Darkness." Hister replied, "Very good Lord Gorgo. I am finally beginning to find some good help around here. I will commend you to King Dragos, after the piece is in your possession and you are clear of Egypt. And does Zaphenath-paneah still serve the Pharaoh? Only he could stop us now Gorgo!" The Gargoyle replied, "No Dread Lord Darkness, he does not. He has passed beyond the vail and our chances of success have increased from near zero to sixty percent at least Master." "Well that is indeed good news. Avoid his people in Goshen at all costs and see to it that you do not fail Lord Gorgo!" Gorgo bowed his head down and replied, "By your command Dread Lord Darkness."

CHAPTER XVI

The Scorpion's Den

From the Skald's Tale

So high a tower is that great monument of Pyramid shape, built in the dim times by the Lord Mizraim himself. Yet even its majestic body, were it alive, had no hands whereby to stop the minions of Loki, from the thievery of the treasure hidden within.

Four days passed and Operation Pyramid began. The moon was still dark as the raiders moved under the cloak of night toward their target. The one hundred Gargoyles flew to the south side of the pyramid and landed along its steep side, where they crept like dark menacing shadows around to the east face where the entrance was located. The rest of the force moved in from both the south and north faces of the pyramid, five hundred Gnomes in each troop and the Philistines equally divided as well. Hector, who was of dark complexion with bushy black hair and brown eyes and standing six feet tall commanded the northern force and Dunsel the southern as they stealthy made their way toward the target like creeping desert insects.

Lord Gorgo's men suddenly came upon the six entrance guards from above and in the flickering torchlight, cut their throats open. Gorgo cupped his hands over his beak-like mouth and hooted like an owl to alert everyone else that the guards had been killed. Dunsel gave a hand signal and he ran up the ramp with twenty Gnomes and six Philistines. The Philistines stripped the dead Egyptians of their uniforms and quickly changed clothes, and then ruthlessly tossed the poor unfortunate soldiers over the side of the ramp and down into the sand. In the meanwhile, Hector and his forces secured the dock at the canal, killing all the guards swiftly and quietly. Hector and his men remained quiet as he searched for any signs that they had been detected. "So far so good," he said and they settled down to wait for Dunsel to retrieve the piece from within the belly of the Great Pyramid.

After opening the door Dunsel and six Gnomes took spades, picks and a pry bar and made their way by lamp light down the long sloping passageway. Being of the race of Dwarves they had no problem with low ceilings or crawl spaces, and it wasn't long before they passed the entrances to the upper chambers of the Pyramid. A Gnome asked, "What directed now Captain Dunsel?" He replied, "Down into the earth according to the word I got from Dread Dark Lord Hister. The Elf scum took it down deep they did."

It wasn't long before Dunsel and his men were through the door and inside the lower chamber. No one had been down here for years, not since the days of Zaphenath-paneah. Dunsel searched the walls for the door that he had been told to look for, and for a while it was in doubt that he would ever find it. The other Gnomes searched as well but in vain. "Wait just a minute," declared Dunsel. "Hister said when he came to me on the night journey, that the walls of this room were rough and unfinished. But this room has smooth walls of plaster. Even the floor is clean and smooth." Another Gnome with a grim face and red beard replied, "Maybe this is the wrong room Captain. Maybe it is up top in the other chambers somewhere." Dunsel replied, "No Eeegar, Hister was specific that it was down below and not up top. Maybe there was a door before this one that we missed Captain." "No Eeegar, there was not door that I saw. Quick lads, bust the plaster off the walls and try not to stir up to much dust. The door is a small one down in one of the corners, or so I was told."

With Dunsel and Eeegar supervising, the workers began breaking away the plaster. It was hard work and the Gnomes were forced to tie rags over their mouths to avoid choking on the dust. Their work paid off for soon the small door in the lower western corner was revealed. They found that it had been sealed with mortar which they were forced to break through. It was then that a black scorpion ran out of the small tunnel and stung one of the Gnomes on the arm! It felt like a hammer hit him and he screamed in agony! Eeegar shouted, "Gadzooks!" as he swatted the insect away while Dunsel smashed it with a spade! The poison was deadly in any case and the Gnomes are small, so his comrades carried him to the other side of the room.

Dunsel looked over at the other Gnomes and said, "Alright! One of you blokes crawls in there and find the piece!" No one wanted to go in there now and Eeegar grunted, "Come on you bloody Waugs! Hop to it!" He grabbed one by the beard and said, "I says move now! Hop to it! No time for a bug to stop us! We're running out of time!" The one that he grabbed took a lamp, and then upon drawing his dagger, bent down and crawled into the tunnel He didn't have too much difficulty seeing that he was a

Dwarf, and he slowly made his way down the tunnel keeping a sharp eye out for scorpions.

Dunsel and Eeegar waited at the door while the others tended to their scorpion wounded friend. But it was no use! He went into convulsions of pain and agony and the others tried to keep him quiet but to no avail. Then there came a voice from out of the tunnel. "Captain, I think we found it. Here it is, a large flat crystal stone wrapped in a sheep skin hide! This thing is too heavy for just one!" Dunsel and Eeegar crawled through the tunnel with their lamps and stood up inside the small, tomb-like chamber. "That is it lads, the next piece of the All Seeing Eye. Let's get it up and out of this scorpion din," said Dunsel.

The three of them drug it back through the low tunnel and into the chamber. Seeing that there was nothing to do for their comrade, the rest of the Gnomes gathered together and all of them heaved the stone up and carried it up and out of the pyramid. Their wounded comrade struggled to make his way behind them but was dead before he could make it to the surface.

Once outside there were more people to deal with the stone. Lord Gorgo looked at it and said, "I hope this thing is worth all the trouble we spent to find it and all the trouble it is going to take to get it back to Kol Oba. We will take it down to the boats where Hector is at and prepare it to be flown north. Let's snap to it lads!"

In the flickering lamp and torchlight, this force of evil carried the piece down the ramp to where Hector was waiting at the canal dock. It was rigged into a pack, and then tied to the back of a Gargoyle named Memmelkhan. It was heavy but this Wing Trooper was very muscular with tremendous upper body strength. Lord Gorgo said, "You and these five Troopers will go north with this! Take turns and make with all due vigor, for Dread Lord Darkness waits. Fly northeast back to the cost and then follow the coasts of Canaan past Joppa, Sidon, Gebal and Arvad. Fly to Samal and avoid the country of the Dwarves of Tubal. Go across Kappodakia and over the Kingdom of the Hittites of Hattusas. Then go west and pass over the Hellespont near Troy. From there, go north along the coast of the Dark Sea and then on into Dakkia. Memmelkhan, do not be tempted to take shorter flight paths across the seas. We cannot risk the loss of the piece in the depth of the ocean. Fly clear of storms as well. Now fly brothers!" "By your command," replied Memmelkhan.

Memmelkhan spread his mighty wings and his team lifted into the sky and was soon gone. Lord Gorgo, turning to Dunsel and Hector said, "Gather all your warriors into the boats. When the Egyptians discover that this raid has taken place, they will be after us in force assuming that the stone is on board one of these vessels. But they will not know at first by whose hands this deed was done. So we will go north on the Nile to the Sea, and thence to Gaza." Dunsel replied, "Yes and we will depend on you Wing Troopers to terrorize these stone stackers. I want to stop off in Sin and take care of a personal matter with that nasty port authority Amunsnefru!" Lord Gorgo replied, "There is no time for you to stop to get revenge for his mocking you Dunsel. For from Gaza we make our way to Delphi!"

By the next morning at the changing of the guard the burglary was discovered and the Egyptians were out in force. The army received reports that vessels had exited the pyramid canals at the Sphinx and had traveled north on the current well before dawn. The garrison was alerted and word sent to Pharaoh Khahotepre himself. "What? Stolen in the night by burglars! That stone cannot be allowed to leave Egypt. If Zaphenath-paneah were still alive he would have made sure something as dangerous to the world as that stone, would still be safely buried under the Pyramid! Alert the garrisons of On, Pibeseth, Pithom and Tanis! Get our ships moving on the river to run them down and send word to Amensnefru in Sin that the harbor is to be sealed! Nothing gets in or out of Egypt until the stone is found! Mobilize troops to block the passes in the Sinai and everyone and everything is to be searched! Leave no stone unturned!"

As Lord Gorgo and his people approached the entrance to the port of On, they were fully on alert, expecting the Egyptian River Navy to intercept them. But the bad guys managed to slip pass the city before the alert could be raised. Just as they floated by, the Egyptian ships were being loaded with soldiers and weapons! Armies of horsemen and chariots were closing in on them on both sides of the Nile!

As the Egyptian boats came out onto the river, Lord Gorgo and his Wing Troopers took flight out of their two boats and flew into a sudden attack against their pursuers! To say that the men of the Nile were shocked at the sight of Gorgo and his Troopers would be an understatement. For them, such creatures had not been seen since ages past, and then only in legend. They just did not know what to do and so they did nothing as ninety Gargoyles attacked two vessels from the air! Gorgo and his winged devils landed amidst the astonished and terrified, boyish soldiers and began cleaving them asunder with short swords of hardened steel! The officers were slain and thrown overboard and became the feast of crocodiles!

Meanwhile, chariots bearing dispatches of alarm rode out as Pharaoh had commanded, and he himself suited up in his royal armor and took to the field. As he rode out of the city with banners blowing and trumpets blaring, the people were bowing to him saying, "Pharaoh is Egypt! Egypt is Pharaoh!" His generals were there and one asked, "Great Egypt is all this force necessary to retrieve one simple piece of blue crystal?" The King answered, "I would not think so General Osnpunk-sneferu had not the venerated Zaphenath-paneah taken me to see the stone when I was a child. He explained what it was and what it would do to the world if reunited with its other pieces in the wrong hands. This is part of the famous All Seeing Eye that was in Babylon and we must make every effort to secure its return." "Great Egypt, why just not destroy it when we get it back?" Pharaoh replied, "No force known to man can do such a thing. It cannot even be melted. We must get it back! I must not fail my old teacher Zaphenath-paneah!"

The army knew about how fast the thieves could go on the river, and so messages were sent to Tutonkhoras who was the commander of the Garrison at Sin, to dispatch troops and vessels to the mouth of the eastern Nile Estuary in case they managed to get that far. Ships and ground troops were to be placed at the fork on the Nile where the river splits into eastern and western estuaries.

As they marched north out of On, a report came in which greatly disturbed General Osnpunk-sneferu. "Great Egypt, the scouts are saying that the thieves' number about seven or eight hundred tiny little men called Gnomes. Apparently this group entered Egypt in the company of a Philistine named Hector of Gaza a few days ago in order to trade for papyrus. But that is not what concerns me Great Egypt. The fleet at On has been attacked by strange flying creatures! They are like flying dragons sire yet they fight like men. The soldiers are terrified of them! They say they are demons!" Pharaoh replied, "Demons or not, if they bleed, they can die so onward General!"

The Egyptians had a system of military mail chariots stationed at five mile intervals, whereby a dispatch carrier could swiftly switch vehicles and continue his mission, and so the messengers of Pharaoh soon outpaced the escaping thieves, allowing the army to set up its interception plans. The Gargoyles and the Gnomes had gravely miscalculated that their escape down the river would be better than overland.

By the afternoon the Pharaoh himself was closing in as fast as he could and the armies from On and Pibeseth were in place at the Nile fork on all shores. The Evrite people of Goshen wondered what all of the fuss was about as they worked their crops and tended their flocks.

"Would you look at them all Gorgo!" declared Dunsel. "They've got both forks blocked!" "We'll have to scrap our way through every bleeding one of the blokes!" shouted Eeegar. Someone from the other boat shouted, "There's more behind us!" Dunsel said, "What do we do now Lord Gorgo? Your plan is amok!" Gorgo replied, "Shut your trap shorty! We've got this well in hand! Come Gargoyles, follow me!" As Gorgo and his troops took to the air, Eeegar said rudely, "All we've done is stick a stick into the hornets' nest!"

There were eight boats anchored to block the eastern fork of the river and Gorgo and his troopers swarmed into the two on the eastern end of the blockade! The reaction of the young, inexperienced Egyptians troops was mortal terror! "There be demons here!" a teenaged soldier shouted.

Gorgo and his troopers were vicious and as they cleaved the bodies of the soldiers asunder they tossed them bleeding into the river! A swarm of crocodiles came out and began feasting and eating the wounded alive in a madman's melee!

The solders on land began firing arrows at Gorgo and his troopers, who soon leaped into the next two boats. An arrow hit one of the teufels in the neck and pierced an artery! Blood sprayed in a shower, soaking a group of Egyptians in a reptilian bloodbath! The Gargoyle fell into the water and was immediately beset by a feeding frenzy of wild crocodiles! An older, more battle experienced Egyptian sergeant said, "Be of good cheer soldiers! Buck up and face the daemons, for they bleed and die like men! Fight I say, fight!

The Gnome boats now sailed into the blockade and they began fighting from boat to boat. Were it not for Lord Gorgo, the Gnomes would have been dead already! But Gorgo and his troopers saved a good many Gnomes in the first boat. The second was overrun by that same Egyptian sergeant who had rallied his young soldiers to the cause! Looking upriver, the sergeant caught sight of his King and shouted, "Look men, for Pharaoh is here! "Pharaoh is Egypt! Egypt is Pharaoh! Pharaoh is Egypt! Egypt is Pharaoh!"

On both banks of the Eastern Nile Estuary, hundreds of soldiers assembled into well-organized lines of Archers and continued to send a hail of arrows into the Gnome boats! "We are defeated Lord Gorgo!" cried Captain Dunsel. Lord Gorgo shouted, "All Gargoyles, retreat! Follow me men!" Gorgo still had a sword in hand and he fought his way through twelve Egyptians, finally reaching Dunsel. He saved the snarly little Gnome, and then grabbing hold of him, Gorgo lifted into the air, taking a hasty flight north with all of his troopers. The Egyptians had never encountered such creatures before and had lost a hundred dead and two hundred and fifty were wounded.

Egyptian soldiers brought a Gnome and a Philistine prisoner before Pharaoh. They forcefully threw them to the ground and General Osnpunksneferu said, "Kneel before Great Egypt! Who are you shorty?" Hector interpreted and the Gnome answered, "I am Eeegar of the Gnomes!" The Pharaoh asked, "Why have you come all the way to my Egypt to seize the blue stone? What were these flying creatures?" The King looked at the Philistine and said, "So, Hector of Gaza. We meet once more."

Hector bowed down even more saying, "Pharaoh is Egypt! Egypt is Pharaoh!" Eeegar replied, "Oh spare me Great Egypt, for I am a mere pawn in this game. The flying creatures are common in our part of Midgard. They are Gargoyles of King Dragos the Green." Was it he who sent you to invade Egypt?" No Great Egypt. There is a powerful Wizard in the land of Dakkia, far to the north of even Hellas and the Dark Sea. He is Dread Lord Darkness, Hister the Black! We were ordered here by him Great Egypt! He is so powerful, that he is able to project himself in visions and no one can escape his power! He wishes to reassemble the All Seeing Eye Great Egypt, and he knew that long ago, the Elf Melchizideck placed part of it in the care of your great ancestor, Ra on Earth, Pharaoh Sobekhotep." Pharaoh Khahotepre replied, "I will allow you and Hector of Gaza to live Gnome, on condition that you tell me every single bit of information that you know about this Hister, and all of the people north of the Dark Sea! Egypt will prepare to face any threat!"

When Eeegar and Hector had been shackled and taken away, Pharaoh Khahotepre turned to his General and said, "General Osnpunk-sneferu, it appears that those Gargoyles have gotten away with the talisman. Because of this, we all have failed the memory of my old mentor Zaphenath-paneah. Now the world is in extreme peril, and along with it, our Egypt and all Great Mizraim wanted to achieve when he first came to this land. Come now, let us return to Noph." The Armies of Egypt disappeared back to their garrisons in clouds of dust as the people of Goshen looked on.

CHAPTER XVII

Bittersweet

From The Skald's Tale

We Visigoths, who sit here in this Mead Hall in Merida, have known loss and hardship and suffering, yet we have also known love and there is nothing more sacred than the love and the trust of a child.

eobalf and Borsippah had a beautiful wedding in the home of Shalmaeser in the custom of the Evrite people, reciting their vows and signing a *Ketubah* (wedding contract) followed by a seven day celebration and honeymoon. The feast was grand.

When the time of the feast had ended *on the fourteenth day of Gói and Ein-mánuðr in the five hundred and ninety eight year of the first age of Midgard,* Shalmaeser fitted out pack mules with provisions for a long, long journey north—for the time had come for Teobalf to return home to his people. He and his bride and her brother were given the finest horses that could be obtained in Assyria along with weapons and an escort of soldiers, for Shalmaeser had the ear of the King of Assyria. And so in the spring of the year, Teobalf set forth from Nineveh on his long journey to Thorstadt. The parting was bitter for young Aisha for she loved her uncle Teo dearly.

They were all gathered around for Teobalf to depart. Borsippah and Calah hugged everyone and were soon upon their horses. Shalmaeser and Teobalf gave each other the traditional Assyrian hug of departure and the Forge Master said, "May the God of Noach bless thee and keep thee. May he lift up his countenance upon thee and give thee peace. May thou be blessed with many sons and daughters and may thy house prosper and flourish."

Teobalf bowed and kissed the hand of Bashemath, whose eyes had tears in them. She said, "Go in peace Teobalf, and take care of Borsippah and Calah." "I shall indeed M'lady." Peleg gave Teobalf the same hug his father had given him and said, "I hope to see you again Uncle Teo. I have learned so much of your world these last few years and I want to see it." Teobalf replied, "Peleg, I will be honored for you to someday come and visit us in Tervingia. You can teach our people about your people here in Assyria." Calah replied, "I shall endeavor to do so someday uncle Teo."

Teobalf came to Aisha who was looking down at the ground in silence—a girl with quivering lips, so sad was she. Teobalf knelt down to speak to her and when she looked at him, he could see that her eyes were red from crying. She had a gift for him made of gold. It was a tiny statue of a little girl attached to a leather cord. She placed it around his neck and with a wavering voice full of pain she said, "This is to remember me by

Uncle Teo. I made it just for you." Teobalf looked at the fine craftsmanship and replied, "Aisha, I will keep it close to my heart always, and know that you live within my heart forever, my beautiful niece and special Aisha."

The child could no longer hold herself back from crying. She grabbed hold of Teobalf and hugged him hard while sobbing bitterly on his shoulder. In between sobs she was saying, "Oh please don't go Uncle Teo? Please don't go, just stay with us forever uncle Teo!" She kissed the side of his head and he felt the wetness of her tears on his ear. He took her small face in his large hands, and looking at her he was in tears himself. He replied, "Aisha, I must go and carry the secret of steel to my people, so that they may defeat the sorcerer. I shall see thee again Aisha. Someday when it is possible I'll return to Nineveh— or you may someday come with Peleg to see me in Tervingia. If it's ok with thy father you may ride with us to the city gate." He looked back at Shalmaeser who smiled and nodded his approval. Bashemath was watching the whole scene and the sight of her daughter in so much pain was causing her to weep with a rag over her nose and mouth.

Teobalf, seeing that the soldiers were ready to get moving, let go of Aisha and mounted his horse. He reached down and pulled the little girl up onto the horse in front of him and together they led the way to the gate. Shalmaeser and his wife and son walked along beside them and in about an hour of slow travel through the crowded city streets, they exited the northern gate and could see the wide Tigris River to their left. Teobalf wrapped his arms around Aisha from behind and said, "I love thee little one. Now go to thy mother." He kissed the top of her head and handed her down to her mum. She was silent now as she watched Uncle Teo ride away to the north. When he was no longer in sight, she wept bitterly in her mother's arms.

CHAPTER XVIII

Giorsal and Pappa Elf

From the Skald's Tale

Many were the scars in the mind of Giorsal Rhydderch but she for whom destiny had brought such horror, now much life was her rich reward. For of her human ancestry blended in marriage to an Elf, would come the diversity in elvish folk needed for their very survival. Twas strange indeed the path she had to first walk, yet out of death there had come life and a continued spring season for the Elves of Midgard.

In the middle of things far away in the north, another child was having problems. This was young Giorsal, who had formerly been of the draugr. *Dan Ene Gud* had brought her back to life from out of the shadowy realm of the undead and she was so traumatized that only Yoshael and Zakarah could help her. Therefore these wonderful Elves had adopted Giorsal as their *Oskmaer*, or *Wish Maiden*, and had been raising her ever since.

In the twenty years before her resurrection the poor child had been cursed to walk among the undead of Myrkvidr, and when she had been resurrected four years ago, she resumed the same age she had before falling prey to the draugr. Giorsal was now as a child of fourteen and almost every boy and girl her age was terrified of her, rejecting her out of fear. Parents were responsible for this fear, with their gossip and their wagging tongues! Siggy and Eileza and Lilia had never rejected her and were practically the only friends she had. Even Aestrith and Borghild were cold to her and all of the children of Master Thonan including Birgitta would have nothing to do with poor Giorsal.

Zakarah knew that someday she would be able to send her adopted daughter north to Alfheim to complete her healing. Only afterwards would she be able to return to her people in Manching—but the Lady of Urtharbrunnr had been given word from the Holy Spirit of Asgard that Giorsal Rhydderch's destiny was to be the salvation of the Elves. The Angel Gabriel had come unto Zakarah one day that week in the Thorstadt Stonehenge with these words for her, "Oh Lady of Urtharbrunnr, the Risen Child shall be the salvation of the Holy Elves—for indeed tis her blood that must infuse the Elves by marriage lest the flesh of thy children fade in the recessive death—for then death will come to the Elves. Men and Elves are the children of God and so he created them in similarity in order that both may prosper together and can be given in marriage one to the other. El Shaddai has said that the gift of death has been given unto mankind and he is appointed once to die. Loki knew this and so thought prevention lest the Elves prevail and he be bound into outer darkness. But El Shaddai has given her life from out of death and now she is the Maiden of the Elves and her blood line is the continued spring for the Elves. Also there shall come another mortal woman into the House of the Elvarim, the wife of Samael—but she shan't have to die to marry—and nor shall other mortals be required first to die in order to marry an Elf, for Giorsal was the innocent lamb, the sacrificial gateway for your physical salvation in Midgard, therefore she was given the first fruits of the resurrection so that the Elves may fulfill the will of El Shaddai—lights shining in the darkness of Midgard and be the pathway whereby the children of the one God can be as one and then both shall live." Gabriel vanished in a blinding flash of light and behold Zakarah told it all to Yoshael in the journeys of the night.

Giorsal was taken twenty four years ago by Vandals in a raid, and even now her sister who was now a woman full grown, mourned not knowing Giorsal's fate. Her sister was Aoibhe and she was the wife of Sezengedrix who was the Arch Druid of Manching. Their parents were Eanraig and Frangag Rhydderch and were aging, still mourning for the loss of Giorsal. The Vandal Lothar had seized the child when she was a mere ten year old girl, intending to sell her in the Scythian slave markets and he returned east with the Faun Army in pursuit. But he and his warriors succumbed to the Huldra and, well you know the result. Lothar however turned on the innocent child Giorsal as his first victim, cursing her to walk in the realm of the undead. She was never given the choice of following either good or evil until being restored to the living by *Dan Ene Gud*.

At this time Yoshael and Giorsal were visiting King Togrobeg and the very morning after he had received words on the winds of the night from Zakarah he spoke with their Wish Maiden saying, "Giorsal, my dear Wish Maiden, I am so glad that you came with me to Ariemel to see the Dwarves in their new Kingdom.". She smiled at him as they walked through King Togrobeg's Halls to take in lunch at the table of the king. She had grown to be quite a beautiful girl with radiant white skin and thick locks of light blonde hair and her eyes were emerald green and she showed no outward signs of the draug that she had once been. She was dressed in a very long blue dress that Zakarah had made for her of pure elvish cotton and she wore soft leather boots which came up just past her ankles. She had even begun growing once more and stood about five feet eight inches tall. On her head she wore a crown of woven white flowers. A gift of healing herbs and elf medicine were already manifesting themselves through her hands.

"I am glad to Pappa Elf. I had to get away from Thorstadt. All the girls there either hate me or are terrified of me. All the boys except Sigmund taunt me and make teeth faces at me. Little children run away when they see me Pappa Elf. The girls in the court torment me with their gossip father, especially Aestrith and Borghild, the Ladies in Waiting for Queen Gwynnalyn!" Yoshael sat down with her at King Togrobeg's table and were served a meal of good vegetable skause with no meat but with all kinds of vegetables with sides of berries, nuts and fruit and fresh hot flatbread. Giorsal was a vegetarian (except milk and eggs) and even the thought of meat or blood made her sick. She loved the taste of the three grain bread that the Dwarves made and their fresh butter was so delicious. She was given a cup of hot mint tea which was a favorite of Yoshael.

He smiled at her through his long pointed beard and said, "The lesson you are learning Giorsal from them all, is the kind of person that you do not want to be. We as the people of Shaddai must have empathy with one another. What you find that is hateful to you Giorsal; do not inflict it upon others. I know that it is hard because those people don't want to let you move beyond your past—and the tongue of the gossiper is as poisonous as the bite of a serpent." She sighed and said, "Pappa Elf I don't even remember what I did when I was a draug. It is like waking up from a dream and then forgetting about it. Even Siggy asked me one time about what it was like being a 'walking corpse' and I couldn't tell him because I just don't remember it Pappa Elf. I don't want to remember it! I still see things in my dreams—faces that I don't know and many ones that I think that I do know. I just hurt inside father and without you and Mumma Elf I couldn't live! I would die again!"

Yoshael replied, "Do not think about death child. We are made in the likeness of El Shaddai and when we kill ourselves, we are attacking the likeness of God that is within us. Someday I will take you unto Alfheim Giorsal, my beloved Wish Maiden, where you will complete your recovery amongst my children and then perhaps you will wish to return to Manching and find your family. Lord Raedwald promised your sister he would find you for her. She was saved by the changelings from Lothar and has her own family. Your true parents are yet alive and will be glad to have you back. You will even grow up and get married and have children of your own one day Giorsal." She replied, "I hope so father, but if I do find a husband someday, it won't be in Thorstadt or in Manching—for

I know it will be an Elf. The only decent boy in Thorstadt is Siggy and he loves another." Very true Giorsal. But come. Let us eat this wonderful soup before it gets cold. I do wish these Dwarves had crumpets Giorsal. I do so miss having tea and crumpets every day at four like I used to in Alfheim." She replied, "Yes Pappa Elf and I can't wait to go there with you and Mumma Elf, to have some with you. I love both of you so much and to be your Wish Maiden is like a dream come true. Like waking up from a fairy tale dream, and finding that it was all for real after all."

CHAPTER XIX

Centaurs

From The Skald's Tale

We sit here people in this glorious Mead Hall in the presence of a glorious King, the great Roderick. Asgard smiles upon his reign, as it did Sigurd's. But sometimes even great kings such as these are unable to protect everyone. And so it was for Sigurd as the forces of the wicked sorcerer closed in with an evil, heartless scheme involving creatures that Sigurd had only heard of in legends or out of an insane man's nightmare!

In the month of *Gói and Ein-mánuðr on the twenty fifth day, in the five hundred and ninety eighth year of the first age of Midgard* with the early spring flowers in bloom, Shamus O'Hurleyhune, his wife Molly along with the laddies set out from Thorstadt on an ambassadorial mission to the Court of Ullich, Khan of the Magyars. The Magyars were a powerful nomadic tribe of horse archer people who lived on the central Midgard steppes and their king, known as a khan, was very friendly to the Tervingians and his hatred for the Scythians was legendary.

Argyle was along as well with Princess Riona who was still the Ambassador from Gergovia and their now three year old son Averngedrix. This boy was the pure delight of his grandfather Dithranti and grandmother Boudicca. Argyle and Riona had wanted leave him behind in Thorstadt in the care of Gerda and the ladies of the mead hall at first but since Molly was taking little Liam, Riona insisted that Averngedrix come along to keep the high strung Liam company. Averngedrix, whom Liam simply called Vern, was a toddler three and a half feet tall and weighing fifty pounds. He had long locks of blonde hair which fell to the tops of his shoulders and sparkling blue eyes. Along to represent the Fauns were Woodwose and Amberwose and their son, the now four year old Rockwose was along and the Faun child delighted to be with his friends Liam and Vern. But the boys sorely wished that their best friend Rony could have come along, but alas the queen forbid it.

This grand entourage was escorted by an armed body of Tervingian knights led by Lord Sigmund on his first mission as a knight and a leader. Volsung had wisely chosen to assign Sergeant Hardrada and his company of one hundred men to the young Duke, knowing that these older men were battle hardened and well trained to deal with any kind of threat from the Slaughter Wolves. Also along of course were Princess Eileza and Sigmund's childhood friends Gustav and Lars and fourteen year Raugust, son of Lord Snaevar. All in all twas quite a merry group that would be heading east away from the Scythian battle areas of the west.

Sergeant Hardrada said, "Duke Sigmund, I don't like having all these children along on this quest. They should have been left behind because they are in danger and alas they make us vulnerable to the Slaughter Wolves and the Ogres." Sigmund shuddered at the thought and then answered, "Ogres! I didn't think Ogres lived east of the Rha Sergeant Hardrada!" He replied,

Ogres live all over Midgard young Duke. Morag is just the centre of their activities—and there are Trolls to beware of east of here. Recall you the story of Sir Horsa and his knights at Troll Springs?" "Yes I do Wachtmeister but we shan't be nearing that place as far as I know." Hardrada replied, "One never knows where we may end up M'Lord but the children will slow us down and will be in grave danger. Forget you not that we're still at war Lord Sigmund." Eileza was quick to the rescue as she rode up beside her fiancé on her long shaggy silver colored pony named Silvertopp. "Oh Siggy, don't listen to Grumpy Gramps! We'll be fine, Ogres Schmoegers Sergeant Hardrada!"

They crossed the River Rha on the ferry rafts and made their way east into the Hyrcannian Steppes going towards Ariemel where they would join with King Yoshael and give official recognition to Togrobeg's new city in the names of the rulers of Cluricawne and of Gergovia. From there they were to travel far to the east to the Altai Mountains to make official contact with Ullich Khan and the Khanate of the Magyars. The Khan had been in contact with King Sigurd for quite some time but the alliance between the Magyars and the Tervingians was not completely assured.

Shamus had really matured over the last four years and took his office quite serious, although they had been out of contact with King Nemed and Queen Clodagh since their departure. There was talk of at least two of the laddies, Aonghus Killian and Ruairi O'Flannin going home under the escort of two of Sigurd's knights to carry news and dispatches to King Nemed. Molly was a huge and an indispensable help for Shamus—for she became his scribe, recording all of the details of the trip since their arrival in Thorstadt four years ago. She had produced two scrolls so far, which eventually they would submit to their king and queen as reports. After this journey to the Altai she planned to send the second copies of their scrolls west somehow to Erin so that Cluricawne would know what was happening—and as well to let their families know that they were safe; and especially to tell them of the birth of Liam Connor O'Hurleyhune—this is where the talk of sending Aonghus and Ruairi home was coming from.

"This is just what we've been waiting for!" snarled *Taxiarchos* Adrastus. He was the Centaur Force Commander and his rank of *Taxiarchos* was the equivalent of what some kingdoms in the west in the third age of Midgard would call a *Brigadier*. These creatures had the bodies of horses but where the horse would have a head and neck, a Centaur has the upper half of a man including arms and they were speaking creatures! Adrastus and a whole unit of Centaurs, numbering about one hundred along with a Phalanx of Horse Mounted Satyr Hoplites, or Dragoons, were there and these numbered about one hundred as well. A Dragoon is an infantry soldier that rides to battle on a horse, but fights on foot like infantry.

The Satyrs are strange race of beings inhabiting the forests south and west of Dakkia. They are a branch of the Faun race with a few physical differences from those of Agara who had split from their people and went away to become workers of evil. They were very similar to the Fauns in that the males have horns like those of big horn sheep and the females like those of mountain goats but with more human appearing lower extremities than the Fauns, who are like more like goats. A Satyr had pointed ears like the Fauns but unlike their Agaran relatives Satyrs had black wool instead of white or brown and long black tails like that of a horse. The males also have long pointed beards—more so than the Fauns. The Satyrs were led by King Memnos with whom the Scythians had forged an alliance once it became known that the Fauns were in league with Sigurd and that the Lord High Elder of the Fauns was also the White Wizard of the Centre Midgard. They counted themselves in the full service of Adawulf Hister Carpathia and considered the Vanier to be gods; although they referred to them by the same names as did the humans of Hellas.

The Satyrs here were led by Tagmatarchis (Major) Eurbiades but Taxiarchos Adrastus had overall command of this expedition, which was part of Hister's plan to gain control of the Heart of the Sea. "You mean we don't have to try and sneak into the city disguised as Fauns after all?" replied Major (Tagmatarchis) Eurbiades. "No," replied Adrastus. Look you hear sir. See what I can see. Riding on that tiny little horse is a Leprechaun girl. She has to be a Leprechaun because she doesn't appear to be a child and she has her baby with her beside her on the seat of the cart. Leprechauns are much smaller than Gnomes or Dwarves. We have enough troops in both our Phalanxes to attack and overcome them in an ambush somewhere along the road between here and Ariemel! The tiny woman must be Molly O'Hurleyhune and the shorty with her Ambassador Shamus of Cluricawne. She is the one who carries the Heart of the Sea, and if we can kill her out in the open and take the gemstone, there will be no need to kidnap her child and take him all the way to Cyclops Island and hold him for the ransom of the talisman—which was the original plan!"

Eurbiades smiled and said, "Very good sir—I didn't much fancy dyeing me wool white—and would you look at that. Down there among them is a family of Fauns! King Memnos would much like to hear of any Faun killed! Aesop their Lord High Elder is our blood sucking enemy and our King would love for us to bring back the woman to him." Adrastus replied, "You seem to have forgotten that Aesop is a Wizard! We get what we came for and nothing more!" Eurbiades replied with a voice which sounded like a low grunt, "There's a better way to handle a Wizard! We have our own Wizard do we not?" Adrastus replied, "Yes we do. I supposed that their Wizards will all be after us soon enough. Very well, you handle the Fauns and kidnap their woman. We can use her to take care of the Leprechaun brat as well as her own child—assuming she survives the attack and three hostages will be better than one if we fail to kill the O'Hurleyhune woman and secure the Heart of the Sea!

CHAPTER XX

The Bad'uns

From the Skald's Tale

To harm a child or to purposely use one for unholy schemes of any kind reeks of soul death and we great men of King Roderick of Visigothia like Sigurd of old, love the children and to harm or exploit them is the highest form of infamy. The same can be said of those who teach their children to hate! Even worse are those who kill them, born or unborn. Indeed the highest crime in the universe is to murder a child—for they are our future. The Slaughter Wolves of Scythia were of this nature and were reserved the lowest depths of the underworld of Halja, Halls of the dishonored dead whilst some were cast into Hel to be frozen in ice. Twas Sigurd who was sent to protect and defend those ancient children of the elder days from bad'uns like Hister and those who plot schemes with kinderlings as their pawns!

A s Grand Duke Sigmund and his people made their way east across the Hyrcannian Steppes they suspected not that they were being shadowed by the forces of evil. In the meanwhile the Princess Aubriel and a force of Elves on Reindeer, having made their way off of the ice flows descended the valley of the Rha, making their way down to Thorstadt. She remarked to those near her, "The glaciers have melted even more than I thought. The last time I was down this far south, we still would have had sixteen and a half leagues (fifty miles) more on the glaciers, but now see where the cliffs are?" As they looked on, great pieces of ice were falling from high off of the cliff face, crashing in thunderous roars and eerie cracking noises into the River Rha, which was flowing in torrents down a canyon of ice. They quickly took cover among the rocks in a boulder strung field as four enormous flying reptiles made their way south. Looking back Aubriel saw a family of white ice bears on top of the frozen cliffs peering down at them. The ice bears saw the flying dragons and headed for cover, for the great she bear made ready to defend her cubs. However the common dragons ignored the bears and headed towards their far away rookery.

It is approximately one hundred and six leagues or so from Thorstadt to the Yural River along a relatively flat plain which rose gently up from the Hyrcannian Sea. Making about twenty miles a day it would take those around sixteen days to reach the Yural River. Once there they would turn north toward Ariemel.

They halted at a spring along the trail around which grew a small grove of trees and a lot of salt cedar. Molly was holding little Liam in her lap as they were taking in a midday meal on the sixth day out of Thorstadt which was the *first day of Ein-mánuðr and Harpa (Easter-mōnaþ / Easter month) in the five hundred and ninety eighth year of the first age of Midgard.*

Siggy and Eileza were having a quiet conversation over some bread and dried beef while sitting on some rocks. Woodwose and his family joined Molly and Shamus and little Rockwose came up and asked, "Can Liam play Aunty Molly?" Molly looked all around and as the sun glinted off of her hair she saw Sergeant Hardrada and his men all around. "Aye Rockwose he can. Liam, finish up ye bread and ye can play here in the camp with Rocky." "Aye Mummy." replied Liam. Just then Averngedrix skipped up to join his friends and Amberwose warned, "You children are not to stray from the camp." Argyle, Riona and Gladvynn were soon there and sat down to eat. Riona handed fresh bread to Averngedrix and said, "Not so fast little prince—eat first and then you can play!" "Aye Mum," he replied as he took the bread and bit off a generous portion.

Siggy was so taken up by his conversation with Eileza that he failed to properly post the centuries and had it not been for Sergeant Hardrada, everyone would have been in real danger. Even Eileza's eyes were so full of stars at the moment for her Siggy Wiggy that she'd let her guard down. Once again they were lucky to have Austri and Vestri along to keep a wither eye out for treachery. Gustav, Lars and Raugust felt totally abandoned by Sigmund right now, and in fact were a bit jealous of Eileza. So the three of them kicked back under the shade tree and took a nap.

Liam jumped off of his mother's lap to be with his friends and although the Celtic boy and the Faun boy where quite a bit taller than Liam he seemed to be the leader of the group. They found sticks and started playing knight and dragon, with Rocky pretending to be a Sail Dragon. Liam was sure tiny but he was so fast and his reactions so quick that he was running circles around the other boys. They could not keep up with him as he rolled and dove between Vern's legs and then jumped over top of Rocky and shouted in fun, "Aye me lads! I'll show that dragon a thing or two! I'll slay the dragon and ride a Mammoth like Siggy did in the old day's mates!" That caused Siggy and Eileza to look up and smile and Eileza said, "Well Siggy Wiggy. You've gone on to be famous!" Sigmund looked at the boys and smiled while in remembrance of the days when he himself played at such games with Gustav and Lars and the other lads of Thorstadt and to even younger days back in Wodenburg.

Liam said, "Hey me lads, we have to make a dragon cave! Let's get some bushes and wood!" Molly said, "Oh no ye don't Liam! Ye boys aren't to go straying past the ponies! Ye hear me?" "Aye Mummy," replied Liam who was now covered in dust. Molly said to everyone, "He's a wee bit hard to control. The boy is a wild sort he is." Argyle replied, "Aye that he is. He's more like his mummy than his pappy I dare say." Shamus replied with a smile, "Aye Argyle, ye got that one right." Molly smiled and tilting her head to one side said, "Oh know laddies. He's much more of Shamus when it comes to a rampage. Have ye heard of the Shamus Rampage? Queen Clodagh was at her wits end and nearly sent him and the laddies to mine in the peat bog. Who could ever forget the fire after Shamus played a trick on poor granny Maolmhuire?" Gladvynn smiled saying, "How could we forget?" She handed some jerked beef to Fearghal Bronach who was close beside her. In spite of the obvious size difference, the two of them had an obvious affection for one another.

The boys went over by Sergeant Hardrada and the horses and tried to arrange the packs, which had been placed on the ground to give the mules a rest, into some sort of a fort. The packs were heavy so the laddies came to help, Fearghal Bronach, Aonghus Killian and Ruairi O'Flannin. Liam looked up and asked, "Uncle Feargy, can I have a barley stalk to chew on?" Fearghal took one from his pouch and handed to it the child saying, "Aye Liam. It's me pleasure it tis me lad." He handed a stalk to Liam and the tiny boy happily placed it into his mouth as the other laddies stacked the packs into a fort. Liam asked, "Uncle Feargy. I heard 'em saying I was like pappy. What is this *Shamus Rampage* they be talking about?"

Fearghal told Liam the entire history of his father and how he used to be the greatest prankster in all of Cluricawne—until it got out of hand and had it not been for Dithranti, Shamus, Aonghus and Ruairi would've been sentenced to hard labor pulling sod out of the peat bogs. Liam was wide eyed trying to imagine it all for never had he laid eyes on Cluricawne, Erin or any other Leprechauns save the laddies and his own family. "So Liam, that's the infamous Shamus Rampage. But that happened way home lad and not here in this land. On Erin there's no war and the consequences of things there aren't as severe as is here Liam. Ye mustn't ever go on a *Liam Rampage* because here it's life or death on a lee shore with bad'uns a plenty. Ye pappy saw the sense in growing up and he loves ye more than the entire world Liam. So ye must always do as ye pappy and mummy says. There are Ogres and other creatures here Liam that would as soon a draw and quarter ye as look at ye. So promise me that ye'll not be such a rascal, especially out here on the trail. But if something ever happened and some waugs took ye away, use all ye smallness and scampering feet that ye have to make fools of the big folks and escape—but never as a prank or a joke Liam only in a real situation. This is a big world after all Liam and we little folk must keep our wits about us if we're to survive. Promise me now Liam?" The tiny little child replied, "Aye Uncle Feargy—I promise all of it." Fearghal hugged him and when he'd released the boy he said, "Aye there's a good lad now—run along and play."

Sergeant Hardrada walked over to where Sigmund's friends were snoring away under the tree. He snarled, "Up and at it ye slackards I got you bang to rights!" There could be Ogres here about or worse! Raugust, you go keep an eye on those toddlers by the packs and don't let them out of your sight for an instant!" Raugust shouted back, "You can't talk like that to me! My father is Lord Snaevar so don't get your knickers in a twist!" The other boys cringed when Raugust challenged this old army sergeant. Hardrada replied, "Yes I know and he put me in charge of you! You're in the army now boy now hop to it before I get your knickers in a bloody twist!"

Hardrada knew that he was going to have to establish his authority very firmly. He reached down and grabbed Raugust off of the ground hard forcefully and snarled, "You get this through your head boy! There is still a war going on and if anything happens to those children there'll be hell to pay for you before you see Thorstadt again! If those children are lost it'll throw a spanner in the works!" The fourteen year old Raugust was stunned and fearfully replied, "Aye sir! I'll hop to it!" Hardrada let go of him and replied, "Don't you 'Sir' me boy! I'm not a toff! I work for a living! You will refer to me as Sergeant! When I speak to any of you boys in training, you will say either 'Yes Sergeant' or 'No Sergeant! Is that understood?" "Yes Sergeant!" replied all three of them who were standing at attention." Hardrada replied, "Good then. Raugust go guard those children while they're away from their parents. You two brothers go tend the horses." All of the older soldiers were smiling about the whole thing, knowing full well what Hardrada was trying to accomplish. He had to turn these boys into men.

Seeing all of this from a distance Molly asked, "Did he have to be so hard on the lads? Is he a nutter?" Argyle replied, "Aye he did Molly.

That old sergeant is just the man to teach them what they need to know to survive the war. If it weren't for men like Hardrada, there would be no kingdom. He's the farthest thing from a nutter as there can be."

Sergeant Hardrada, who was in full helm and hauberk and was now clean shaven (except for his big gray handle bar moustache), strolled over toward Siggy and Eileza and the two of them stood up in his presence for they greatly respected him; he was polite and said, "Duke Sigmund, you're the officer in charge of this outfit and you must lead. You must take charge or the soldiers will become an undisciplined rabble. I know those lads are your best friends, but unless they get serious they're going to die before the war is over and take a lot of people with them that have no need of dying. Your father and Lord Snaevar both know that as well as Lord Thonan and so my company was assigned this mission with you. They and you will learn by the numbers and I will teach you. You're the Duke of Wodenburg now, and when we return home you'll have to go down to it and take charge of the city and the garrison there. That is down on the Goblin border M'Lord and so anything I have to teach you from all of my years of experience, you and the mates would do well to learn." Eileza chimed in saying, "Sergeant Hardrada, don't think you're leaving me out of this training! I will someday be his Duchess and I know how to weild a sword. But I want to learn more, and no one is leaving this Dwarf out of any training!" Hardrada replied smiling, "Aye, that's the kind of attitude I like to see!" Sigmund answered, "Well if my father assigned you to me then I want to learn as well Sergeant Hardrada." Hardrada replied, "Good M'Lord. We've got a long trip ahead and a lot of work."

Raugust was angry embarrassed and humiliated and at that moment he hated Hardrada. He stomped over to the packs to, as he saw it, babysit the toddlers. He passed groups of soldiers sitting in circles on the ground, all clad in armor like Hardrada, minus the red sash that the old Sergeant wore as his insignia of rank. Arriving at the packs he saw the Leprechaun men were no longer there but had joined Argyle and Shamus over eating lunch. He saw that there were guards posted and that Gustav and Lars were over wiping down the horses with damp rags and feeding oats to them.

But he didn't see the boys anywhere. He was mumbling angrily, "That Hardrada's a blag artist!"

Adrastus and his forces kept themselves well back and hidden, hoping to find an opportunity to strike, and seize both Molly and Liam at the same time. Major Eurbiades kept under the cover of the thick salt cedar in the area as he and his hoplites dismounted to get as close to the Tervingian camp as possible without giving themselves away.

Sergeant Hardrada went over to his men and was eating dried beef and bread, when he saw a flock of quail take flight from the salt cedar south of their day camp. Then he noticed that no other birds were singing in the grove of trees at the spring where they were resting. Something was wrong and he could just feel it. He stood up saying calmly, "Look lively lads. Keep alert because something is wrong." He looked around and everyone seemed to be there except Amberwose.

Not seeing the children where they were supposed to be, Raugust could see that their tracks were leading away into the salt cedar. But instead of alerting anyone, he was so terrified of the reaction he might get from Sergeant Hardrada that he set out on his own to find the wee laddies. He expected them to be a short distance away, playing and in no danger.

Amberwose had gotten up after eating her meal and, needing to answer a call of nature in the grove away from the others, she walked away. Passing the guards she traveled a short distance for privacy. When she had accomplished her task, sudden a wooly black arm grabbed her from behind around her mouth and yanked her backwards onto the ground! They pulled a blanket over her head so that she could not see who it was and then the Satyr's quickly wrapped a rope around her and dragged her away! As they did so they frightened a covey of quail, which quickly took flight—the same one seen by Hardrada.

Raugust found the boys playing with a horned toad under some big salt cedar thickets about one hundred yards south of the spring. He startled them and said, "Ok laddies! Back to camp with you all! You three were supposed to be playing at the packs."

Back in the camp Molly noticed that the children were not where they were supposed to be either and she made this known to the others. Shamus said, "Its ok Molly. They probably saw Amber walking away and followed her." Molly replied, "Not likely Shamus. Women are private about toilet matters and don't want their wee youngers along. She'd have sent the three of them back Shamus." Riona replied, "We best find them quick. Come on Argyle, Gladvynn, and Fearghal, let's go."

A Mace flew from out of nowhere smashing into Raugust's head! He'd not been wearing his helmet as instructed and the wooly black Satyr knocked him out cold! Liam screamed as two big hands grabbed him from behind! Two other Satyrs came from under the brush and one grabbed Rocky and the other seized little Vern! Rocky screamed in terror, kicking and biting at the Satyr! Vern kicked and screamed and bit the Satyr hard on the end of his nose and then raked the Satyr in the eyes with his thumbs! "Why you scroungey blighter!" bellowed the Satyr. Vern slipped his grip as the Satyr put his hands up to clear his eyes!

The soldiers were started and jumped up upon hearing the screams of the kinderlings! "Look lively lads we're under attack!" bellowed Sergeant Hardrada! Molly ran towards the pack with the others trying to make it to her child in time to save him! Shamus and the laddies were right behind her as were Woodwose, Riona, Argyle and Gladvynn!

"Secure the horses mates and form a line!" shouted Sigmund! He turned to Eileza and said, "Help find the younglings, and hurry darling!" Eileza ran quickly to join Molly and shouted, "Don't run into the brush alone, stop Molly!" At that moment Vern ran up screaming and crying, Mum, Dah! Black wooly goat men grabbed Liam and Rocky! There's bad'uns all over!" He jumped into his father's arms and Argyle asked through heavy breath, "Wooly goat men? Like Fauns?" Yes but different dah with wooly black hair and horse tails! They were mean and they're all over in the bushes!"

"Stop Molly, don't run into the bushes! We're being attacked by Satyrs!" shouted Woodwose! Sergeant Hardrada and Duke Sigmund formed up all of the men, half on foot to defend the camp and the other half on horses. Then a horn sounded and they fell under attack by a wave of black wooly Satyrs led by Major (Tagmatarchis) Eurbiades! They swarmed the camp and suddenly Gustav and Lars were fighting for their lives! "Blinking heck—What'n the name of Asgard is those creatures?" asked Sigmund as he saw the Centaurs for the first time. "They're half men and half horse!" "It's the Centaurs!" warned Argyle with a shout. "But they're well beyond their range!" cried Gladvynn. "Tell that to them!" shouted Molly.

Molly would not be held back as she ran to find her little Liam. Behind her were Shamus and the Laddies. Seeing her, Eurbiades grabbed Molly and threw her over his shoulder and as she bit kicked and fought back hard he ran away with her into the brush! "All horsemen to arms, the Centaurs are attacking us from the salt cedar!" shouted Hardrada. No sooner were the cavalry mobilized then a force of Centaurs attacked the camp led by Adrastus himself. The fight locked in the chest of bitterness too horrible to tell as the combatants resolved to destroy one another.

Two Satyrs came at Gladvynn and a third came after Fearghal with an axe! She blocked the sword of the first Satyr with her own and then with a spinning back kick, she smashed the face of the second Satyr! She then stabbed the first Satyr in the eye with the tip of her sword piercing his skull and killing him! She was just in time to save her little Leprechaun from the axe wielding Satyr, by stabbing the creature hard in the buttocks. Fearghal rolled to the side as the Satyr fell forward and stabbed it in the side with his dagger. He was quickly on his feet and said, "Why I thank ye m'lady—ye're a really good help when a man is in a fix." She replied, "No Satyr is a taking you today m'lad—the shitehawk's got me in a chuffer!"

A Centaur ran up to Adrastus and said in a deep gruff voice, "M'Lord we have everyone we came for!" He replied. "Well then. Sound the withdrawal." The horn sounded and the Satyrs and Centaurs withdrew into the thickets of salt cedar as fast as they had come. Shamus saw a Satyr throw Molly into the arms of a Centaur. He ran at the Satyr and coming up from below, stabbed the creature square in the bullocks with his sword shouting, "I'll make of ye a eunuch as the queen so famously says!" Molly

saw him trying to save her and shouted, "I'll save ye from them Shamus!"
She bit the Centaur in the nose and thumbed him in the eyes! Then she
pulled out her dagger and stabbed him between the seams of his armor as
he now held her upside down. He wore armor to protect his human half
and another kind to protect his horse body and between the two Molly saw
a small gap which she exploited, plunging her dagger into the beast's naval!
He dropped her and as Shamus rolled out from under him the screaming
Centaur went to the ground in agony for his castrated groin and was soon
overwhelmed by Eileza—who stabbed him through with her sword in the
same spot as he wreathed in agony on the ground. Molly found herself free
from the wounded Centaur who soon bled out dead in the brush. Molly
jumped from off of the ground and looking at the dead Centaur she kicked
it and spat upon it shouting, "Ye bloody egit!"

Molly turned around and ran shouting, "Liam me darling! Ye can
come out now! The Wooly men are gone! Liam. Liam, Liam! Where are
ye me darling boy! The bad'uns is gone! Liam, Liam! Liam O'Hurleyhune!
Come to mommy now me darling" Woodwose was shouting for his wife
and son as well but to no avail! They soon found Raugust unconscious
on the ground and far in the distance they could hear the voice of Liam
screaming for his mother as the forces of Adawulf Hister carried him away!
Molly fell to the ground weeping bitterly and Shamus was there with her,
taking her into his arms, his face bitter and mournful and his eyes running
red with tears!

Suddenly an arrow flew their way and stuck into a tree. On it was
a note written in runic writing. Gladvynn hoisted Fearghal up onto her
shoulders and he stood up on her and retrieved the note. Jumping down
he handed it to Argyle who read it.

To the rebel who calls himself King Sigurd;

**We have the Leprechaun child, the Faun woman and
the Faun boy. We will hold them until you, Molly and
Shamus O'Hurleyhune of Cluricawne; bring the Heart
of the Sea to us in the Sea of Hellas, on Cyclops Island.**

**Any rescue attempt will result in the execution of the
hostages. You will have ninety days to bring Molly
with the Gem to Cyclops Island. We know the true
gem and its power so any attempt at deception with a
false talisman will result in cruel retribution against
the child Liam. By your calendar today is the sixth
of day of Ein-mánuðr and Harpa. Your people have
until the 12ᵗʰ to get home to you and deliver this. Then
you will have until the twelfth day of Sól-mánuðr and
Heyannir to be on Cyclops Island with the talisman
and the Leprechaun. Once there, we will exchange the
gemstone for the hostages!**

**Signed
Brigadier Adrastus, Centaur Force Commander.**

He handed it to Sigmund whose face fell in crestfallen horror as he
read it.

Meanwhile back in Thorstadt, little Rony had been taking his midday
nap. He was lying in his bed with Grandma Gerda sitting in a rocking
chair beside him knitting a sweater for him. Rony sat bolt upright in bed
screaming, "Liam! Liam! Liam!" Gerda jumped up and ran to him and
took him into her arms to calm him down. "No Rony. It is ok child. Liam
is with his parents. He's ok Rony." "He was crying and said, "No Grandma
he isn't alright. Some big horsey monster men and some hairy goat men
got him Grandma!" "No Rony. It was only a bad dream child." Her voice
was so kind and Rony embraced her. She took him to her rocking chair
and began rocking the child as he cried saying softly "There now Rony.
It's alright—grandma is here."

At that moment, the queen and Greta, Lilia and Galorfilinde walked
in and Gwynnalyn asked in a start, "What's wrong with Rony Mum?
We've heard his cry from all the way down the hallway." Rony reached
for his mother and when she had taken him into her arms he said, "I
saw it Mum! Just like it was here right now and I was there. Some big

bad horsey monster men and some goat monsters took Liam away from his Mommy!" She remembered the mystical connection that had been established between Rony and Liam while they were yet unborn. Everyone here knew that Rony was a special anointed child of promise for the Tervingian people and that he had been born with many spiritual gifts such as second sight. At that moment the king entered the room.

Queen Gwynnalyn said to their son, "Tell me what you saw Rony." The child explained in vivid detail the battle far away in which the Centaurs and Satyrs had kidnapped Amber and the Children. In conclusion he said, "Mummy, Dah it really happened! I saw it all like a dream, but it wasn't a dream."

Gwynnalyn replied, "We believe you Rony. Mommy and Dahhy believe you son." The king asked, "What does it all mean my Heart? Is it symbolic or has something actually happened to Sigmund and his group?" The queen looked at Galorfilinde and asked, "What do you think it means?" She answered, "Prince Ronan saw a vision of something real because of his bond with Liam. I believe that Liam has been taken by the Centaurs for some evil, sinister purpose at the behest of Hister. We'll know in a few days when Sigmund returns—for surely now he must." The looks on everyone's faces were dire and grave. Rony reached out for his father and when the king had taken him the boy said, "Dahhy we've got to get Liam back." Sigurd replied, "Indeed we shall son. But for now, we must train. Come Rony. We'll go down to the bear pits and train with swords and learn how to fight off horsey men and goat monsters." The queen smiled as Sigurd left with his son in his arms to go teach him swordsmanship and to bond with his boy.

CHAPTER XXI

Soul Searching

From the Skald's Tale

My people, when events such as those of that terrible day so long ago in the mists of the first age we all blame ourselves. We ask, "Could I have done more?" Or, "Would that my sword hand had been faster, and my blade sharper!" No, sometimes my Visigothic brothers and sisters, we must pick up the pieces and resolve to go on no matter the cost, and to put it all back together as best we can, just as these heroes of old did. So today, let us resolve to be like them, shining example to our beloved children.

Shamus and Molly could not be consoled over the kidnapping of little Liam, nor could poor Woodwose, whose son hadn't only been stolen but his beloved wife as well. And so it was in bitter agony that the Duke of Wodenburg ordered an end to the mission and commanded a return to Thorstadt. Five knights however went on north to Ariemel to inform the Dwarf Lords of what had happened and a squad of dragoons tracked the attackers south towards the Hyrcannian Sea.

On the first day of the return march, Sigmund and Eileza rode at the head of the column and the wagon train. He was so glad that Sergeant Hardrada had been there to take charge for he knew that he had much to learn. "Leeza, I have failed on my first mission. It is my bloody fault for being so relaxed. I am not a real Duke Leeza. I allowed a woman and two, almost three children to be kidnapped from under my nose Leeza! The king will never trust me again. No one will."

Eileza replied, "Siggy, no one could have foreseen what was going to happen. All of us thought that Centaurs were just legends and I had never heard of Satyrs before. You snapped back pretty darn well when the chips were down Siggy. At least I think you did and so no matter what anyone else thinks, I am the woman who is going to marry you whether you are a Duke or a Pauper. I love you Sigmund the Volsung and I trust you—I trust us and what we have will not be shaken by a few Centaurs my love!"

He replied, "Leeza, I love you to so very much. We can't sit still for this Leeza. By the Lord of Asgard I plan on going to this 'Cyclops Island! But it won't be to give up the talisman but to get the children home and to slay those infernal dimmocks! Are you in for this darling?" Eileza replied with a big smile, "Now that's my Siggy Wiggy that I know! You darn tooting I'm in!" Then, having been so reassured by his wife to be he said, "Wait a minute though. There's Ogres out there." "She laughed and smiling said, "Oh Siggy, Ogres schmoegers!"

They made camp for the night. No one was going to be sleeping much and the watch had been doubled. Sergeant Hardrada had said, "Lord Sigmund, those nasty equestrian mutants won't be back. They got what they came for. They'll not as like attack us, wanting us to be able to carry word to the King that Centaurs are on the loose and will expect us to take

Molly's gemstone to that infernal Cyclops Island." Eileza asked, "Where is that place anyway? What is a Cyclops?" Sergeant Hardrada replied, "I only know about them from hearsay from the Hellenes of Byzantium. It is somewhere in the Hellene Sea they say, and the Cyclops are a nasty race on one eyed trolls." "Eeegads, Trolls are gross," replied Eileza.

In their small tent, Shamus and Molly talked that evening in camp. "Me darling Molly, we'll go after those bloody fiends and get our boy back!" Molly replied, "Oh Shamus, I will give that Hister this stone if it is the only way to get Liam home safe." Shamus replied, "Aye the thought has crossed me mind all day as well, but somehow I don't believe that giving him the Heart of the Sea will bring our boy home or the Fauns either. Like as not Hister will pull a double cross." She replied, "Right ye are Shamus, and if the king and queen don't have a good plan to get the children home, then we'll go ourselves Shamus! I feel helpless right now and I hate the feeling so! We have been violated in the cruelest way Shamus! Violated in the sanctity of our home and family and I canno just sit still for it!" They wept in each other's arms.

Woodwose sat alone and watched the sun setting in the west. He was talking to himself saying, "Woodwose you stupid idiot, why weren't you there with your boy when the fiends took him and where were you when they made prey of your wife? What kind of a father and husband are you? You're nothing, and because you are nothing, your family is in the hands of Satyrs! Satyrs of all people are the arch enemies of the Fauns!" He held his flute in his hands and then threw it far over his shoulder and into the salt cedar saying, "I will never play the flute again!" He thought for a few minutes as the last part of the sun sat red on the horizon and then said to himself, "Woodwose, the only way that you can make up for this is to go rescue all of them, no matter what anyone else does, because even if Molly gives up the Heart of the Sea Hister will never allow anyone to leave Cyclops Island alive."

Gustav and Lars watched as several soldiers tended Raugust's wounds. He had woken up briefly and was now sound asleep. The two of them left the tent and as they did, Woodwose's flute landed in front of them. Lars picked it up and handed it to his twin brother. Gustav took it and said, "We'll keep it for him Lars. Someday he'll play again. Sergeant Hardrada was right about all of us! We haven't been taken the war or life seriously and look what it has cost us. Innocent women and children kidnapped right from under our noses!" Lars replied, "From now on we take this war serious Gustav. I don't know what anyone else is doing, but if no one else comes up with a plan, we should go find this Cyclops Island and rescue the children! We'll kill every last Centaur on the whole bloody Island Gustav! What say you brother?" Gustav replied, "I'm in Lars. Even if they decide to give in to the Dark Lord's demands, we'll go and rescue the hostages ourselves!" The two of them gave each other their secret handshake, and then tucked away Woodwose's flute.

Sergeant Hardrada came up to them and the brothers snapped to and said respectfully, "Sergeant!" He replied, "Stand at ease boys. You requited yourselves well in the fighting. There's hope for the two of you after all. Join the guards on the first watch of the night and then get some shut-eye." "Yes Sergeant," was their immediate reply. As he walked away, Hardrada smiled, seeing that some of what he had been trying to teach them was sinking in.

Argyle had taken a few good sword cuts today and Riona took care of them. Little Averngedrix lay under the covers in their sleeping role, still terrified to sleep without Mummy and Dahhy there with him. "Oh Riona, we very nearly lost him today because I let him wonder off." She replied, "We are both at fault Argyle. We were eating lunch together and everyone agreed that the boys could go play. It was just in a quick space of time and they hadn't gone very far at all love. It's Vern we are to be proud of him for fighting the way he did, for was he not the first one to alert the camp?" Vern sat up and his parents both hugged him, and he felt safe and secure between the two of them.

They lay under the covers and Riona sang to him a sweet Celtic lullaby and the boy was soon asleep. Outside, Woodwose could hear the sweet lilting music, and he broke into tears. Molly and Shamus could hear it as well and it tormented them, for their child was not here for them to sing to. For them it was the worst night in their lives.

When Vern was sound asleep, and Riona saw his eyes moving fast under closed eyelids she said, "Argyle, this hostage crisis must not stand.

We must not allow the Heart of the Sea to fall into the hands of Hister." Argyle replied, "That is more certain than ever dove. When we get back, my father will know what to do. But no matter what anyone else decides to do, we must be prepared to go down to Cyclops Island ourselves and rescue the children. All a Cyclops is a one-eyed Troll! If we can take down the two-eyed variety, we can take down the one-eyed kind even easier."

The laddies were secure in their tent, but Fearghal was sitting outside near the fire with Gladvynn. "Gladvynn, I feel so rotten tonight. What are we Leprechauns doing here? We're nothing but wee little urchins that all the big folk in Midgard feel they can just pick on and bully! We're just so tiny that everyone either thinks of us as children or freaks for a side show! We're people too Gladvynn! We love, and we dream and we weep when we lose those we love! And I let down Master Shamus today Gladvynn. I let him and dear Miss Molly—who's in that tent over there heartbroken having lost her baby. What am I good for Gladvynn, nothing but a carnival sideshow act?"

Gladvynn said, "I'll tell thee whom thou are Mister Bronach. Thou art the truest, most decent and honorable man that I've ever met. Our size doesn't matter Fearghal. I am a friend who cares for thee and I say that no matter what happens, we're going after those Centaurs, the two of us—and we'll bring Liam and the others home safe." They warmly embraced as friends but with deeper feelings awakening for Gladvynn.

Out with the soldiers, Sergeant Hardrada was fuming about all of this. At the fire he said to his men who were stretching out into their sleeping bundles, "The loss of the kinderlings today was exactly what I was afraid might happen when I saw that the parents were bringing along the poor little tikes! No matter who else does what I intend to pay a very unfriendly visit to Cyclops Island—and cut the throat of the Equestrian Mutant says I! Before it's over, this Brigadier Adrastus is going to die! Even if he releases the tikes, which he shan't by the way, I'm going to cut his throat with my dagger says I—and he who isn't for me is against me!" The soldiers all began to talk at once saying, "I'm in on this to Sergeant!" "Yes, you aren't leaving me out if it Sergeant!" "And us neither you hear Sergeant! We're all in this together and the mutant dies no matter what!"

CHAPTER XXII

The Se'er Stones

From The Skald's Tale

The forces of good will triumph in the end, and we must be assured of that my Visigothic brethren. Though the times seem dark, and indeed are, yet out in the vastness of the Universe, the Armies of Light will someday gather for the final triumph. It was so, even in those far off, long ago times of our fathers, in which I Lothar am telling thee of; here in the Mead Hall of Great King Roderick in this early third age of Midgard. Oh and behold now comes the time to tell thee of the Se'er Stones—those mythical relics of legend.

On the *sixth day of Ein-mánuðr and Harpa in the five hundred and ninety eighth year of the first age of Midgard* the Duke of Wodenburg and his people arrived home in Thorstadt with the tragic news of the kidnappings. The king with Rony at his side looked down at the lad and placing a hand on his shoulder said, "Thou were right son. Thy dream was indeed a vision. Good work lad." The boy looked up at his father with deep sadness on his face and said, "But I wished that I'd been wrong dah. Those bad horsey men have my friends." The king planned to call a meeting soon.

The Wizard King Yoshael knew about the awful turn of events, for the messengers Sigmund had sent to Ariemel arrived safely. He had then gone on a night vision through the power of his own dolman, which he carried with him about his neck unto Zakarah and them twain discussed the situation at hand and what it meant.

Yoshael and Zakarah carried around their necks and beneath their garments and hanging upon chains of star crystal were two very unique gemstones called "*The Se'er Stones.*" These sacred talismans were shaped in the forms of six pointed stars and had been crafted by the *Weylandr*, smithy of the Aesir. Behold when *Dan Ene Gud* had created the Elf and his Elf Mate, Weylandr crafted for them these gifts from his heart—for great was his love for God's new created beings—his guardians of Midgard.

These angelic gems were the size of the hand of a child and were the personal dolmans of Yoshael and Zakarah, enabling them to complete their night journeys while away from the Crystal Star Temple and other dolmans which located in various parts of Midgard in chambers beneath Stonehenges and other megalithic monuments and within the Castle of the Queen of Mirrors, *Chandra* of whom there will much more later in this tale. These personal dolmans were known as the *Se'er Stones* for they were the power of sacred visions. They could also be used in the same manner as the magic orbs were used to see the unfolding of events far away and to concentrate the mind's power for spiritual warfare and they function via the natural power of Midgard and creation all around—life being the source of all such energy—magic.

The Se'er Stones, just like the Heart of the Sea (and the other pieces of the All Seeing Eye) couldn't be destroyed by the hands of man or elf nor that of any speaking creature whether good or evil, save by God or by the hand of he who made them—until the coming of Ragnarok at the end of days. No element could harm them nor any fervent heat melt them, even that of Vulcan's Mountain. The Se'er Stones glowed with the colors of the rainbow and glistened with the holy light of sacred power. When the time came for Yoshael and Zakarah to ascend into the *Halls of the Light Elves,* the Weylandr Se'er Stones were to be passed to Shlomael and Aubriel, who were to be the new White Wizard and new Spirit Maiden of the North. No other person could use the Se'er Stones unless they were given leave to do so by the owners—thus they were no good to a sorcerer. These were also weapons against the draugr and the månenhundene and other forces of evil and could be used during exorcisms to drive out a jötunn and to purify a haunted house. The though had come to Yoshael's mind once that he might be able to use them to perform an exorcism and purification of all Myrkvidr. But alas they had no such power for they simply couldn't channel the magic necessary when the dark powers would be pushing back with the entire might to avoid the abyss.

Now it came to pass that Yoshael was resolved that as soon as Molly was available with the Holy Lamp that the Children of Light should go into the circle and conference as to what the proper course of action would be in the Spirit Realm while King Sigurd tended to earthly matters with his war council.

That night Yoshael, by the power of the *Se'er Stone* about his neck came in the spirit to the circle of the holy people who were gathered in the Dolman Chamber beneath the Thorstadt Stonehenge. The people in the city could see through their open window shutters the bright glow of the blue and white lights emanating from the sacred temple across the river. These Mystics of Light were gathered around and sitting cross legged on the floor with outstretched hands upon their thighs in their deep trances of meditation and calling upon the power of the name of God. Molly was in the circle beside Gladvynn and the Holy Lamp hung outside of her dress betwixt her breasts glowing with its beautiful light—a good sign from *Dan Ene Gud.* They all sat around the *Dolman Orb* which was glowing with soft ambient bluish-white light. Outside of Zakarah's blouse as usual for these events was her Se'er Stone—glowing with the coventental colors of the rainbow.

Their bodies were here yet their spirits were in the *Rakia*, that realm which separates the physical from the heavenly. The Rakia was the dimension through which the Elves traversed in their night journeys and in time did not exist. Spirits could move through it in the midst of Midgard, unseen by physical eyes and like other mysterious forces of creation, it had its dark side as well and could be accessed by sorcerers. There were new souls in the circle now who were there, Galorfilinde, Shlomael and Aubriel, as well as Argyle and Vong the son of Byock. In that realm all of them could see one another and they were clothed in garments of pure light. All was peaceful yet not content—especially with young Molly, whose only child had been cruelly snatched from her in order to extract a ransom. The circle seemed to be hovering in the open universe and in the background the stars went forever in all directions.

Yoshael spoke saying, "The kidnapping of Liam and the others have caused a great disturbance and an imbalance in the spirit realm and this must be set right—for tis the destiny of this lad to be a White Wizard and to be the council of King Ronan. There's more at stake here than the Holy Lamp, for Loki put this plot into the mind of Hister to thwart the mission of Ronan when the time cometh for the binding of Loki—for he knoweth that his time is short." Byock said "Loki will be bound when his own Gotterdammerung comes, but the end is not yet—coming only at the end of days." Dithranti replied, "Aye it shall be indeed but for the here and the now the one thing for sure is that no matter what happens, the Heart of The Sea cannot be allowed to fall into the hands of Hister. For if it does the shadow of darkness greater than what now is shall fall across the land. It will be the undoing of both Loki and Hister as long as Molly retains the Holy Lamp and her goodness through it shall keep that darkness in check—in balance." Vulcrus spoke as well saying, "Dithranti is right my brothers and sisters. If Hister possesses the Heart of the Sea there will be nothing to stop him from his plot—or Loki from his."

Molly had a look on her face of agony as she replied to them all, close to sobbing one moment and filled with wrath in the very next saying, "Aye! I understand that Hister canno have the talisman lest he activate the Eye. But I'll not just let me loving little Liam rot on Cyclops Island! Me boy is coming home no matter what!" Min-Tze said to her, "I know that right now it's hard for you to be of good cheer Molly but you must try. Let not yourself be conquered by anger and hate—for these are of the dark side and Hister knows that if you succumb to them then he will have weakened this circle by causing division. We stand with you Molly in all things that you do that are righteous and holy—so let your anger be a righteous anger. Let it be an anger which seeks justice and not revenge. Byock and I have not seen our son Vong for four years in person, yet here he sits with us in the spirit. You can do the same with the Holy Lamp Molly." Gladvynn said, "Yes Molly, until Liam is home safe, you can go to him on the night journeys and comfort him in his sleep. But beware lest the circumstances in which the lad is held cause thee more pain and anger Molly." Zakarah said, "I will show thee Molly how we Elves accomplish our night journeys—yet since thou art not an Elf, your power will be much weaker and it will seem to Liam that he has only seen thee in his dreams." Molly replied, "At least it's something Matriarch and I thank ye so very much for it—the thread of hope."

Byock spoke once more saying, "We must battle the Vanier that have engineered this evil. So while a quest is sent out for the recovery all three of the victims, we here must combat those wicked spirits within the Rakia. Also two of our number must be part of the quest on the ground, for the powers of darkness shan't sit idly by and watch us defeat their scheme." Yonas and Gleadra nodded in the affirmative and Aesop said, "Yes, and as you know, two of the victims were Fauns; Amberwose and Rockwose. Since they are of my nation and race, I suspect that Hister will try and use them to gain further leverage against this council and against the Fauns as a whole." Boudicca agreed saying, "That will surely be the case and I suspect that Hister feels quite confident and full of himself about right now."

Zakarah, sitting next to Yoshael said, "King Sigurd is meeting with his War Council as we speak." She looked at Yoshael and said, "Melchizedek, what are your thoughts on all of this?" He replied, "Liam, Rocky and Amber must come home and the Heart of the Sea must not be handed to Hister under any circumstances. We of this circle will battle the dark spiritual forces involved in this as Byock has said, and try to blind them to the march of Sigurd's knights. Vong, you will go along on the quest as a Kung Fu Master when thou hast arrived in Thorstadt from Shangra La.

As well there must be a wizard team just as Master Byock has said. Hellas is part of the south and so, Yonas and Gleadra, it falleth upon the two of you to go with them to Cyclops Island. In the meanwhile there is my grandson Samael. He's been in Hellas living a prodigal life and unknown to him right now, all of it was for many purposes—this one as well as others which shan't play out for three thousand years. But this one shan't take so long and Samael will play a role in all of this as well—though as yet it is completely unknown to him. And you Master Dithranti gather in the Druids at the Brython Stonehenge for we need all the combined powers of good in this battle against the Vanier. Boudicca, contact them using the Orb of Erda."

This caused a reaction from the soul of Aubriel who was attending the meeting after her arrival in Thorstadt that very evening in her spirit who said in amazement, "But Grandfather. How can that one, young grandson, the Dark Elf who has sinned and rebelled against all that we hold sacred be of consequence in this matter?" Yoshael, whose face was full of compassion and love for her said, "Little One, those who are lost must be found and even Samael must be rescued for like Liam, Rocky and Amber, he too is a captive—albeit in a different sort of way. I knew that he was destined for this moment the first day he was born and even greater still when he wanted to run away to Hellas and establish commerce. Twas no coincidence that when he went there he went to Delphi, which as you know was one of the places where a part of the All Seeing Eye was hidden by me all those years ago. Someday Aubriel, you will be wed to Shlomael, and the two of you will take our places in the Circle as the White Wizard and the Spirit Maiden of the North when our journey upon Midgard is finished and Zakarah and I ascend to the Hall of the Light Elves, Ljosalfheim; tis a place that all Elves must go little one—whether they live to ascend or whether they die in battle; for we cannot die as other speaking being do—diseases and so forth. Tis a far, far better resting place that we go and indeed shall see all those Elves who've died, and who shall yet die in this war and in those to come. For if we Elves do not ascend, or die in battle, then we are doomed to live until dark despair of the world sets in and we die in spirit. Therefore El Shaddai grants each Elf our own length of days in Midgard, whether to die in war or to live to ascension—that we not wither in despair. So let your light shine forth in forgiveness, for your brother wants to repent and come home and Aubriel my beloved, before you can go to Urðarbrunnr for schooling as a Norn, thou must overcome this bitterness."

Zakarah said, "Yes. All of this has been for a purpose. Not only will the hostages come home but Samael as well shall no longer be a spirit hostage to the dark powers for he too, as the Melchizideck has said is a captive now—in a different way. He will be rescued from the bondage of sin, and take his place among the Elf Lords. From the time he returns home, and is wed to the mortal woman called Miriamne, forces will be set in motion which will see the rise of whole new Kingdoms of Elves—the twelve Kingdoms to come." Turning to Molly Zakarah said, "So Molly you see that Liam has been blessed from the moment he was conceived and is destined to walk the way of the White Wizard, with Samael as his Norn." Zakarah looked at Galorfilinde and smiled, knowing that her daughter needed the reassurance that her first-born son was not lost forever to the world of men and their commerce of corruption. Molly took great heart and from this she received courage for she knew that her son was going to be alright; that he was going to be rescued.

Suddenly they were surrounded by thousands of beautiful Valkyries and the Æsi (Angel) Brigid appeared. Brigid held high her flaming sword and it was struck by a massive bolt of lightning. Back in the physical realm, a storm gathered strength in the night sky over Thorstadt centred about the Thorstadt Stonehenge. Thunder let its voice be heard and lightening flashed all around in the clouds as the rain began to fall. In the Rakia, the Circle of Spirit Maidens and that of the Sons of Light began to turn in a circle around the Dolman Orb in the centre and were soon going so fast that it seemed as if they were a solid ring of blueish-white fire. And far away to the west were the Druids, led by Arch Druid Aodhangedrix who in their hood brown robes were gathering into to the Brython Stonehenge united in purpose for the struggle to come—for indeed Dithranti had already sent them word via Lady Boudicca and her magical Orb of Erda from the first moment they heard of the kidnapping—the game was afoot.

CHAPTER XXIII

Bold New Plans

From The Skald's Tale

During these dark times, the King and the Queen of our people so very long ago, knew that the outrages that had been perpetrated upon them must be met with strong force. Therefore was the Mighty Griffin bold in his plans—just as is our good King Roderick who sits here in this Mead Hall as the tale is told beside the winter hearth.

Thе queen was absolutely incensed and outraged when she found out what had happened and that Ronan's dream had been confirmed—not angry with Rony of course, but with the lowness to which the enemy had now fallen. She had a grim look of determination on her face as she entered the war hall (war planning room) with King Sigurd and her brothers Gedron and Sigmund. All of the *Reiks* of Tervingia were there. These were the Lords Volsung, Snaevar, Sinfjotli, Hodbrodd, Radagaisus, Fridigern, Randver Jarl Godwin, Jarl Gondark and the Jarl Adaire and the famous Lord Raedwald. The Priestesses Byrnhilda and Anke were there as representing the religious orders of Tervingia. Sergeant Hardrada had been summoned as well as many others—these having been called to an emergency meeting of the *Witena Gemot*. Queen Gwynnalyn had in clinched in her angry fist the ransom note from the Centaur Force Commander—which Sigmund had delivered to the king and queen immediately upon his arrival home.

King Sigurd's allies had been called to attend the meeting and so Woodwose and the other Faun officers and those of the Celts were in the room as were representatives of the Elves—Shlomael and the two Elf Generals being honored with seats at the table. Shamus and the laddies were honored with seats besides the Lords of Tervingia as well as the Elves and of those seated at the great and long table were engaged in much excited conversation and speculation as to what was going to happen in light of this ugly revelation brought home by Sigmund.

King Sigurd and Queen Gwynnalyn entered the room with stern looks upon their faces wearing their crowns and their hauberks—for this were to be a working meeting. The table was very long and wide—wide enough so that two chairs could be placed side by side on each end and the king's and queen's chairs were sat accordingly, hers on his right hand. Their chairs were very large with great and high backs with pinnacled points—thrones in miniature in which no one was allowed to sit save them. All those seated at the stood up and together with all those who'd been standing took their bow and said, "Hail Sigurd King! Hail Gwynnalyn Queen!" The king and queen took their seats in great chairs beside one another and King Sigurd said, "Very good M'Lords, now that the formalities are over we'll get to the business at hand."

The seating arrangements were thus. Lord Volsung was around the corner and to the left of King Sigurd. Scap Rolf was seated to the left of Volsung on the same side of the table, followed by Scap Kronos, Lords Snaevar, Regin, Sinfjotli, Hodbrodd, Radagaisus, General Randver and Lord Raedwald—followed by Shlomael, Yoavael and Gidonael of the Elves. Down the right side of the table around the corner from Queen Gwynnalyn sat Lord Gedron, Duke Sigmund, Princess Eileza, Lord Fridigern, the Jarl Adaire and then the Jarl Gondark. Then were Lords Hjalprek and Genersarik, Jarl Godwin, Shamus, Ruairi, Aonghus and Fearghal, and finally Ambassador Althjolf of the Dwarves. The two priestesses sat at the far end of the table side by side and the king and queen could see them down the length of the table. The rest of the people stood around the room and these included Austri and Vestri. Galorfilinde stood in the corner quietly behind Queen Gwynnalyn.

Tanman served up the ale as the king spoke. "What we have here is a grave turn of events. Something that we should've anticipated but didn't and we shan't let it stand." The queen was clearly very angry and said, "Agreed Sire. This slanderous outrage must not and will not stand! We must formulate a response to this attack M'Lords and we're open to suggestions." Lord Hodbrodd replied dismissively and with much contempt saying, "The young Duke should never have been given such a mission to begin with! He is young and inexperienced." Lord Volsung was quick to defend his boy and said, "You cannot blame my son for this Lord Hodbrodd Gunnbjornson! This is why Lord Snaevar and I assigned Sergeant Hardrada to the Duke's military force—and besides all of that, a lad can only gain the experience he needs by actually going out and doing it."

The queen's ire went up—for what Hodbrodd had said had gotten her goad and she said, "Lord Hodbrodd blaming my brother for this outrage serves no one and won't get the hostages back." He replied, "Facts are facts my queen and that irresponsible lad should never have been sent out. He was the leader and so he bears the blame!" Lord Radagaisus took the side of Hodbrodd (to no one's surprise) and said, "Lord Gedron you should've led the mission to the khan or even me! Sigmund has no real experience and he is as Lord Hodbrodd has said."

Sigmund, who was seated between Gedron and the Queen started to say something in his own behalf but Gedron said, "No Siggy. You've done nothing for which you have to defend yourself." Gedron glared at Hodbrodd and Radagaisus saying, "How dare the two of you pass judgement before the facts are in! Especially you Sir Radagaisus—after all aren't you engaged to marry into this family? You weren't there!" Radagaisus made no reply and Gedron cried, "Art thou calling my brother a liar Lord Hodbrodd?" Eileza would have stood up and drew her sword but Sigmund put his arm around her shoulder to hold her down as she scowled at Hodbrodd. Shamus and the Leprechauns were watching it all with wide eyes of alarm.

Hodbrodd started to reply but the mighty Volsung stood up and said loudly, "That's exactly what he's saying! Thou hast offered insult to the House of Volsung Lord Hodbrodd—as head of the family Volsung, tis my duty to defend our honor—in the bear pits!" Queen Gwynnalyn would have stood up as well had not King Sigurd pressed his right hand hard down on her left hand (which she had placed on the table) and looking at her he shook his head, "No." Lord Hodbrodd stood up to accept the challenge and suddenly a very outraged Shamus jumped up on top of the table down on his end and said angrily, "Now see here mates! Tis me own son that was nabbed by those shitehawks and I place no blame on Siggy or Hardrada! If there's any ones with the right to place blame it meself, Molly and Master Woodwose. What say ye Master Woodwose?" The Faun, who'd been leaning in the far left corner of the room spoke loud and clear, "Tis all of our faults lads—no more and no less!"

King Sigurd could see that this meeting was getting out of control and he said to Shamus, "Well said Master Leprechaun and you to Master Faun. And as for the rest of you—enough of this! I tell thee all that we haven't time for duals over honor! Take thy seats M'Lords for there will be no blame assigned, nor will there be any recriminations against the Grand Duke Sigmund or Sergeant Hardrada! I chose the Grand Duke Sigmund for the mission and no one else has any say in which person I chose for I am the king! So any blame belongs to me Lord Hodbrodd! We haven't time for this so M'Lords please take thy seats so we can get down to work and figure out what we're going to do about this!" Shamus took his seat as did Volsung and Hodbrodd and everyone had the feeling that this was only the beginning of troubles between the Volsungs and Hodbrodd and his supporters. Lord Radagaisus wisely stayed in his seat and said not a word. But he was a man with a dark spirit and many people, everyone except the love struck Greta could see it.

King Sigurd toned down his voice and said firmly but smoothly, "Lord Sigmund, give us your report on the mission and how these events came to be." Sigmund stood before the Elders and reported to the best of his ability on everything that had happened.

When he had finished and returned to his seat, the queen looked sternly at Hodbrodd and Radagaisus saying, "So you see M'Lords his report aligns with that of Sergeant Hardrada—I'll hear no more of this ineffable twaddle!" Hodbrodd and Radagaisus backed down and replied in unison, "Yes my Queen. It would seem so." The king said, "Very good Sigmund. Clearly you did the right thing by sending word on to Ariemel and then sending a squad to track the kidnappers and then returning here to Thorstadt."

King Sigurd lifted his mug and said, "A toast to the Duke of Wodenburg and Sergeant Hardrada." As they lifted their mugs and horns to do the toast they all said, "Skol!" The Queen noticed that Hodbrodd done so only reluctantly. He was acting a bit strange here of late and was seen a lot in the Crow's Beak tavern and out in the hemp lodges with Lord Radagaisus. Those two gave the queen a bad feeling but right now she was unable to put her finger on exactly what it was. All in all Hodbrodd was a rather odd and strange old fellow to say the least; not the kind of bloke that one would care to bring home to supper and Queen Gwynnalyn was utterly incensed at Greta for pledging her troth to a man like Radagaisus—who seemed to have a dark spirit around him.

Queen Gwynnalyn joined in the toast with the rest and said "Skol!" She drank from her horn slowly and with dignity. When the toast had been concluded and the horns and mugs removed by Tanman (for no servants were allowed in the war room during secret meetings) the King said, "Clearly we have a vile situation on our hands and right now I want unity from all of you. We cannot afford to tear ourselves apart with backbiting at any time, least of all right now and in duals over honor. Hister has kidnapped the child of the Cluricawnish ambassador as well as the wife and child of Woodwose Faun. We know why they wanted Liam O'Hurleyhune, but why Amberwose and Rockwose?"

Queen Gwynnalyn replied, "My King, I would suspect that Hister and the Slaughter Wolves hope to gain some leverage against High Lord Elder whose territory is west of Dakkia—on account of their victories over the Gnomes." King Sigurd replied, "It seems so since both he and Vulcrus are here and have been for four years now; and because they're the White Wizard and Spirit Maiden of the Centre Midgard." She replied, "My thoughts exactly my Lord King. Hister wants to gain leverage against not only Agara but against the Circle of the Spirit Maidens and the Sons of Light and I dare say, even the Druids. But I know our allies and they shan't yield to pressure like this."

King Sigurd said to all of them. "Right now the mystics are meeting. The circle has been gathered and by tomorrow we shall know the outcome of it. The Heart of the Sea is a talisman of powerfully good magic and I shan't pretend to understand it." He looked at his Priestesses and said, "Ladies, you are wise. Explain this to us please?" Lady Anke rose and began to speak. She told the story of the All Seeing Eye from beginning to end and then said, "This final piece was entrusted by the Elves to the Merwif, by the very hand of the Prince Shlomael and the Princess Galorfilinde who even now honor us with their presence in this room—until the time of the birth of Prince Ronan, the Prophesied Goth King to come. Then it was given by the Merwif to Molly on her way here with Dithranti four years ago."

She motioned and Priestess Byrnhilda rose and said, "My king, my queen, you are both familiar with Molly's Gemstone and the Eye, and you both know that it cannot be allowed to fall into the hands of Hister. No matter how many pieces of the Eye Hister gets assembled up there on his evil black tower, the Eye will not function without the Heart of the Sea—and this is why Hister is desperate to get it. It is the reason why and has gone this far to do so."

"What say you Lord Shlomael?" asked King Sigurd. The Elf Prince replied gravely, "Hister will go much further I am afraid. We cannot under any circumstances allow the Holy Lamp to fall into Hister's hands and it grieves me to say this Master Shamus and Master Woodwose—but no matter what the cost M'Lords, even if it means that the hostages are killed. The power that the All Seeing Eye will unleash in the wrong hands will cause the End of Days! The destruction of Midgard in a fiery holocaust will result and Surt the Fire Giant will walk unchecked. But the Eye, when used by holy hands, like that of an Anointed One brings about the binding of Loki. Even then we will long for the time of the Anointed Son of Asgard to come and only he will bring about the epoch of peace such as it was in the first age when Adam was in Eden—as foretold in the *Scroll of Hanokh.*" Shamus stated angrily, "That's easy for ye to say Prince Shlomael! It's not your wee laddy that's been kidnapped!"

The queen hadn't heard this part of the story before and she replied with a happy look of hope on her face, "Priestess is not my son an Anointed One? Was Ronan not prophesied by the Elves to Conquer evil? Can it be that when he reigns, that he as the Goth King will activate the Eye for Good, and bring about this epoch of peace, this new Eden?" Byrnhilda replied, "I cannot say my queen for that knowledge is hidden from me. Perhaps your Norn will have much greater insight in this than I." Queen Gwynnalyn felt a sense of joy pulsing through her and all of her anger at Hodbrodd was gone and everyone could see it on her face. Hodbrodd felt greatly relieved to see that the attentions of the queen were no longer on him, but in his heart he hated her.

Lord Volsung nodded and said, "Well, let's hope so Priestesses for the world could use an epoch of peace—and who better to usher it in than my grandson. But now we must consider our actions. The talisman must not be handed over to Loki's stooge nor must the hostages be allowed to die—or worse yet rot away on this infernal Cyclops Island, wherever that is. What in the name of Asgard is a Cyclops anyway? And these Centaurs! I never believed the legends about them were true. We must send forth a quest my Lord King to bring the hostages home safe—and we now have less than ninety days to do it."

Lord Snaevar said, "He's right. Believe you me the legends that we've all heard about the Centaurs were true and we've found out the hard way. Volsung is right Sire. We must launch a rescue mission and somehow hide this from Hister, less he have the hostages murdered."

General Randver asked, "Are there any reports of Scythian troop movements? I cannot help but think that King Idanthrsus doesn't also have some game afoot in all of this. It is only a matter of time before the Slaughter Wolves and their horse archers come after Tervingia with their entire horde. Those slaughter wolves are the backbone of Hister's entire effort to wage world war and conquer all Midgard. They're coming soon—I feel it in my bones King Sigurd."

King Sigurd replied, "This is why I've been working so hard these last few years to build an alliance, a Steppe Confederation of our own in order to counter the Empire when it strikes once more." The Jarl Gondark replied, "There has been sire. Cimmerians and Ogres attacked the farm lands west of Oarus River in my lands of Sandfrith ten days ago before I was called here sire—but my men held them in check as I reported to you." King Sigurd looked down the table at the Jarl of Frenwic and asked, "And what is afoot down your way Jarl Godwin?" He replied, "Down my way the Scythians raided the Wodenburg region as well but it was all minor in nature. We are having our normal Gargoyle flybys and there have been a dozen of Huginn's Folk about. My scouts have detected no preparations for a major attack so far down in Frenwic."

King Sigurd nodded in reply and looking at the Jarl Adaire asked, "And what's been happening in Grunewald?" Adaire was leader of the Issedones of the Steppes in the Grunewald area of the former Kingdom of Issedonia on the Steppes of Kuban—great hunters were they and most renowned. Adaire was about thirty eight years old with long hair on the left side of his head while the right side was shaven and covered in blue dragon tattoos. His face was clean shaved except for a big handlebar moustache. He wore dark green trousers and shirt under chainmail hauberk and his eyes were emerald green. He was armed with both short sword and a dagger and was a close friend and loyal subject of the king. His wife and children had come north with him; thirty six year Jarless Alfhild, fifteen year old son and heir Adalheid, fourteen year old daughter Zelda and five year old daughter Asynja who were in that moment in the company of Lady's Gerda and Greta elsewhere in the mead hall.

Adaire replied, "My Liege we've had our fair share of trouble in the last month. Scythians Serpent Maidens have given us quite the challenge. A whole unit of Amazons sire—and most fierce! Shield Maidens led by

Malvina de Scythia. But we've held them and destroyed their camps. Last word was that Malvina had ridden west to join a large force massing at the mouth of the Tanais around the Hellene merchant colony of Palus." Queen Gwynnalyn replied, "I've heard of the Serpent Maidens and this Malvina. I would challenge her if given the chance." King Sigurd replied to her, "I know that you are the greater shield maiden betwixt the two of you my heart." Looking at his Jarls the king said, "Very well then my friend. I want you to keep them at bay down towards the Great Dark Sea—both you and Godwin as you have been and lose no opportunity to inflict upon the slaughter wolves the greatest of harm while you Jarl Gondark shall be doing the same up north on the Oarus against the Cimmerians, the Sarmatians and as well the Ogres. Wade into those Ogres and spill their blood with your horse archers Jarl Gondark!" Gondark with his wild hairdo replied with a smile, "It shall be my pleasure Mighty Griffin."

The queen said, "I suspect all that the empire's strategy will change in the near future whether or not Hister has the Heart of the Sea or not. If he gets the talisman this year, the Slaughter Wolves will launch another invasion in full force—and if not, then it will come by next spring." The King answered, "Yes you speak the truth. Four and a half years ago we launched this rebellion and won our independence. Then we united all of Tervingia under one monarchy and established the Eagle Throne. For narcissistic kings like Idanthrsus and Krosis such a thing cannot go unchallenged and indeed it hasn't—what with all of this see-saw, back and forth campaigns out on the steppes. But the reports tell of great numbers of Ogres and Gargoyles gathering around Kol Oba and Gelonus as well as at Palus. I feel that the hordes Morag will soon be unleashed upon us. I feel that we have been living on borrowed time—bought for us by Molly and the Heart of the Sea."

Lord Volsung said strongly, "So much the better for us my king for in spite of the invasions and counter attacks it has given us time to firmly establish this kingdom and build up our arms and our economy." "Right you are Lord Volsung," answered King Sigurd. "And so here is my plan to start with M'Lords. We shall send forth a quest to find this Cyclops Island and return the woman and the children home safe. Shamus, my son Rony loveth thy son as a brother, as he does thy son Woodwose and thine wife, dear Amberwose as an aunt. So we shall go forth and save them. This is the pledge of King Sigurd Rothgarson, direct descendent of King Tyrfingr Ashkenazsson and who wields his reforged sword unto all of thee." The group replied, "So say we all. All hail the Mighty Griffin."

The king stood up and placing his arms behind his back he paced back and forth. Hanging on the wall was a huge map of Midgard, at least the parts that they knew of—which had been inked on the hide of an Elk. Everyone was silent and the queen; seeing the familiar looks on his face of 'I have an idea' she knew that something big was forming in his mind. He unsheathed his sword Tyrfingr and planted the point of it square on Kol Oba. "Now here's part two of my plan. Methinks that it's high time I paid Herr Hister an unfriendly visit—with an army! This Kingdom has been on the defensive long enough! Two can play this game of raiding and attrition but I want full scale invasion. General Randver, gather your staff and come up with a plan for an invasion in force behind enemy lines with the aim of freeing the thralls of Helmgard! Helmgard is far west of the Scythian Capitol and this attack will draw Idanthrsus and Krosis away from our territory. I want us to free the Gutthiuda thralls—after all they are our Tervingian brothers and I am most displeased that they are still being held captive, forced to build Hister's evil tower! We'll bring with us siege engines and ballistae and wind lances and I shall field the greatest army in the history of Tervingia, putting an end to the Midgard War once and for all." Seeing the looks of approval on all faces present King Sigurd said, "I also would enjoy the input of my allies in this—Prince Shlomael of the Elves—Captain Cathal of the Celts and definatly you oh great Heraclius of the Fauns; and lastly but in no way in the least, you Lord Althjolf and the Dwarvish officers in planning this. So let it be written, so let it be done." The group replied, "So say we all. All hail the Mighty Griffin."

There was an immediate look of excitement on the face of Lord Radagaisus and he replied with a much changed tone of voice, "I am with you Sire and I want to go with this force. General Randver said, "But Sire, I agree that we need to attack Helmgard and even Kol Oba, but how will we get past King Dragos and his Gargoyles? And if the reports be true, Morag Ogres in unheard of numbers are gathering for an attack even as we speak? They will see us coming for miles and then alert the Scythians who'll move to intercept us." Radagaisus never gave the King a chance to reply and said, "Sire we can slip in through Myrkvidr."

There was immediate unrest at even the suggestion of that route for men greatly feared what was lurking in the depths of it dark, sinister forests but Lord Raedwald said, "Lord Radagaisus is right. We defeated Myrkvidr four years ago sire and if needs be we can do it again." The queen replied to all of them saying, "Nonsense Lords!" Did not Master Dithranti come through it four years ago on his way here? The Fauns know their way through it." "But what about the armies of Lothar the Defiler and the draugr?" asked Gedron? The queen smiled and said, "I would take out my dagger and make of them eunuchs, were I going! However I am not going on that mission. I will go to help rescue the children though!" The King replied, "My queen, somehow I knew that you would want to be along on that one." She replied, "We shall indeed go, for this is an issue of mothers having had their children stolen and I, as a mother shan't sit this one out my Lord King." Sigurd replied, "So let it be written, so let it be done my queen. You shall lead the quest to Cyclops Island. Well it would seem we have preparations to make for two missions. Tomorrow we'll meet with the wizards and mages here in the war room. All of this is to remain top secret M'Lords—for our ears only!" "Aye Sire," was the reply from everyone and then all said, "So say we all. All hail the Mighty Griffin." The King dismissed the meeting.

183

CHAPTER XXIV

Prophecies Concerning the Goth King

From the Skald's Tale

The things foretold of the Goth King have come to pass back in elder days that I am telling thee of here at the tale fire. Twas foretold of him of powerful deeds and how mighty his halls would be. All spoken of in signs given in the stars concerning his birth and I have told thee oh King Roderick in tale fires past of those things. Now tell I thee of more things which were told of him unto his mother who was the Shield Maiden Queen of legend and lore. Only her womb could have given birth to such a hero as was the Goth King Ronan.

The queen slipped away and after nightfall she met some strangers in the darkness of Osrik's Tunnel by the light of flickering lamps. These were odd and mysterious folks, part of her web of spies which she had in every city in the kingdom. What was said in these dark shadows was never revealed for such is the nature of cloak and dagger. She was becoming quite powerful and very dangerous to anyone she considered to be an enemy. The sound of the trap door opening and soft footsteps on the steps coming down into the tunnel was heard and the flickering of another lamp could be seen by the queen and these three dark cloaked strangers. "Away now and see to it that Hodbrodd doesn't know he's being watch north those in Grunewald. Away with you and quickly," whispered Queen Gwynnalyn and the three shadowy strangers vanished in the darkness, feeling their way out to the exit, where they vanished into the salt cedar and river side forests—for the queen had arranged for the tunnel guards to be silent and to let these odd folks pass on into the shadows of the night.

After that strange bit of cloak and dagger someone came into the view of Queen Gwynnalyn in the light of her lamp. The mysterious person's face was revealed by the lamp in the person's hand and when the queen hand recognized who it was she was much relieved saying, "Oh it's just you Galorfinde—I was worried that some other person had come down and I should've had a bad time explaining it all. Galorfinde replied, "The Spirits told me that you would need me tonight in a private place Eowythane and so I have come to you dear one—for I know that the talk of chosen ones and prophecies have opened questions in your mind. I am here for thee Eowythane, just as even now my brother Shlomael is explaining these things to thy brothers—for he is their Norn.

Gwynnalyn her Galorfinde sat down cross legged on the sod floor of the tunnel with their lamps between them and the queen asked, "Dear Galorfinde, today they spoke of an *Anointed One*—the Son of Asgard. I must know. Is my son he?" Her dear Norn replied, "Ronan is *An Anointed One* but he is not the one spoken of by the elder scrolls. Ronan is anointed for the earthly salvation of this kingdom and this part of Midgard and indeed he shall be *The Goth King*. When the third Midgard War has come and he is the victor, the Goth King shall lead your people and many others into a promised land beyond the northern reaches of the Oster Sea called

Gothia—and then shall the Æsir bind Loki until the coming of Ragnarok. In Ronan's time all of your people will come to be called *The Goths* and my father's vision foresees a time in an age yet to come when there will be two nations of Goths—the Visigoths and the Ostrogoths—all of who will be ruled by the descendants of you and Sigurd—and *Ronan the Goth*. But no, Rony is not the Son of Asgard, or the Son of God Eowythane. That son shall come forth in a far distant age."

Gwynnalyn sighed with disappointment and said, "Well I had hoped that he'd be that one as well but I am heartened by the thought that he could play part in the binding of Loki. I am happy because I know that my son shall be the refounder of our nation and that our dynasty is secured but a land north of the Oster Sea? How can that be? They tell us that the Oster Sea is naught but ice the further one goes until it becomes part of the Land of Forever Ice. The Hagobards in their dragon ships have sailed out of Eikengard and can only go so far—for the ice starts and is impassable. Shall it be a magic land? Is Gothia like Alfheim?" Galorfinde answered, "No, it's not like Alfheim Eowythane—at least not right now. But it can be when it emerges from under the glacier. It will be a new frontier for Ronan to take the people to and there build a nation. You see something wonderful is happening to Midgard—the ice is melting. All of this ice was made by the great world flood—that destroyed primeval Midgard. *Dan Ene* Gud changed the nature of Midgard—the climate as we Elves call it, from the way it had been before in elder times when there were no high mountains and all Midgard was warm. The world that emerged after the deluge was new and forbidding at first to all life—but we survived and are thriving. The top quarter of Midgard froze as did the bottom quarter below Cushan Midgard. The world is blessed now that the circles of seasons are becoming less turbulent and it is warming. New lands are opening and new lakes and rivers are forming. In one generation, that which was frozen shall be warm and full of life—Gothia emerging from under it to grow life—a land which will flow with milk and honey. And then shall the Land of Forever Ice retreat into the uttermost parts of the north and the Southern Ice even now retreats into the bottom of Midgard. Soon the glaciers surrounding Alfheim will be gone and we Elves shall no longer have need of our magic invisible dome—for it will be warm enough for us to live without it. The River Bifrost will flow free and clear all summer long without need of its shelter."

Gwynnalyn replied with childlike wonder at it all, "Such a wonderful time it is Godmother—to be a part of making the new world." Her tone now changed to one of worry and she said, "But yet I worry. You spoke of the third Midgard War; what of the second my Norn?" Galorfilinde replied, "My father hasn't revealed to me the second—only to say that it will be a time of weeping and of gnashing teeth for all of our peoples Eowythane. Let not thine heart be troubled about this Eowythane—take comfort that your son shall be the salvation of us all—at least as far as this world is concerned. Tell this to Sigurd and let him be reassured as well."

Gwynnalyn thought and then asked, "After the binding of Loki, will there still be evil in Midgard?" Galorfilinde replied, "Yes Eowythane, unfortunately there will be." Gwynnalyn shook her head and asked, "Then why bind him then? If nothing is different—then why bother?" Galorfilinde answered, "*Dan Ene Gud* created every speaking creature with inclinations to both bad and to do good, so that each one has its own free will. Those who are evil make a free choice to be so—but yet they always blame it on Loki saying, 'Loki made me do it.' His binding is to show that Loki the treacherous is master of those who chose to do his bidding." Gwynnalyn replied, "And so then afterwards, people will chose some other dark spirit to blame."

Her Norn responded by saying, "Truly thou hast grown wise Eowythane. But after the binding, those who claim the excuse will no longer find it valid at the end of days when judgment is falling. But yes, thou art right and my father has foreseen that in Midgard, tis the Witch King Thrain who shall rise to power when Hister is in the dust." Gwynnalyn was appalled by the very thought of such a thing and drawing her own conclusion said, "So then it is Thrain that the world will face when Loki is bound. My son will face him—and vanquish him." The elegant lady Elf replied, "Indeed. But now the hour is late and so we must go and rest."

"You're right Godmother," said Gwynnalyn with a yawn. They twain stood up on their feet and walked to the bottom of the staircase. Gwynnalyn mounted the staircase and began walking up with her Norn behind her. Just before they reached the top she turned and looking back at Galorfinde with deep affection she said, "I love you Galorfinde, my dear godmother. You are my wisest council and beyond my husband, the dearest friend that I've ever had." She stepped down and embraced Galorfinde who returned the love with an equally warm embrace, and they kissed one another upon their cheeks before heading up and out of the tunnel. When they'd emerged into Osrik's old bed chamber, Gwynnalyn closed the trap door and said, "Goodnight dear one, I shall tell my husband everything that thou hast told unto me this night." They parted company for the night.

A short time later in the royal bed chambers, with little Ronan sound asleep, the king and the queen spoke. Sigurd was deeply concerned about Gwynnalyn going off to Cyclops Island. They cuddled like two spoons, warm and snug in their blankets. Her head was tucked under his chin and he said, "My heart, I don't want thee to go off on the rescue mission. What kind of a king sends his queen off to war?" She replied, "My hunter, I am a shield maiden of Thorstadt or am I not?" Sigurd knew where she was going with this and replied, "Indeed you are my heart—the best that there ever has been in the history of our people." She answered, "Twas not my sword the Gwynnian Scythe, when given to me blessed by Thor to protect the innocent children?" He replied, "Yes, it is so My Heart."

She rolled over and facing him, kissed him and then said, "And that is why I am going my hunter. Not because I am merely a shield maiden, but because my sword's blessing tasks me to do so. In the meanwhile my hunter, thou art going off on the invasion of Helmgard and shall fight battles which will be sung of in lore and legend—fights that will determine the fate of our kingdom. But we need a wise man to oversee the affairs of the kingdom in our absence—one that can be trusted not to usurp us. And that leaves out that shitehawk Hodbrodd! So place Scap Rolf in charge while we are away. I would suggest my father but I know that he will not be kept away from such an adventure. I trust Rolf and even Kronos—but that Hodbrodd I mistrust and detest. I think that he will someday betray us for some reason. Take him with you my hunter, and do not leave him in a position to plot against us."

The king was amazed. "Hodbrodd is plotting against us? I grant that Hodbrodd is a somewhat a boor, but a traitor? How know you this My Heart?" She said, "He schemes to replace my father as your military advisor, and Scap Rolf as your Chief Steward and he's a lot in the company of Lord Radagaisus—that damned Radagaisus! For the life of me I cannot see why Greta loves him! Hodbrodd wants to gain your trust so completely, that he can plot a putsch and seize the Eagle Throne for himself and betray us all to Hister—and Radagaisus must be involved as well! They're divisive creatures and bad hearted—so heed my warning. Take them both with you, and if what I say proves true, execute them—that would at least rid us of his marriage to Greta. I feel Hodbrodd and somehow even Radagaisus are hangers to our son and the survival of our dynasty for that glorious future prophesied for our Rony."

Sigurd replied, "Yes, and Hodbrodd commands a large following among the Issedones. But Radagaisus not so many and he, if what thou sayest is true my heart, would be a spy and anything said in the presence of Greta, she'd tell it him and soon it would find it way to Hodbrodd. So that's why he's so intent on marrying Greta. I will listen to you My Heart, for we are one person. How know you this?" She replied, "I'm not without my eyes across the kingdom—my *black watchers of the night* shall we say for lack of a better word." King Sigurd replied, "What a deadly resource my heart. You never cease to amaze me." She replied, "I had to move with the utmost secrecy after Greta's engagement to that black knight and since you have thine own spies to watch among our enemies, I knew that with the threat of Hodbrodd looming, that we must have such within our own kingdom lest you be taken unaware into a traitor's snare. Everything that I do My Hunter is for you and for the sake of our son—who must rule this kingdom as prophesied and no waugs like Hodbrodd can be allowed to tear this United Kingdom apart."

They twain were cuddling like a pair of spoons, Sigurd's all-embracing arms pulled her tight against him and he said, "Right you are My Heart. For anyone who betrays us I'll see their head on the block. But I can't just come out and accuse them without proof. Such a thing could turn the Issedones against us and tear their entire shire away in a rebellion in the midst of the life or death struggle that we are fighting against the Slaughter Wolves. Therefore I see the value of what you have been doing and I support it thoroughly My Heart. But if it is found that Sir Radagaisus is plotting and he goes to the block, Greta will hate us forever. In such circumstances can she even be trusted. We've no word yet as to the fate of my mother Aslaug and my brother Rognir—and yet Greta seems to have forgotten all about her engagement to Rognir, writing him off as dead. This grieves me but I know a young woman can't wait forever for marriage."

Gwynnalyn answered, "She already resents me Sigurd. See how she trains as a shield maiden and she plans to challenge me in the tournaments—should the war allow us to have any. But methinks that I love her and though deluded, Greta has a true heart and I shan't ever believe that she would betray us. Like as not if she discovered that Radagaisus was plotting with Hodbrodd or anyone else, she herself would swing the executioners axe. She's a true Volsung and a shield maiden of Tervingia. In spite of her rivalry against me, for me to believe that Greta would choose a traitor over our family and this kingdom I'd have to see it for myself."

Now that she had the full support of Sigurd for her *Black Watch of the Night* network (The Black Watch or Black Watchers) Gwynnalyn told Sigurd everything that Galorfilinde had spoken of in Osrik's Tunnel and he was greatly moved by it all and Sigurd said with satisfaction. "I know that the purposes spoken about by the Elves for our son is true—it had to be after all that happened at his birth. She would say nothing of the Second Midgard War? I can't say that the prospect of further wars thrills me My Heart—but a time of gnashing teeth and weeping? I shudder to think it My Heart. She replied, "Worry not my love for our concern now is of the war we are now fighting."

Gwynnalyn sat up and blew out the lamp for the night and rolled into the blankets with her husband in quiet but passionate romantic rapture.

CHAPTER XXV

Ronan's Mystical Map.

From The Skald's Tale

As I look around at all of your faces here in this Mead Hall, I see mothers and fathers who love their children more than life itself. This is because we know that all human life is sacred, especially that of a child, especially those still carried by their beloved mothers. How sad it is that in our world life has become cheap and short, taken with ease by the edge of the sword—for many who were slain could have been like little Prince Ronan for even in youth the Goth King had the gift of visions and twas at this time that these began to manifest—in dreams from which he drew a map of Cyclops Island for his beloved mum—the first quest map.

The next night after supper while the king was tending to last minute matters in the court the queen took Rony to his bath and readied him for bed. She herself tended the lad this, not any servants or nurses or her ladies in waiting. Often they did tend him as well as Gerda and Greta but not tonight. After she had him cleaned and dressed Rony asked, "Mummy, I'm glad that Uncle Siggy came back and glad that Uncle Shamus and Aunty Molly are home. But Liam and Wocky (Rocky) and Aunty Amber are gone Mummy—but I know where they are. They're on a big water in boats bouncing on waves in a storm mommy. And I saw where they're being taken—to a dungeon beside of a smoking mountain and it's an awful place with one eyed trolls! They're not there yet Mum but with my every dream they get closer. Everyone so sad—especially me and in my dreams I see the boats and then it's like I fly away o'er land and lots of water. Then I see this big castle made of stone beside of a mountain with fire in the top. I don't want to see it mummy because I know that Liam and Wocky are going to be in a dungeon in that scary place."

The queen was intrigued by this and said, "Here, take this hide and feather pen Rony. Dip the ink and draw this island. It shall be your dreams which lead me to this place to save your friends and Aunty Amber." There in the lamplight Rony drew a map as best he could of the forbidding fortress and the island. She was amazed at how complex and how detailed the map was and when the lad had finished he said, "Alright Mummy, here it is." She looked at it with a look of triumph on her face and said," Tis by thy dreams my child that they shall they all be saved. You've helped us so far more than anyone has son and I thank thee my dear heart." Rony replied with much unsurety, "I'm glad those nightmares are good for something."

But the child had other thoughts besides the map and said, "Uncle Woody came back and is so sad because Aunty Amber is taken away with my pal Wocky—with Liam in those boats—stuffed in wine barrels they are! Herr Woodwose won't say anything about it to me either Mum but I know that the bad horsey men took them all away and they're on the way to that mountain in the water. I dreamed it again last night and I know when I go to sleep tonight I'll dream it again Mum. Liam's eyes in my dreams look like he's been crying and so do Wocky's and Aunt Amber's Mum. I dreamed that the black fauns stuffed them away in barrels on as boat and that's how they're getting to that place Mum. Are my vision really real Mum? Did it all happen for real?"

Gwynnalyn knew that her boy was seeing what was happening to the hostages and was slightly tempted to take him along for that reason and especially since he had mystical foresight concerning Cyclops Island. But logic, common sense and better judgment prevailed and so Ronan would be staying home—but his map would be going along. "Yes, indeed it was Rony and that's why thou wast able to draw this map," she replied. "And while your father and I are away to rescue them, tell all of thy dreams to Grammy Gerda, so that all the people here may know what has become of our friends my dear heart." "Yes Mummy," was the lad's sad reply.

No one else was there. It was just mother and little son there in the royal chambers, sitting at the table eating freshly ground oatmeal and cow's milk for a late evening appetizer. His hair was dark red and very long and he could easily have been mistaken for a girl had he been put into a dress. But it was the custom of these people to let their children's hair grow long whether they were boys or girls and during tender age years it was their clothing which set them apart. Only when reaching past tender age and into their teens were Tervingians children allowed to select their own hairstyles as the young folks established their identities as individuals— and indeed those styles were quite diverse. Tattooing of children was not a custom among the Tervingians but after their first battles as adults many did tattoo themselves with runes and other images. However among the Elves tattooing was expressly forbidden by the law codes and was abhorrent to them—for they considered the practice to be quite uncivilized and within the purview of savages and barbarians.

As he ate, his mum brushed his hair and then tied it off down his back in a ponytail. She answered him gently saying, "You'll like as not hear it around the mead hall from loose lips so I'll tell thee Rony." He interrupted her asking, "Mummy, what is 'lose lips?'" She smiled and answered, "The kind of person who can't keep a secret, and tells everyone around—and we have to beware lest there be spies that hear the loose lips—and then go and tell it to their master." He took a few bites of his food and then replied, "That's not me Mummy! I don't have loose lips. You can tell me the secret

Mum—and no spy shall hear it from me either." He held up his left fist and making a stern look upon his tiny freckled face saith, "I give spies a beating—I'm a fist of legend!" He then growled like a big dog and his mother, being moved by his cuteness when making sich faces and sounds laughed saith, "Indeed Rony methinks the secret is safe with thee my son."

She sat down beside him and said, "Rony, its ok for you to have loose lips around me or dah, or Grandma and Grandpa. It is ok for you to have loose lips around any of your uncles or Aunty Greta, especially if someone tries to do bad things to you and hurt you, and then bully you into swearing to not tell. "What kind of bad things Mummy?" asked the child. When she had explained it to him in full she looked him direct in his eyes and strongly said, "Thou must always tell mummy and dahhy so we can protect you and be on your side. Promise me that you will Rony." He took her cheeks in his hands and kissed her under her eyes and said, "I pwomise Mummy."

She said to her little boy, "I loveth thee so much Rony," as she kissed his forehead. "Rony, just like you saw in your vision, some pikey's came and stole Liam and Rocky and Aunty Amber. Those horsey men are called Centaurs. Those black fauns that are in thy dreams are called Satyrs. They and the Centaurs are the servants of the sorcerer Hister, and by his command they took them away to that awful Cyclops Island—just as you have been seeing in your dreams. And those big one eyed monsters that thou art seeing in thy dreams are a race of evil Trolls called the Cyclopses."

Rony interrupted her with another question, "Mummy, what's an island?" She replied, "It's a piece of dry land, a mountain or other piece of land surrounded by water, like in a river or a lake. That big water in thy dreams is called the sea or the ocean. But fear not for them because Mummy is going to go there and get them back—and I'll bring them all home safe to you here in the mead hall. Soldiers and Knights are going to help me; Uncle Gedry and Sergeant Hardrada, even Uncle Siggy and Aunty Leeza. And when we find the buggars they'll be done up like a kipper—I'm going to give those infernal Centaurs a pasting that they'll never forget."

Rony looked worried and scared, "Will the pikey's come steal me away while you're gone Mummy?" She took him into her arms and a lump filled her throat so much so that she could hardly speak. But forcing herself she replied as tears filled her eyes, "Oh no Rony. No pikey can ever get thee here and steal thee away from mum and dah—not ever my Little Hunter for it is your destiny to be the next king." "Will Dah be here? Will the pikey's get you Mummy?"

She sat down with him in her rocking chair and cuddled him. She said, "Rony, Mummy is a shield maiden. Those pikeys are really going to get quite a pasting for stealing our friends away, and indeed thou shalt be safe hear with Grandma and Aunty Greta—even old Dithranti will be here to tell you the stories of Celtica. This is all a secret of the kingdom Ronan so whisper not a word of it. Dahhy has to go with the army to another place and save some people from the sorcerer." Something else was bothering Ronan and as he curled up in his mother's lap he stated sadly, "Mummy I wish I didn't have visions like that." Rony wept.

She replied, "Don't wish that love. You are a miracle child, the anointed one destined to be the king when your father has gone to Valhalla. The Wizard King has called you a *Man Child.* So fear not your gift of second sight son—embrace it and learn to use it for the good of us all—just has thou hast done this very night and made for me the map." Then he asked, "Mummy what is a *Man Child,* a boy baby?" His mother answered, "No Rony, not merely a boy baby. A *Man Child* is a term that the Elves call a son who was born by the will of the One God to fulfill a great roll or a destiny that shapes all of Midgard for a good way. Another word that they use is *Messiah* which means an *Anointed One* and that refers to any person that the Elves have blessed by anointing with sacred oil by placing it upon the forehead betwixt the eyes of the chosen one. Galorfinde says that someday *Dan Ene Gud,* who is the creator God, shall send his son as the ultimate Messiah to be King over all of Midgard. But until then there are other human, elf, faun and merwif anointed ones such as the wizards and spirit maidens, and you Rony, when thou art become king." He replied, "But I'm just a little boy Mummy and all that is—well I just don't understand what I have to do and I'm scared about all of that."

Gwynnalyn said lovingly, "Fear not little one, for thy destiny unfolds a little at a time—one bite at a time just as mine has and that of thy father. Just like it took four years for Asgard to give thee visions and magic dreams—the time when twas the greatest need for those who thou lovest Ronan, so shall it always be. And besides all of that, mummy is here and thy father also to guide thee. Someday the Elves will send thee a Norn, just like they sent to me when I was a little girl. That was Galorfinde and I'm sure whoever the Wizard King sends to thee shall be a fantastic friend and teacher; just as Galorfinde has been to me and Shlomael to Gedry and Siggy."

Mother and son embraced and her heart was breaking at having to leave him behind. She wept on his head and her tears wet his hair and the brave little boy said, "Don't cry Mummy. It's ok. Let not thy heart fall down." She rocked him to sleep with the elvish lullaby:

> Good night, sleep tight, go to sleep my dear baby—good night, good night—go to sleep in my arms. For thy mommy is here, drives the cold far away. Good night, sleep tight—go to sleep my dear baby—good night, good night, for thy mommy is here.

Later in the night King Sigurd returned to the bed chamber. Little Rony was sleeping soundly and Queen Gwynnalyn lay under covers in her sleeping gown with her hair down. He removed his weapons and hung them on the wall in their place next to his shield and then he saw Rony's map lying on the table. Walking to it he said, "From whence cometh this map My Heart?" She replied, "From our son. In visions Ronan has seen Cyclops Island and so I had him draw this map." Sigurd sat down and looked at it in the lamp light and marveled at the detail. "Tis a miracle indeed and he is an anointed one. Since the events at the gathering concerning his birth for years ago there haven't been any signs of his power until now and this is the first sign since then of our son's gifted life." Sigurd laid the map down and walking over to Ronan's bed, he leaned down and kissed his boy on the forehead with deep love and pride. He then changed into his sleeping clothes, blew out all but one lamp and then cuddled with his wife under the blankets.

CHAPTER XXVI

Justice for the Shield Maidens

From the Skald's Tale

We Visigoths have among us many shield maidens. Our fighting women have slain dragons and have ridden with King Alaric in those years that ended the second age of Midgard when he sacked the city of Romulus and humbled Imperators of their evil western empire. But it was not always so my king. Twas in those elder days before King Sigurd when shield maidens couldn't lead men but by his enlightened rule and because of those elders of a bygone age that a Visigothic woman may rise to heights of power and glory as great as our men can; because of the decree of the shield maidens brought them justice and honor for their many sacrifices for the kingdom..

ith the rising of morning's yellow sun King Sigurd up and out of the bedroom. He led his Thanes on a thorough search of the mead hall in all nooks and crannies for any Huginn's Folk that might be lurking about lest Hister have a spy in their midst and they not know it. There were none about that they could find and King Sigurd breathed much easier. "So Captain Gauron, keep the Thanes on the alert and if any Huggins are found, slay them. We cannot afford for Hister to get word of our plans.

While all of this was going on Queen Gwynnalyn's ladies tended to her and helped her into her dress and then braided her hair. First two long braids over the ears. They Borghild then took those two braids and formed them into one long, very thick braid which came down the centre of Gwynnalyn's back.

There was a knock on the door and the queen said, "Enter." Two maid servants entered with breakfast for the queen and the prince—new ground oatmeal and a pitcher of fresh cow's milk and their because of this noise, the young lad began to stir. When the servants had departed and closed the door behind them, Rony awoke. Sitting up he yawned and rubbed his eyes. His long red hair was a tangled mass on his head and Lady Aestrith took the lad by a hand and gently tugged Rony out of bed. His long white dressing pajamas fell down to his ankles and the lady sat him into a chair and began brushing the tangles out of his hair over his whining protests. When she had brushed and braided the lad's hair, (one long braid down the boy's back) the Queen said, "Very good ladies. I'll tend to Rony for now so go and have breakfast." The young ladies bowed in courtesy and said in unison, "Yes my queen."

When Aestrith Tanmansdottir and Borghild Tanmansdottir had departed Queen Gwynnalyn got her child out of his pajamas and into his day clothing. After their meal she washed his face up good and made him brush his teeth with mint leaf oil and then eat a few mint leaves. Then with Rony's map, rolled up in her right hand it was off to the War Room with her son riding on her shoulders. Greta and Galorfilinde met her in the corridor and she handed Rony to her sister and the boy moved easily from her shoulders to those of Greta while she and Galorfilinde made their way to the war hall. Guards were posted at the door, Sir Arnlaugr and Sir

Arnthor and Captain Gauron was with them. He saw her coming and said, "Make way for the Queen," whereupon he opened the door for her them.

The room was already filled with murmuring people including her father and the king was seated in his chair, but not at the table this time—for the chairs had been placed on the small dais which was located at the far southern end of the room below a new and very great map of Midgard—inked upon large elk buckskins which had been sown together. She took her usual place at his side and handed Rony's map to King Sigurd. Looking around she saw that all of the Reiks of the High Council were there—Sigmund as well as Eileza along with Gustav and Lars. Sergeant Hardrada and his twenty men also as well as a new face from the east, Vong, son of Byock and Min Tze had arrived as had Aubriel the Elf maiden who was sitting next to Shlomael. All of the wizards and the spirit maidens were there, except Yoshael who was still at Ariemel. Gedron Argyle and Princess Riona were there as was Shamus and Molly and the laddies as well as Clovis and Merovinge in their human forms. And finally, Woodwose and Captain Heraclius were present.

The Hellene Demetrius was there as well for he was known as Midgard's foremost linguist and also he was the ambassador at large from the King Byzantium to the tribes of the steppes. He knew the way to Cyclops Island and had enough connexions to get any rescue party passed Byzantium and Troy—the great powers of Hellas who controlled the sea lanes in that part of the world. Demetrius was fluent since childhood in all the major languages and dialects of languages in Midgard (which was why he was employed by the Byzantines) from Elvish to Dwarvish and Celtic to Gomerian; Hellene to Aramaic and Egyptian; Cushan to Cathayan and Hoduan to Persian, Assyrian and Chaldean; Dakkian to Etruscan; even the dialects of the speaking creatures. He was truly an amazing genius within the sphere of languages and the Elves felt that *Dan Ene Gud* had created him for such a time as this and not for base commerce—although it was a great gift to have as a tradesman and he certainly was that.

The languages that he detested was the dark speech of the Ogres of Morag and the black speech of the Goblins—languages of foulness and curses. Nor did he approve much of gargoyle for it was a tongue of hisses as if of a serpent. No one other than Demetrius could comprehend it and there was really no need because the Gargoyles were a multilingual species and although (with a few exceptions) evil they were quite intelligent. The one language he wasn't fluent in was the bird speech of Huginn's folk, for he simply couldn't duplicate the caws snaps and sqwalks of the raven people. But again twas no great loss for the Huggins were another species which had mastered the arts of other creatures speech—including their much smaller raven kinsfolk—birds which hadn't been created with the great intelligence of Huginn's Folk but yet have their own primitive form of communication as do all the creations of *Dan Ene Gud*.

Queen Gwynnalyn motioned her hand and said, "Ambassador Demetrius, come here for a moment." The Byzantine lord in his toga approached and the king handed him Ronan's map and speaking quietly so that others in the room couldn't hear saith, "Thou hast told us that thou hast been to Cyclops Island. Take a look at this and tell me whether it be accurate or not." Demetrius unrolled it and looking it over and was quite impressed and asked "From whence cometh this map? Sire tis quite accurate indeed and the only thing missing are the names." Queen Gwynnalyn said very low and quietly but with pride burning in her eyes, "My four year old son drew it last night—from his visions." The Hellene's eyes went wide as coins and in utter amazement saith, "By the gods?" King Sigurd smiled and said, "Yes indeed. Say nothing of this map when you return to the company of the others. Later on today I shall call upon thee to fill in the place names on the map." "It shall be my duty as well as my pleasure King Sigurd," Demetrius replied as he bowed and stepped away to return to his place. Everyone was wondering what had been said for they were unable to hear the private conference and Hodbrodd had strained to hear it but to no avail.

The King called the meeting to order as Tanman and Sandilin and some kitchen help brought in hot mint tea with fresh hot bread and butter. "I'll start this meeting by reading the ransom demand sent to me by that, 'Equestrian Mutant,' as Sergeant Hardrada so aptly refers to him as," stated King Sigurd. Everyone in the war hall listened as King Sigurd read the outrageous letter and on their faces was looks of anger. Sigurd turned the letter over and sat it on his lap and there was silence in the war hall as they waited for the Mighty Griffin to speak. The king looked at Molly and Shamus and said, "My friends, rest assured that we're resolved to get Liam back from the Centaurs!" Dithranti remained quiet but nodded approvingly. Sigurd looked over at Woodwose and said, "We're going to rescue Amberwose and Rockwose from Hister's clutches Master Faun and we have a plan." King Sigurd looked back at Molly and then over at Byock and the holy people he said, "And we shall do this without handing over the Heart of the Sea to Hister. We all know what will happen if we do that so, Molly, to hand over your gemstone is out of the question. What we say and do here this morning have to be kept in the utmost secrecy." "That is most wise," said Byock.

King Sigurd looked to his wife and saith, "My queen, draw thy sword please?" Queen Gwynnalyn stood up and from the sheath on her side she brought forth the Gwynnian Scythe. As she did so all in the war hall were silent. She said, "I was given this sword to protect innocent children. Our innocents have been kidnapped as pawns in a twisted and sick power game and we shan't stand for this outrage of Hister's! This blade will go forth to cleave asunder those responsible for this outrage and mark my word that someday Hister will fall, consumed in the flames that he himself has started."

She turned to the large map of many elk skins with her sword in her hand at her side and said, "See here this map? Master Demetrius has been updating it for us." She walked to the left side of King Sigurd and pointed her sword at an island in a sea that had been previously unknown to them and said, "This is Cyclops Island." She took away her sword and going back upon the dais she found Thorstadt on the map and pointed to it saying, "This is Thorstadt M'Lords." There was murmuring among those gathered and Lord Hodbrodd said in incredulity, "Given what I know of the distances here in Tervingia, that island must be more than four hundred leagues distant my queen." *(One thousand two hundred and twelve miles)* What're the chances of success?"

Queen Gwynnalyn extended her left hand and King Sigurd gave her Rony's map. She sheathed the Gwynnian Scyth and said, "The chances were always slim from the start Lord Hodbrodd. But see you here this map? Tis a map of Cyclops Island—a map drawn by my son; he's sees the place in his dreams and from it cometh this map." Hodbrodd replied in disdain, "Are we to trust the fate of the hostages to the whimsical dreams of a child—really my queen? How are we to know its accuracy?"

There was an angry look on the face of King Sigurd but before he could chastise Hodbrodd the queen spoke to the issue. She said, "Demetrius of Byzantium has traveled to Cyclops Island M'Lords. He knows both it and the seas that will take us there. Lord Demetrius? What say you of Ronan's map?" Demetrius replied, "I have indeed been to that terrible place and I know it all too well. The Crown Prince's map is the most accurate depiction that I've yet seen M'Lords—save only that the place names are missing. I shall write them in myself in both your runes and in Hellene script." The queen replied, "So thou all hast seen a witness who's been there has proven that Prince Ronan's visions are truly from Asgard." The she said dismissively, "Does that quiet thy concerns Lord Hodbrodd?" He replied, "Indeed my queen."

King Sigurd looked at Hodbrodd and said, "I trust my son Elder—and so should you in this matter." He replied with a bow of his head, "Forgive my impudence Sire" Once again Hodbrodd had caused himself to be humiliated in front of the Reiks and he was embarrassed with hate growing in his heart.

The king said, "A plan has been made and my son's map has much to do with it. I've gathered all of thee here to seek volunteers for a quest. Those going forth on this great mission are to be called *'The Knights of Viðarr (Vitharr)*. Our stories tell of a hero among the Aesir who is the lord of justice and righteous vengeance and I dare say that we need his help for this quest. All on this quest all shall be knights be he lord or knave—be he noble or commoner or ne'er so low. Let this be a new order of knighthood in our kingdom henceforth. *The Order of the Knights of Viðarr*, whose Grandmaster is to be Queen Gwynnalyn—for she is a mighty shield maiden and so her sword is for vengeance upon those who've preyed up our younglings."

Lord Radagaisus was put out and said, "But Sire, with all due respect to our great queen as a shield maiden, no woman has ever been made grandmaster of an order of knights. It's not traditional among my tribe to do such a thing. Shall we send out women with child to die like warriors?" The queen burned hot with anger as did her father and brothers but before she could chastise Sir Radagaisus King Sigurd answered calmly,

"Lord Radagaisus, when we formed this kingdom, this United Kingdom of Tervingia we became one people. We're no longer Getic or Gepid, Gutthiuda, Issedone and Thyssagetae, but Tervingians—named after the father of all of our tribes, King Tyrfingr. In war many traditions peculiar to one tribe or another have become obsolete and the one that thou speakest of is one of these. In my kingdom, shield maidens to may be knighted to serve."

Queen Gwynnalyn said calmly, "Women in our society are free to own property and to engage in commerce—to own land and to go to war; even free to divorce and seek a new man and in the past, shield maidens have had battle sport in the tournaments. These are all laws passed in light of the war and the changes in our way of life since the new kingdom was founded—all laws passed by this noble assembly and so methinks it absurd that a woman be unable to command armies in battle or to lead an order of knights! But I agree that women carrying babies such as I did, have no place on the battlefield for the life of infants who are the future of our kingdom is paramount."

She looked angrily at Sir Radagaisus and said, "You of all people should support this! Art thou not soon to be married to Lady Greta—my sister who is herself a shield maiden?" Radagaisus relented saying, "Indeed my queen, thou art wholly right and it is my honor to be her chosen." Gwynnalyn glared at Radagaisus and said coldly, "I should hope so!" "Here-here—the queen is right!" argued Lord Volsung and Hodbrodd mumbled, "Why doesn't that surprise me!" Now Hodbrodd grew irate and ignoring both the queen and Volsung said, "Sire, only by vote of the elders can such a law be made and it's contrary to our traditions as Lord Radagaisus has said!"

"Very well," replied King Sigurd. The king is not above the law—but rather the chief enforcer of the law. Scap Rolf is the Lawspeaker. What say you Lord Rolf" There was angry mumbling and murmuring among those in the room and King Sigurd was angry that this entire meeting was going off of track—but he quickly saw the opportunity presenting itself to propose a new and just law to the Witena Gemot, the law making body of the kingdom. In fact he had been discussing the wording of such a law in private with Scap Rolf and Scap Kronos for some time now.

The aging First Steward of the King with his long gray hair and beard and wearing his elegant gray flowing cloak over blue shirt and trousers and rune stave in hand walked forward to the dais and said, "Tis true my lord king. Such a fundamental change in our society cannot be simply decreed by the king and Lord Hodbrodd is right—as is Lord Radagaisus in that such a law cannot be made simply by a decree of the king. All decrees of the king are subject to recall by the Witan if they so choose. The king is not above the law, as King Sigurd has rightly pointed out. Rather he is the chief law enforcer as speaker of the witan. All of the Reiks are present and we have a quorum. What say you M'Lords? Shall this be a new law of our people or not? Shall a woman be allowed to lead armies in battle and in times of peace and shall women be allowed to be knighted to serve—be she commoner or noble? And shall women be allowed to lead orders of knights? Shall women be allowed to be enforcers of the law in these new roles? And shall this new law be for our entire society and kingdom? Husbands shall not be able to order their wives not to serve in war—except if that woman or shield maiden is with child, her husband may forbid her to fight. If she is a widow and is with child, her father, brothers or living cousins be they men or women my forbid her and restrain her if necessary from going to war. Pregnancy doth not retrain a woman in her role as a grandmaster; however she may not go to war nor fight in the tournament while with child. No woman with child shall fight in the tournaments. When a woman is not with child and she is of age, not in her father's house, husbands and relatives may not be allowed to order their wives, daughters or sisters not to serve as knights or grandmasters of knights. Shall this new law be made so that no *witan* (parliament) or king in years to come may overturn it? I call for a vote."

The vote was almost unanimous excepting Hodbrodd and Radagaisus and the Lawspeaker declared, "Then by the will of the Witena Gemot, women may be knighted and can serve as grandmasters of orders of knights and may lead armies in time of war and in times of peace and may service as law enforcers—and this law is forever and shan't be able to be overturned by anyone; and husbands shan't be allowed to prevent their wives from doing so. Sire this law also is enforced upon thee in regards to the queen. So let it be written; so let it be done."

The queen and all of the women in the room were quite happy at this sudden turn of events. It was a move that King Sigurd had wanted to make in years past—but he just needed the right set of circumstances and his wife looked at him and smiled, so proud was she of her husband this day. She said, "This shall raise even more support for you among the people my king—truly you've learned much from the Elves and are the most enlightened king in Midgard." He replied, "In this life or death struggle we need every sword we can get. It matters not if they're men or women—I need the best people we have." King Sigurd addressed the Witena gemot and said, "Very well then M'Lords—all's in order. Lord Rolf, see to it that this decree of the Witan is written out and posted in every public meeting place in our kingdom and in every camp, every village and every town."

CHAPTER XXVII

The Knights of Víðarr

From the Skald's Tale

What would any of us do to save the life of our child? I dare say that those of us who truly love our children know that they are gifts to us from Asgard, and would go to extraordinary lengths to put their lives above are own safety. The tales of the Aesir speak of one who was a lord of justice and righteous vengeance called Víðarr (Vitharr) and twas in his name that the shield maiden led her quest to wreak havoc upon wicked kidnappers—creatures of the vilest sort.

They finally returned no to the reason that the meeting had been called and King Sigurd said, "We now have less than ninety days to affect the rescue and therefore we must proceed with all due vigor. What wizard and what spirit maiden shall go forth on this quest?" Yonas the Dwarf, White Wizard of the South and the Spirit Maiden Gleadra got up and walked over, taking their place in front of the dais. The king was pleased and said, "I have heard of you Vong. Your father and mother have told me much of your mystical fighting skills, honed to razor edge in the Temples of Shangra La. We need you and all your skills. Will you go with the queen on this mission and be a Knight of Víðarr? Vong stood up in with a polite bow he said, "This is why I have come here, oh Great King," saith he as he took his place in front of the dais. (The dais was high enough so that everyone could see the king and the queen with an unobstructed view if people were standing in front of it.)

King Sigurd said, "The queen will need the best warriors that we have, and so Lord Gedron, and Sergeant Hardrada wilt thou twain be bound into the Knights of Víðarr?" Now Hardrada's company of twenty elite warriors was there in the war halls as well and heard it all." Gedron and Hardrada stood up and took their places in front of the dais saying, "We shall sire and by your leave." The company of twenty came forth one by one and each man said, "We also shall become Knights of Víðarr and pledge our oaths to the quest."

General Randver, Lord Raedwald, Lord Snaevar Lord Regin and the three steppe Jarls stood up without being asked and Randver said, "My king, I will go on this quest and do my duty sire." "As will I," stated Snaevar. "Count me in as well my king," said an enthusiastic Sir Regin. Lord Raedwald said, "My liege, twas I who led the western quest and I desire to be on this one as well. Those kinderlings must be brought home." But the king said, "M'Lords I know that all of thee are brave and would contribute much to the quest. But there is a part two of this plan and I shall need all of you brave men at my side—to help my do what I must to try and end this war once and for all—to win this war. And I know that you my Jarls, dear Godwin, brave Adaire and mighty Gondark would also gladly go with the queen and even thou oh mighty Raedwald to whom we owe so much. But I need the seven of thee serving for me up here as part of my plan to win the war." They nodded and Gondark said, "My horse archers are at thy pleasure my liege." "As are mine," said Godwin. "Mine also!" cried Adaire. Lord Raedwald bowed his head and said, "My desire is to serve thee in whatever capacity that I'm needed my liege. The seven of them sat down as the entire room erupted into cheering at what King Sigurd had said about winning the war. The king raised his hand for everyone to be silent.

King Sigurd was quite happy now and said, "Parents have the right, yes even the duty to go and rescue their children from evil clutches and to exact justice and righteous revenge. A man must be allowed rescue and avenge the honor of his wife and save his family. Master Shamus and Lady Molly, will thou twain take thy places in the quest and become Knights of Víðarr? You will need help from your own kind as well. Ruairi, Aonghus, and Fearghal, wilt thou also join your master and become Knights of Víðarr? Shamus and Molly and the laddies with no hesitation at all took their place, standing in front of the growing group of quest warriors.

The King smiled and said, "And you Master Faun, Herr Woodwose, wilt thou also take thy place on the quest as a Knight of Víðarr—so that thou mayest save thy family from bondage?" The noble Faun was already coming toward the dais as the king spoke and said, "I shall indeed Mighty Griffin and if I do not my duty to them, then let me not return alive." Woodwose quickly took his place with the others, standing beside Sergeant Hardrada.

Sigmund and the boys were beginning to worry that they weren't going to be called on to volunteer for the quest and were looking quite dejected at that moment. Sigmund was just about to come up on his own when they heard welcome words from the King and their spirits were lifted on high. "Sigmund, Duke of Wodenburg, you deserve the chance to go as well to rescue the children. You did your best to rally your forces when the attack happened. You will need Gustav and Lars as well. The queen is the grandmaster of this new noble order, and under her is Lord Gedron. Follow the instructions of Sergeant Hardrada and continue to learn the art of war. Learn from Yonas as well. Wilt thou Sigmund the Volsung, and you Lars Thonansson and thee Gustav Thonansson, take thy places here before me as Knights of Víðarr?" Siggy and his friends were quick to join the rest of their comrades at the dais. The king saw the look of "What about me?" on the face of Princess Eileza and said, "Rise Princess Eileza Andavarsdottir of Ariemel. Behold thou art a warrior princess, a shield maiden and soon to be the Grand Duchess of Wodenburg. Wilt thou also take thy place at the side of Queen Gwynnalyn as a Knight of Víðarr?" Eileza practically leaped from out of her seat for to join and ran to the side of her Siggy Wiggy.

King Sigurd said, "A Princess cannot go without her most trusted and faithful guards—Dwarves who've been with her since she was born—Dwarves who pledged to the late King Andavar and to King Togrobeg that they would guard Eileza even unto their own deaths. Oh Austri and Vestri, brothers of east and west, wilt thou join Queen Gwynnalyn and Princess Eileza and become Knights of Víðarr—if it is so then come forward to the dais." Without hesitation and with smiles on their thick dark haired heads and bearded faces these two most famous twins strode forward with their mighty battle axes in hand to become Knights of Víðarr.

The King looked at Lady Zakarah and said, "Oh Lady of Urðarbrunnr I thank thee for all the council and support which thou and the Melchizedek have given to this Kingdom and to this family. Therefore I ask you to give your blessing to those of your blood which may want to become Knights of Víðarr." Zakarah already knew who was going and so she replied, "It was their destiny to go King Sigurd, according to the word of King Yoshael." The King was pleased by that remark and she said, "Galorfilinde and Shlomael. You have been Norns to Queen Gwynnalyn and Lord Gedron since they were mer kinderlings. Shlomael, you've taken Duke Sigmund into council and understanding as well for these last four years. Aubriel, you've come to Thorstadt for such a time as this. So will the three of you to join the quest?" The three Elves rose and took their places beside Sigmund in front of the dais.

The King said, "It is important as well that the allies in the west be represented, and that the laddies have along their master and trainers. Therefore, Argyle of Brython and Riona of Gergovia, wilt thou also take thy places at the dais as Knights o Víðarr? Gladvynn Dithrantisdottir you too are a Spirit Maiden of the Celts as well as a Shield Maiden of Brython and it is right to ask that, if thou wilt, wilt thou also become a Knight of Víðarr?" She who was so tall blond and elegant walked forward to the dais and said, "I pledge my service for this quest to Queen Gwynnalyn Volsungsdottir," whereupon she took a bow. Argyle and Riona did so as well.

Looking over at Demetrius the Byzantine the King said, "And we need you as well. You know where Cyclops Island is at, and you speak all known languages. We are friends with King Byzas of Byzantium. You've had dealings with the Centaurs in the past I take it?" Demetrius replied, "Ah yes, the Centaurs. Unfortunately I have sire. I have met the Centaur Force Commander Adrastus—who's quite an unpleasant fellow to say the least. As well I know of the other creatures in that sea such as the Minotaurs and, even the Cyclops who are a race of one-eyed trolls. They are led by the most wicked, cannibalistic and barmy king ever to rule at Mandraki—King Minus. " King Sigurd replied, "Very good then Demetrius. I shan't ask of thee a pledge to be a Knight of Víðarr unless thou wilt—but I will contract with thee for your services as interpreter and guide. What say you sir?"

Demetrius, clad in a white toga rose up and took a polite bow and replied, "I'm already pledged to the service of King Byzas, and a Byzantine is only allowed an oath to a new king after he's been released from the service of his rightful king. So while I cannot accept the honor of being a knight, I'm free to contract with you, for a price—to go along for as long as Queen Gwynnalyn needs me and so I say, yes. King Byzas wished our two peoples to be strong allies and trading partners, and he will stand with Tervingia against the outrages of Hister and his allies—he knows the danger already and so this was why I was sent. The Scythians are no less a threat to Byzantium as to Thorstadt. I will gladly go along and take the beautiful queen and her knights to Cyclops Island. But please, just call me, Demetri." He walked over and took his place with the quest warriors.

The King looked over at Clovis and Merovinge and said, "Your skills at changing form have been priceless my friends. Please, wilt thou also go with the queen on this as she has requested and become Knights of Víðarr?" As the two of them took their places in the group Clovis said, "Well we wouldn't miss this for the world. We'll give those bloody Centaurs what for we will." Merovinge said, "The nerve of those beasties to kidnap the children! We're on the job your Majesties."

Then the King rose looked over to his wife and smiled. Turning his head back toward the others he said, "All those standing who've volunteered, turn and face the dais and kneel." When they'd done so he said sternly, "Hear ye then! Let it be known that Queen Gwynnalyn will lead as grandmaster, this Order of the Knights of Víðarr." The queen rose from her seat and then kneeled in front of King Sigurd. He stood up and then taking his sword Tyrfingr, touched her on the head and bother shoulders saying, "I hereby knight thee oh Gwynnalyn Volsungsdottir as Grandmaster of the Order of the Knights of Víðarr. Thou Gwynnalyn Volsungsdottir havest my full confidences in thee that thou wilt succeed and return safely home. Rise now and dub thy knights oh Grandmaster."

What shall be the standard of the Knights of Víðarr? It's coat of arms shall be the image of Víðarr, foot on the neck of the Fenrir Wolf, slaying him with his spear, a symbol of the triumph of justice over criminality—which has already been embroidered on a banner and which shall be inscribed upon the shields of all those who today are dubbed Knights of Víðarr. Rise up my queen and dub thy knights."

She rose and then one by one she touched each of them once on their heads and both shoulders with her sword the Gwynnian Scythe saying. "I dub thee Knight of the Order of Víðarr." When she had completed the dubbing of all those kneeling before the dais she said boldly and strongly "Let us swear the oath. We live in the east, just on the edge of the Centre Midgard and so I ask you Master Byock to give us the blessing. The White Wizard of the East, wearing his long white hooded robe walked forward and stood upon the dais beside King Sigurd and he waved his staff back and forth as if over the knights and said in his oriental accent, "Everyone repeat after me:

> "I do give my solemn vow before God and before Asgard and pledge my service to the Crown of Tervingia and to the Order of oath freely and of my own accord I vow my service until released by word of the Grandmaster—so help me God. So say we all! So say the Knights of Víðarr on this noble quest to rescue the innocent, defend those who are weak, and to free the oppressed. I take this we all! So say we all."

He gave the blessings of the Holy Order over them saying, "May El Shaddai bless thee and keep thee; El Shaddai make his face shine upon thee and be gracious to thee; El Shaddai lift up his countenance upon thee and give thee victory." Everyone in the room cheered. Even Hodbrodd and Radagaisus joined outwardly the praise but on the inside there was envy in their hearts.

With all of that done the King said, "All this must remain a secret. No one must know of this. We will develop a cover story regarding the absence of the queen from the public and whoever speaks of this to anyone about this outside of those here in my mead hall will be charged with treason and if convicted, executed on the block as a spy. In the meanwhile, I will form an army and attack west past Myrkvidr and then unto the Guithuidaland—it's what we should have done long ago. I will march to Helmgard and free the Gutthiuda Thralls from their shackles of bondage and try to bring this Midgard War to a final resolution this summer by attacking Scythia from the other direction and perhaps even Castle Kol Oba. While my queen and I are away, you Scap Rolf, being my *Chief Steward* and *First Minister* will govern the daily affairs of the Kingdom. In the meanwhile, we must set up a ruse. Send the bravest rider with a message to Herr Hister that we'll comply with his demands. The rider must know nothing of this plan or this meeting, lest Hister draw our plans out of him by some foul sorcery. We will dispatch the rider who will contact the Scythian patrols. Tis they who will carry word to Idanthrsus and he will give word to Hister. I will send a message full of threats as to what will happen to them if they betray us. So let it be written, and so let it be done."

The meeting was dismissed and hope was in the air once more. The rest of the day was spent making preparations and plans. Demetri filled out the place names in Gomerian runes and Hellene script on Ronan's map of Cyclops Island and described it in detail to everyone remaining there and what kind of force they would be up against. He said, "And so here it is my Leprechaun friends—the map of Cyclops Island. Molly saw it and replied, "I canno bear the thought of me son down there in that clinker! Shamus and me are gonna have ructions with those bloody boggers—but with me sword and no with words! I'm ready to go now and tired of waitin!" "Aye," stated Shamus, "I'm gonna show those Centaurs a bit of the Leprechaun sword right up the jacksi!" The other laddies were just as enthusiastic and could hardly wait for the quest to begin. All in all Demetrius was quite impressed by their go getting spirit.

CHAPTER XXVIII

A Night of Fare thee Well.

From the Skald's Tale

Oh long ago night in yonder mead hall in land so far away. Time for fare the well had come. For knights so brave and so bold must away ere the coming of dawn, into unknown dangers—a fate unknown now awaits those who o'er land and sea must gallantly go—to fare away island of belching fire of Vulcan's unholy hearth.

That evening everyone had a hearty meal in the private dining hall, and Tanman served up his best pumpkin ale. They feasted from a great pot of skause made from elk roast and a rich variety of vegetables and mushrooms. It was indeed a fellowship meal of warriors. There was music and dancing as the laddies played their harps and strings. Molly was in no mood for any of it and so retired early with Shamus beside her, arm around her shoulder as they left the dining hall. But for those with the spirit such as the Dwarves, they lifted up their horns of ale and their many toasts were made to the simple word *Skol* as horns and mugs were filled and refilled.

Later in the night at bedtime it was time for Argyle and Riona to explain to little Vern that Mumma and Pappa had to go away for a few weeks. The tiny Celtic boy was heartbroken and scared. "No Mommy. Ye canno go away from me! No pappy ye canno go! What if the hairy goat men come back and get me like they did Liam and Rocky!"

Dithranti and Boudicca were there as well and Riona said, "No, no Vern. Those goat men are called Satyrs and they cannot get to you again. Dah and I are going to bring Rocky and Liam home safe. We're going to get the Satyrs and the Centaurs for what they did to ye friends my love. And besides, you'll be here with Rony to play with and you'll be with Grandma and Grandpa the whole time love." The child replied, "Aye, I guess it's alright Mummy. But I dunno want you to go away. And not dah either. Let me go with you and I'll be a good help dah" Argyle picked his son up and said, "Aye, and a good help you are Vern. But you can't go on this one. Maybe when ye're a wee bit older son and better with a sword or with Grandpa's magic. You have the gift. Stay and learn it all from your Grandfather and maybe, just maybe mind ye, someday you be a White Wizard like he is."

Dithranti was sitting in his rocking chair as Argyle handed Averngedrix to him, sitting the young boy on his lap. Dithranti said, "Vern, let me tell you a story. It is the story of a wizard. The White Wizard of the north, Yoshael." The boy laid his head on grandfathers shoulder and curled up with a blanket that Boudicca had made for him and asked, "I know him Grandpa. Is he a great wizard or is he like you Grandpa?" Everyone in the bedroom got a chuckle out of that and Dithranti looked a little bit embarrassed, rather taken aback by his Grandson's question. He took off his pointed wizard's hat and handed it to Boudicca who set it aside on a table near a flickering oil lamp. Dithranti had long gray hair and a well-groomed pointed beard. He replied, "Ah yes Vern. I think that he is. Yoshael is a very great wizard indeed. Let me tell thee about him and where the Elves come from Vern. I will tell thee of their magic and how it is used for good." "Absobloodylutly marvelous!" was the instant and happy reply of the boy.

Meanwhile, Vong and his parents were having a heart to heart conversation. Byock was saying, "I've missed seeing you my son." "Yes my father," replied Vong. It has been four years since you and Mother departed Yerpa. Not long by the reckoning of the heavens, but long for those of us who are mortals." Min Tze brought hot tea and the three of them sipped it sitting at a low table, the kind of which is customary in Midgard's Far East in the lands of Cathay, Shangra-La and the Isle of Shoguns (Nippon).

"It is so good to see you Vong," said Min Tze. "You arrived at the appointed time and then all too soon, you must go away from us on this quest." Vong smiled at his beautiful mother and said, "I am sure mother that when I return there will be much more time for us to spend together as a family. It's my hope that my wife Meiying and our daughters Lihua and Chuntao—and our son Changpu can join us as well." Byock replied, "The grandchildren. I miss them so much Vong. Lihua is eleven now and Chuntao seven and our little Changpu is five. I know that it was very hard for you to leave them Vong." He replied, "Indeed it was father. But I know that they are safe in Shangra La. I know that what we do here in the west will determine their fate." "You have grown wise my son. You have mastered all of the mystical fighting skills of Kung Fu. You are becoming a wizard as well and we are most proud of you my son." He replied, "I am honored father."

The King and Queen put Rony to bed and he quickly fell asleep with Gwynnalyn singing the sweet elvish lullaby to him. When she saw that Rony was in a deep sleep, she cuddled with her husband for the night and said, "I shall miss Rony and thee so very much My Hunter. But I know that this quest was meant for me. I've trained for battle ever since I was a toddler with father in the bear pits." He kissed her and said, "You haven't been on a mission in quite some time. I've to admit that as a husband I dread the thought of thy departure on such a dangerous quest. But I know that I cannot hold you back My Heart—and now it's law that I cannot hold thee back. I married a warrior princess and I wouldn't have thee any other way." Filled with love she replied, "Oh My Hunter I love thee so much. I know we've been waiting but methinks that when I get back I shall be ready to have another child." Their eyes met and their gaze locked and they rubbed noses. Turning to look out of the window at the moon and stars, they said their soft goodbye as theirs eyes filled with tears. They soon found themselves in love's romantic passion.

Sigmund and Eileza talked for a while in the dining hall after everyone had departed and she felt safe and secure in his arms as they embrace whist sitting upon the bench at the dinner table—a table which brought back so very many dear memories for the young couple. Twas then that Lila came in and sat down beside them. She felt like an intruder when she saw them but she had come to talk to Siggy. She sighed sadly and said, "Siggy, you and I have been brother and sister since forever. When you and Leeza get married, shall I still be your little sister? Will you still love me like the old days?" Eileza looked at Siggy and said, "This one is a keeper Siggy. You better set things right with her. She adores her big brother." He let go of Eileza and held his arms out for Lilia. The ten year old child cuddled him and he hugged her like it was the end of the world. "Lila, no matter who is here you'll always be my baby sister. I'll always protect you from Ogres or anything else and I'll always love thee, even more than in the old days."

Eileza was so moved that her eyes filled with tears and she thought how wonderful a Pappa that Siggy would someday be. Sigmund and Eileza, due to the age in which they lived and the circumstances of the war and the daily struggle to live in such a tough world, were far older and wiser in mind and in spirit than the mere years of their lives would suggest—looking back upon them from the third age.

Sigmund continued speaking to Lilia using formal language saying, "And besides, when Leeza and I are married, she'll be thy sister as well and if it is ok with mum and dah, thou canst come live with us in my new mead hall in Wodenburg—after we get back from the Quest." She replied, "I want to go with you on the quest Siggy. Just like so long ago when we ran away through the secret tunnel. It was so fun but a bit scary that night."

He moved her head from off of his shoulder and looking her in the eyes he said, "Baby Sister, this quest is an army mission this time, and you just cannot go. It will be much too dangerous for thee. You're not yet a page or a squire, much less a knight and you haven't been called into the Order of the Knights of Víðarr. We already have Aunty Amber and two of your friends missing. I don't want anything to happen to you. Thou must stay here this time. And when we go, thou mustn't follow us through the tunnel Wish Maiden. We shall be gone for a few weeks, and I want to know that thou art safe and snug here at home. In the meanwhile, thou knowest that by the new law, women and girls can be knighted and even rise to be grandmasters. So train here with Greta and someday Lila, thou shalt be a shield maiden and a knight." She protested saying, "I thought I was your page Siggy?"

Sigmund knew not what to say and so he looked to Eileza and she had no answer other than a shrug of her shoulders. Sigmund said to Lilia, "Indeed thou hast always been my page but much training is still ahead of you. Learn from Greta whist I'm away. She's a powerful shield maiden just like Gwynnalyn." She replied with some consternation, "But Greta is so twitterpated by Radagaisus till she thinks of nothing else—least of all poor little me. "It's always,' Raddy this and Raddy that! He's a pikey and a bad'un Siggy and I'm frightened of him. " Eileza answered that saying, "Not to worry Lilly because the bad'un is marching off to war with the king so he shan't be here to interfere." "At least something is going my way these days," replied Lilia.

Lilia's were quivering lips and her eyes slowly started to cry and she replied between sniffs of her nose, "Very well Big Brother. I'll stay home. But if you get hurt or get killed, that will be the end of it for me. I'll sit in ashes forever and ever!" Eileza leaned over and said, "Lilia, I promise to you as Asgard as my witness, that I shan't let anything happen to your big brother. I'm a shield maiden of the Dwarves of Ariemel and I'll guard him for the both of us." The three of them shared a group hug and Lila with tearful eyes saith, "Yes Aunty Leeza. Fare thee well."

To Be Continued

A King sat Sigurd; carven silver, raiment gleaming, rings and goblets, dear things dealt he, doughty-handed, his friends enriching, and his fame upraising

Volsungakvida En Nyja
Edda Sigurdarkvida en Mesta

LAND OF FOREVER ICE
EIKENGARD
GUNDERBAD
AURVANDIL
VANDALIA
SKOFINGA
MYRKVIDR
KIMMERIA
SARMATIA
OARUS R
SANDFRITH
GELONUS
DANPAR R
SCYTHIA
HELMGARD
GNOMES
DAKKIA
Tanais R
PAULUS
VINGIA
RIVER RHA
THORSTADT
HYRCANIAN
STEPPES
THE STONEBELT FELLS
THE MAGYAR KHANATE
KYZUL KUM Desert
Wodenburg
HUMANBORG
THE GREAT DARK SEA
LOFTY MTNS
HYRCANIAN SEA
SATYRS
BYZANTIUM
Troy
DOMINIONS OF THE SONS OF HETH
KAPPODOKIA
HELLAS
Delphi
Athens
Gobekli Tepe
ASSYRIA
NINEVEH